The Viking's Highland Lass

The Highlanders

Book 7

TERRY SPEAR

ISBN-10: 1-63311-012-5
ISBN-13: 978-1-63311-012-0

DEDICATION

To Sandi Carstensen, my prayers go out to you and I wish you every success. Keep your chin up, lassie, and my thoughts are with you as you go through radiation treatments. Big hugs.

ACKNOWLEDGMENTS

Many thanks to Donna Fournier and to Vonda Sinclair who helped to make Gunnolf and Brina's story so much better!!! Thanks, ladies. If I could, I'd send you both a braw Highlander to thank you too.

PROLOGUE

1097, England

A thick fog coating the whole area, Gunnolf drifted in and out of consciousness. At the age of five and ten winters, he was lying on the ground in the wet grass, a sword wound in his side hurting something fierce. Was this how it felt to die?

Somehow, he'd always imagined he would just…die. Quickly.

"You will be lost to us," Gunnolf's amma, his grandmother, had said before he had left his homeland in the north with several of his kin in longboats to rescue one of his older brothers captured by the Sassenach. "Many will be lost to us."

Her words of warning had haunted him the whole way to England and now, lying here, gasping for breath, he couldn't put them out of his mind. His amma knew things no one should have known.

But if he fought well, he would die a warrior's death. He welcomed it, was ready to join his kin that had fallen this very day and those who had died in the past. He had been going on raids since he was ten winters and he really hadn't thought he would die this day or any other. Such was the hazard of youth.

"Will I die in battle?" Gunnolf had asked her, not really believing he would die in battle, but he had always questioned her visions, and she had seemed to appreciate that he didn't readily believe everything he was told.

She had shaken her head, her white hair braided, her wrinkled face soft, her blue-gray eyes saddened. "You will be lost to us."

Now as he lay bleeding on his back, a piece of cloth tucked against the sword wound on his side, he stared up at the mist cloaked sky in the lands of the Sassenach. The woods all around him where he had crawled were quiet, except for a falcon calling out a rasping kack-kack-kack-kack from a nest somewhere high above.

"But you will not die this day." His amma's words whispered in his ear.

Tomorrow then, he thought, as he felt he would surely die soon while the pain rippled through his weary body. Then he heard a horse snorting nearby, pawing at the ground. A rider-less horse?

Or had one of the Sassenach survived or had more arrived and they were looking for the injured among the dead? If they found him, he would disprove his amma's words and he would die this day.

He couldn't see his fallen kin from where he'd crawled to, but he'd seen them struck down, saw the life leave their eyes. He'd captured his father's gaze at one point, willing him to fight well, to be proud of who he was.

Then a gray-bearded Sassenach, bloodlust in his narrowed blue eyes, stabbed Gunnolf in the side, and he had fallen too. He thought he had gone to Valhalla, but he hadn't remembered being led by the Valkyries into the great hall. When he had opened his eyes and seen all the carnage and felt the pain, he knew he was still alive.

But then his older brother Hallfred had appeared before him, his red hair dangling in Gunnolf's face. Had his kin freed him? Or had Gunnolf just imagined his brother leaning over him, his blue eyes hard as he stared back at Gunnolf, their gazes locking, his hand on Gunnolf's chest as if he was ensuring he was dead.

"Is Gunnolf dead?" another man had shouted.

"*Ja*. He no longer breathes. He has gone to Valhalla," Hallfred had said. "Brave warrior that he is," he added, sneering.

Then Hallfred had run off and Gunnolf had slipped away into blackness.

Now, he was well awake, in agony. Had he

really seen his brother? Gunnolf couldn't be sure. He finally managed to grab hold of a low tree branch, and get to his feet, but jagged sharp jolts pained him something fierce. He sank to his knees, gasping for breath.

God's wounds, he had to get to the longboats before they left. He had to leave with the rest of his kin who had survived, if any had, before the Sassenach arrived, if they were not here yet. He heard no voices, no sounds of dying men, just of the pounding of the waves upon the shore below the cliffs. Except for the horse and the falcon, he felt all alone.

Shouting in the Sassenach tongue from a distant place spurred him to get up off his knees and leave…now.

Unsteadily, he staggered to his feet, pressed the heel of his hand against a tree and lowered his head, everything spinning beneath him. Finally able to see the fallen leaves on the ground more clearly, he raised his head and saw the white horse as a silhouette in the mist. No rider anywhere. The horse was watching him, brown eyes soulful, and he moved toward him. He meant to do so carefully, cautiously, but he couldn't manage as much as he was hurting, and stumbled over fallen branches in his path. Even where there were none.

He spoke quietly, reassuring the horse as he made his slow, painful progress to close the gap between them. "I will not harm you," he whispered. The horse's ears twitched.

He continued to speak softly when he was able to grasp its reins, and brushed his hand over the horse's neck. Then he attempted to climb into the saddle, once, twice, and the third time finally managing to seat himself in the leather.

He nudged the horse in the direction of the sea, but when they reached it, he saw the longboats off in the distance sailing home without him.

"You will be lost to us," his amma's words whispered on the chilly breeze.

He believed then he would not die this day.

***

Midday, a low fog clinging to the loch and pine trees surrounding it on the warm summer's day in the Highlands, Brina Auchinleck saw a beautiful white horse eating grass nearby. Her quiver of arrows at her back and her bow slung over her shoulder, she'd been searching for birds to hunt. But she hadn't expected this. A horse so white, she'd never seen such a sight, as if he was a gift from the old gods themselves.

A branch snagged her hair, yanking it and hurting, instantly snapping Brina out of the vision she'd been having. She quickly looked around the area, the same place where the vision had occurred, the blue loch before her, no breeze stirring so it was glassy and reflected the pines surrounding it. A low lying fog covered part of the loch and clung to the pine trees. Then she looked to the north.

And saw the white horse. He was real.

Panic filled her breast as she feared an enemy clan was in the area. But where was the rider of the beautiful beast? What if the horse was just…lost?

She moved toward him.

He lifted his head from eating grass and watched her approach. Her heart beating hard, she paused, afraid she would spook it. Gathering her courage, she moved closer and saw the sole of a boot in the tall grasses and gorse. She came to a dead stop. The rider was sleeping in the grass? But wouldn't he have heard her approach? Was he dead then?

She knew this was a dangerous idea, but she had to see. She had to know. Her da had always said she was too curious for her own good.

On the other side of the gorse, she saw the lad belonging to the boot—a lad who looked to be not much older than she. Blood soaked his tunic, his eyes were closed, and he wasn't stirring at her approach. Was he dead? She observed him further and saw that his chest was rising and falling and heard his labored breathing. A sword was sheathed at his waist, a dirk in his boot. Was he a young warrior?

She had to do something. She rushed forward then and secured the horse's reins on a gorse bush. The lad groaned, and she jerked her head around to see him looking wide-eyed at her.

She quickly pulled off a blanket rolled up behind the saddle and then rejoined him. "Where are you wounded?" His side, it appeared, though he was a bloody mess.

Had he stolen the horse? Only he'd gotten

away after a swordfight?

His eyes studied her. They were a sky blue that pulled her right in until he lifted his hand to his waist, and she remembered her duty. She hurried to pull out her dirk and cut a strip of the cloth from the blanket to bind his wound. "What is your name?"

"Gunnolf, son of Gustavson," he hoarsely whispered. "Are you the goddess Freyja?"

"Goddess?" She smiled, but she didn't recognize his strange dialect. The words, but not the accent.

Then she struggled to help him to sit up. He groaned, and she feared he was going to pass out on her the way his eyes rolled back in his head.

"Nay, nay, dinna pass out on me. 'Tis too difficult to get you up."

Her words seemed to bring him back to this time and place, and she quickly secured the strip of cloth around his waist to help to stop the bleeding. Then she pulled her flask from her belt and lifted it to his lips. "Drink."

He was so fair haired when she was not. While he gulped the ale down, some of it streaming down his chin, she observed him further. His dark golden hair fell about his shoulders, curly, beautiful as if kissed by the golden rays of the sun. He wore no whiskers, but his arms were well-muscled, his brown tunic embroidered with strange black stitching, a fur brat secured at his throat.

No one had ever likened her to a goddess. But

she'd never heard of that goddess either and frowned at him. "Can you stand? Mount your horse? 'Tis your horse, is it no'?"

No matter what, she couldn't help a horse thief get away with stealing a horse, yet he was so beautiful, so injured, she wanted to save him like she had done so many times with birds, a wolf pup once, even a wild cat, and aye, men who had been wounded in battle.

Gunnolf lay back down as if unable to sit any further and stared at her with a look of peace in his expression. She feared he was dying. She'd seen that look before when a warrior no longer felt any pain and was ready to leave this world behind, had accepted his fate, and was ready to move on.

"Can you stand?" She was determined to get him to her shieling and from there, she would run to the castle and get help for him. Before she ran off though to get more help, she would do what she could for him like their healer had taught her.

He didn't respond, just stared at her as if she was just as beautiful to him as he was to her.

"Come, I must get you to my shieling." She tried to lift him, but he was heavy and too injured he couldn't push himself up. "Gunnolf, you must help me."

"Is...this...the field of Fólkvangr," he rasped out.

"Where are you from?" She had never heard of such a place.

He closed his eyes, and she was again afraid he

was near death.

Then she stared again at his clothes, the furs he wore, and the strange markings on his scabbard. Heart pounding, she shifted her gaze to his face. "You are a Finn-Gall," she gasped, her skin chilling at once. Her kin had fought the Norwegian Vikings who had raided their land last winter and killed her grandfather. Yet he spoke her language, even though it sounded strange to her ears. And he seemed to understand her.

Were the Vikings near her lands again? But her people hadn't been fighting anyone or she would have known.

She was torn. She knew she couldn't take him to her shieling or she could be cast from the clan for aiding a Viking warrior, lad that he was, if she was caught caring for him. It was her duty to tell the chief a Viking lay bleeding near the loch.

If her da wasn't on the mountain with the sheep for the next several days…

She glanced back in the direction of her aunt and uncle's shieling. She couldn't see it for the distance, but she was to call on her uncle or his son, Christophe, her older cousin by four summers, if she needed help. Even Lynette, who was his age, raised by her aunt but not truly kin, could help. Though her da had forbidden her to see her after Brina's mother died. And she didn't want to get Lynette into trouble.

So why was she now running to get a cart in the byre, fully intending to take him to the shieling and aid the Finn-Gall further?

***

Gunnolf watched the beautiful lass run off into the woods, her dark hair flying behind her. Thought about her warm hands on his cold skin, the way her blue eyes had caught his gaze and he'd fallen right under her spell. Breaking free of the image of the lass, he knew he couldn't stay. She might be willing to care for him, but when she had called him a Viking, he assumed her people must have had trouble with his kind. He was certain her people would kill him, or chain him up in a dark, dank dungeon.

He struggled to get up, and somehow through sheer willpower, despite the way his vision was blackening, he finally managed to get back on the horse and headed north again. Somehow, he would reach his home. He glanced over his shoulder, but he couldn't see the girl or the shieling she had spoken of.

He'd rested long enough. Thankfully, the ale and food in the packs on the horse had kept him alive or he would never have made it this far. He just hoped the girl wouldn't alert her clansmen before he was well on his way. Better, if he was well out of their reach. If he was to die anywhere, he'd rather do it while he was free than lying half dead on the ground, chained in a dungeon.

CHAPTER 1

Ten years later, the Scottish Highlands

The impending battle looming, Lady Brina's da and his men were eager to fight with the Vikings over yet another dispute concerning territory and livestock again The Norsemen had settled near their lands less than a year ago and as soon as her people had their first clash with them, Brina had wondered if the injured lad she had found near her shieling so long ago had survived and was living among them. How the world had changed. Her da was no longer a sheepherder but the chief of their clan. She still couldn't believe how her father had become chief either, after such a humble beginning as a sheepherder. But he'd been so ruthless in battle when called to fight and so good at rallying their clansmen, when she was four and ten summers, he'd been elected chief of their clan upon the death of the other.

She'd always wished her mother had lived to be the lady of the keep, but she had died when Brina was two and ten and the newborn son along with her. Brina still missed her mother.

Now her da wanted Brina to wed a man who had been elected Tanist, the chief who would take over when her da no longer ruled, Seamus MacDougald, whom she despised.

Brina had felt the battle would be like any other, until she had the vision. She'd just left her bedchamber and was hurrying down the narrow winding stairs, intent on serving the first meal, when the candles lighting her way dimmed. The sun had not even risen in the morning sky when Brina's vision grabbed hold, the world in a blur, like a dream, but not a dream. A vision of a future happening.

Men dressed in plaid in a glen a long ways from home fought against their enemy, furs and tunics, the embroidery work that of the Norsemen, swords clashing, clanking, powerful swings, and thrusts aimed at cutting down their opponents. Horses rearing and whinnying. Men fighting on foot. In the midst of battle, a man struck a mighty blow at her da on horseback.

Her heart in her throat, she gasped.

It was as if nothing else was there, no one else, no ongoing battle, no more men or horses or swords or targes, just her da falling from his horse and landing on the rocky ground. She wanted to run to him, to care for him, protect him, even if he didn't care about her. But he was her da. Worse, if he died, she would be forced to wed a brigand who had no heart.

And then the scene changed. She was running down several flights of stairs from her tower room to the door that lead to the inner bailey but it was locked. She bolted to another door, intent on reaching her horse in the stables and riding her onto the battlefield to see to her da. But she couldn't find it as if the door had just…vanished.

"My lady," one of the cooks said, and Brina stared at the stout woman, wondering how she'd gotten from her bedchamber all the way to the kitchen without ever realizing it, while lost in the vision. "Are you all right?"

"Aye."

"We are getting ready to feed the men going into battle," Salora said, directing the kitchen staff to serve the porridge and bannocks.

Brina's skin still prickling with concern over the vision of her da, she reminded herself she had not seen him dead. Only knocked from his horse. Brina took a deep breath and let it out, then as she usually did, she carried some of the porridge to the waiting men where they were already drinking ale and eating bannocks, serving her da and his second-in command.

"May I have a word with you?" she asked her da as she placed his porridge on the trestle table, hoping to warn him of what would befall him on the battlefield and to be prepared.

His nearly black beard was streaked with gray, the same with his long hair, now tied back. His brown eyes studied her for a moment, then he said, "You are late in coming to the hall. Salora had to serve my bannocks this morn. You sleep in when others are busy preparing for battle?"

She shook her head.

"Do you want to wish me well then?" He asked the question with a sneer, as if he knew she wouldn't care if he lived or died.

Which wasn't true. She did care. Just because he didn't seem to have any feelings for her, didn't mean she felt the same way about him.

The problem was she had never told anyone of her visions. Not her da or anyone. Would he think her mad? But she had to tell him. She would never forgive herself if she did not warn him when maybe her words could help him in seeing the danger before the man struck him from his horse.

"I worry about you on the battlefield. You must be extra vigilant this day."

Her da smiled in a mean-hearted way. "You have never worried about me before. I am always vigilant. How do you think I have managed to live so long? Be off with you so I might visit with my men before the battle."

She couldn't tell her da exactly what was on her mind. He would think she was cursed, a witch, maybe dangerous to him and his people. "Just…be careful."

"And me?" Seamus asked, his golden hair hanging about his shoulders, his brown eyes challenging her. "Should I be careful too, Brina?"

"You will be fine." *Unfortunately.* She set Seamus's porridge in front of him, then hurried off. She had tried to warn her da, but she was afraid to do much more than that. She caught Lynette's eye. The woman was about four years older than her and served as her companion. She knew nothing of Lynette's family, but the woman was mindful of her position as Brina's personal companion, and nothing more. It bothered Brina that they couldn't have been equals and truly friends, even sisters. But every time she'd pushed for more, Lynette had stepped back as if not wanting the friendship, or afraid of having it.

They had practically grown up together, her uncle and aunt, who had had also died, raising Lynette at the shieling not far from her own. And when her da hadn't been around, Brina and Lynette had played like sisters. But that had all changed when Brina's mother died. Her da had forbidden Brina see Lynette, but wouldn't give a reason. That was until he became chief, Brina became a lady, and Brina's uncle and aunt died of a sickness. Their son, Christophe, had joined the guards in service, and Brina's da allowed Lynnete to be her companion.

Brina was delighted, hoping they could become fast friends now, but it hadn't happened.

Lynette never seemed to find any pleasure in a man's company, nor did she seem to enjoy any of the festivities her da would have from time to time. Brina thought she was like her in that respect. Lynette's hair was a light brown, but her eyes just as blue. Lynette was the same height as Brina, maybe a wee bit taller.

The one thing they did enjoy doing together was plying their talent at archery. Not just for a social pastime either, but as a way to defend Anfa Castle if they needed to.

Brina never confided in anyone about her feelings concerning her da or Seamus and his men. Not even with Lynette. Likewise, Lynette never discussed how she felt about anything either.

Though they both had their roles to play in regard to the running of the household, Brina thought Lynette was distant acting about belonging to the clan. She'd tried to talk to her about it, but Lynette wouldn't or couldn't tell her anything about herself. Maybe she'd been too young when Brina's aunt and uncle had taken her in.

Yet there was something even odder about her. The way Brina would catch Lynette watching her and Brina wondered if she knew that Brina had a gift. Maybe she was afraid of Brina. She wished she could confide in someone, but she dared not.

As soon as thirty of the Auchinleck clansmen ate their fill and left the castle to fight with their neighbors, a group of Vikings who had settled near their lands, Brina was filled with dread. Every time they fought, she feared her da would be injured or killed. Since she had seen him fall from his horse in a vision hours before it could have happened, she feared what would become of the clan under Seamus's rule. And what would become of her.

Her da was a difficult man to live with, his temper triggered by anything—but it was the man he had taken into the clan that she dreaded most since her da had declared Seamus would marry her when it was time. If her da had truly died and not just been injured in the vision she'd seen, she knew Seamus would force the marriage as soon as he could.

She had hoped the time would never come. That instead, Seamus would fall in battle.

But she was always packed and ready for the eventuality because as her da grew older, it was inevitable. Could she escape the confines of the castle without anyone being aware of it though? That was her biggest fear. Seamus would want to kill her, she was certain, if he should catch her stealing away.

She finished her duties downstairs, supervising the kitchen staff and then the rest of the household staff for hours, before she headed up to her bedchamber to make last minute preparations to leave.

She had every intention of doing so and finding her way to her mother's family—the MacAffin, who had allied themselves with the MacNeills. Making it there by herself would not be easy, but she was bound and determined to do it. And hope they would take her in and not return her to her da for his disposition, believing he might still be alive, and she was his responsibility.

She had just reached her bedchamber when she

felt the strangest sensation of falling. *Her arm burning, she was lying on top of a man garbed in furs, his beautiful blue eyes staring back at her. He looked shocked and then his very kissable mouth curved up just a hint.*

Where had she seen those beautiful blue eyes before? Like a brilliant sky after a refreshing rainstorm?

She came back to her senses and realized she was having another vision.

Who was the man? She'd never seen him before. Yet there was a vague familiarity about him nudging at some distant memory — his eyes that had held her hostage and wouldn't let go. Because of the vision, she suspected their paths would collide when she escaped the castle. Would it be a good thing or not? She couldn't get the vision of his blue eyes out of her thoughts when she heard the men returning then to the castle, horses' hooves pounding the ground in the inner bailey, shouts for help, chaos. Weeping women cried out when they learned their loved ones had been wounded or killed.

Brina hurried back down the stairs to find to her da when she saw some of the battle-weary men in the keep. They refused to look her in the eye as if afraid to acknowledge her unpleasant fate or maybe their own. They were dirty, bloodied, and a couple of the men limping.

She hated the fighting. Forever, she'd feared this day would come. Her da had been a hard man, having lost his wife, her mother, when Brina was younger. She'd always wondered if her mother had lived, would her da have been any less cruel.

"Where is my da?" she asked several of the men.

Everyone shook their heads. She rushed outside and searched all over the inner bailey, looking for her da, but other than a handful of wounded men, and two men who died after being brought back to the keep, her da was not among them.

"Where is my da?" she asked Seamus as he dismounted and a lad led his horse away.

She didn't wish to speak to the devil himself, but she had no choice since no one else would enlighten her.

"He is dead." Seamus smiled a little as if amused to see her distraught over the matter.

"Where is his body?" She wouldn't believe it until she saw him for herself. What if Seamus had ordered his men to leave her da on the field, injured and dying so that he could take over?

"Several of our men were left in the glen—all of them dead. A winter snowstorm approaches. We will bury our dead when we can. Prepare yourself to be my wife on the morrow." Then Seamus headed inside the keep, two of his men joining him.

She hurried into the room off the kitchen where they'd taken the wounded men, and helped to clean and bind their injuries. And then she slipped away to her chamber and paced across the rush-strewn floor, the fading light disappearing from her narrow window. She couldn't leave until Seamus was celebrating their victory with the clan.

She prayed another man would step forward and show the clan he had the courage and skill to fight Seamus and stand up for her people. But everyone seemed so ill at ease after returning from battle that she assumed no one had the mettle to challenge him. She couldn't say that any man truly made her heart sing. If her cousin, Christophe, returned and became chief, he would take a wife of his own and then she would be without a position. Better that than having to wed Seamus, she reminded herself.

But Christophe was gone again, not interested in clan politics, maybe even dead. They hadn't heard from him in two years. She assumed his leaving had to do with the way her da had favored Seamus over him. Mostly because he wasn't heavy handed like Seamus was. Now, she almost wished her da had wed her to some other clan chief to strengthen ties between the respective clans, rather than leave her to this fate.

She pulled on her brat and headed back down the stairs, intent on finding her da in the glen and ensuring he had not been left wounded on the field to die alone. She would do what she could for him.

As soon as she hurried outside and headed for the stables, one of Seamus's men roughly seized her arm, stopping her. "Where do you intend to go, Lady Brina?"

She held her chin high, narrowing her eyes at

him, not to be cowed by the man who towered over her, mud and blood spattered all over his clothing, face, and hands. He was a frightening figure, but she would not be intimidated. "To the glen where you were fighting to find my da. To say my good-byes."

"He is past needing them. Return to the keep as Seamus will wish you to join him at the table. We will take care of your da on the morrow as Seamus has said."

She assumed Seamus wished to wed her because he was from one of the other branches, and he thought marrying her would give him more of a say with her people. Her clansmen had decided who the next clan chief would be. It was not like in the Lowlands where they followed the Norman Teutonic way of naming the chief's son to guide the clan next. Here, the old ways remained. The strongest and most dominant of men would gain the position. Like an alpha wolf would take over a pack, the man who was best at leading the clan into fights—the strongest, most aggressive would be chosen. Which was just why her da had taken over once the old chief had died.

She wanted to shove her way past the hulking warrior, but she knew he would not let her pass and would report her behavior to Seamus. She saw Lynette in the inner bailey then, watching her, as if she knew what she was up to. Brina didn't want anyone to know what she was planning.

Brina stalked back into the keep and headed up

the stairs. She would try to take her horse out again when more of the men were inside the keep, preparing to celebrate. If she could, she would ride out of here, look for her da, and if he was truly dead, she would say a few words over him, then be on her way. But she didn't truly believe she could leave here on horseback. She figured she'd have to walk out, or she would be seen leaving.

The feasting was well on its way and she knew she'd pay dearly for not seeing Seamus in the hall when he had returned victorious from battle and he had told her she would sit with him.

The thought of marrying Seamus left her cold with worry. He wanted her only as a means of taking over the clan. He'd never shown a hint of affection for her, and she didn't delude herself into believing the situation between them would ever change. How could it when she despised him and his men?

She headed back outside the keep, found a couple of men caring for the horses, and some of the women still tending the wounded men near the stables. One of Seamus's men, Corak, looked in her direction as he led his horse into the stables.

She would never get past any of Seamus's men. Probably not her da's either. But especially not Seamus's men.

She began to take care of one of the injured men, giving him some ale to drink and thinking one of these men might tell her the truth about her da. "Did you see my da die in the battle?"

He shook his head.

When she was done, she went to the next man, settling a fur over him, and asking him the same question. And received the same answer.

Then she reached a man with a leg wound who nodded. "I seen him fall from his horse, his forehead bleeding, and he was still as death on the ground. But then I was struck from my horse and I dinna know what happened after that. No' until I arrived here. Seamus will wed you now, aye?" Culain asked. He was their blacksmith, but had been required to fight as well.

But as to the matter of wedding Seamus? Not if she could help it. She bound Culain's leg wound and gave him a tankard of ale.

Even if Seamus suddenly changed his ways, she could not tolerate him. Not after witnessing his cruelty toward others in the two years he'd lived with the clan. No love would ever exist between them. She'd argued with herself all that time over this—knowing this day would come and the role she had to play. Telling herself she had no choice. That someone in her position didn't marry for love. That she had only one role to play: manage the staff at the castle and satisfy her husband's needs, which meant providing him with a bairn.

"Rest," she told Culain, patting him on the shoulder. Had she been in charge, she would never have sent their blacksmith into battle.

If she hadn't intended to leave, she would have come by to check on him later. She wasn't about to give the man false promises.

Boisterous boasting and laughter filled the great hall, the men celebrating their victory with a feast and kegs of ale. She looked up at the gray sky and the mountains beyond. A light snowfall had already dusted everything in white. She'd never traveled anywhere other than the shieling where she used to live by the loch and the surrounding area. Her da had never permitted her to stray very far once she'd found the Viking lad wounded in the glen. Her da and the other men had ridden out there not to take care of his injuries, but to kill him, and she'd been horrified. When the men had returned with word that the wounded lad had made his escape, she'd been relieved, but then again concerned he would have died somewhere else from his injuries.

Experiencing her da's wrath when she'd disobeyed him in a fit of passion, twice, she had earned a lashing each time and so he'd quashed her rebellious nature right away.

Would Seamus be as dangerous if she chose to disobey him? She was certain he would be. He was cut from the same plaid, though he was no relation to her kinsmen. He had always looked at her in a way that was predatory and insulting—as if he knew she was his, and only waited for the day when he could claim her.

She finished caring for the last man and when she returned to the inner baily, she glanced in the direction of the stables. Two of Seamus's men were speaking to one another in front of them. She ground her teeth and hurried back to her chamber. As soon as she shut the door, someone knocked on it, and she jumped a little, dread pooling in every fiber of her being. "Aye?" she called out.

The door opened and Lynette peered in. "I beg pardon, Lady Brina, but Seamus wishes you at the meal straight away."

Torn between wanting to leave and avoid being married to Seamus, but wanting to stay here in her own home, she tried to reason this out. How bad could it get being married to him? He was only a man. Surely, he would see her as the woman who would be his wife and the mother of his bairn and treat her with some dignity and respect. He would not beat her, if she continued to run the household staff as she had always done. He couldn't act any worse toward her than her da had behaved.

Yet her stomach roiled with upset as she envisioned what it would be like now that Seamus was ready to claim the clan as his own and her along with it.

"My lady?" Lynette said, watching her with wide blue eyes. "He wishes you to come now and isna happy that you didna come right away to greet him when he first arrived home like a woman who is to be his bride. He is saying you asked about your da, but not about how he fared. He says he will have to train you to be a better wife. The longer you stay away from the feast, the worse it will be for you, I fear."

Brina could do this. She had no choice but to do this. She nodded, then left her chamber to join Lynette. The maid said nothing to her, behaving like most of the women there, knowing here they had no say in anything that went on. Though Brina's da had been careful not to antagonize Cook because she tended to make him pay for it in the way she could subtly ruin the taste of his food or give him stomach pains.

When Brina reached the great hall, the conversations and laughter continued, and she hoped she could take her place at the head table without anyone noticing her much. Maybe they would think she was just one of the kitchen staff, serving the meal and ale while she made her way to the table. But as soon as Seamus saw her, he glowered at her. She had insulted him by not greeting him as a warrior coming home victorious from battle, and instead had only cared about her da's welfare.

She had further affronted him by not joining him straightaway at the meal and instead taking care of the men's injuries. Everyone would know what had prompted her behavior. And watch expectantly to see how he handled a recalcitrant wife-to-be.

He didn't rise from the table to greet her, just watched her like a warrior who was ready to beat her for daring to insult him. She bowed her head a little to him in greeting, the conversation all around them slowly dying as she felt her heart shriveling.

He would be like her da, only worse. With Seamus, she would have to suffer his abuse in bed.

***

The chilling wind blowing the snow about, the flakes fat and heavy, Gunnolf had split off from a group of the MacNeill clansmen in the snowstorm, checking on those living farther away from the castle. They were concerned for their health in the winter storm, as Gunnolf headed for Wynne's shieling. She was an elderly woman, set in her ways. No matter how many times members of the Clan MacNeill tried to convince her to leave her shieling and move into the keep, she had refused. She reminded him of Helga, his *amma*, his grandmother, the woman taking care of him as if she were his mother when he was growing up. Helga had odd ways, just like Wynne, he had soon learned. Something about the woman touched a place deep inside him, just like his *amma* had done.

Maybe her reluctance to live at the keep was because of her strange ways, and she felt she would not be welcome.

Gunnolf had been gone for over a year, staying with the laird's brother, Malcolm, a laird now in his own right to help him with a fight with his neighbors. And then off to see Angus and the clan he now lived with. He'd only been at Craigly Castle since this morn, so this was the first time Gunnolf had seen Wynne in all that time, and he was anxious to visit with her.

He observed the cold, stone shieling in the

distance, dread worming its way into his blood when he saw no peat smoke curling above the chimney. Without a fire to warm her old bones, Wynne would freeze to death in this chilling snowstorm. She was said to have the gift of two sights or *taibhsearachd*. He'd heard tell of how she had seen the *taibhs*, or vision, concerning James and his discovering the pearl of the sea—the woman who had become his wife. That's how the *taibhsear* would share a vision—in cryptic words, unclear to any of them who heard her message as to what she really meant. Despite his grandmother having the same gift, Gunnolf had been wary of believing in such a thing until the woman James had wed had been rescued twice from the rough sea.

If Wynne could see what future events awaited them, why didn't she look to her own future and know she would be safer living among her clansmen within the walls of Craigly Castle? Maybe her gift told her that she would stay here in her own shieling until she died.

When Gunnolf had asked her a while back if she had ever seen a vision of *his* future, she'd only lifted a white brow. She didn't think he believed she could truly have the gift. But then she had shrugged and told him he would have his own place of honor at the head of his clan. Which made no sense at all. He would never be next in line to manage Craigly Castle. If James died, his son, when he was old enough, would be laird. If James's son died, one of his brothers or his cousin would take his place. Gunnolf would not be the head of anything there. If Gunnolf returned to his people's land, someone else would have taken over his family's farm by now.

Worried, Gunnolf moved his horse into the byre. He gave Beast some oats, then strode toward the door of the shieling and knocked. No response.

"Wynne, 'tis me."

When she didn't call out in greeting, Gunnolf opened the door. The shieling was empty, the sweet smell of heather and other dried flowers and herbs hanging from the rafters scenting the air, her bed covered in furs, neatly made. Everything was in place, the windows shuttered, the gloomy wintry light from outside spilling into the one-room home. A modicum of hope that she might have gone to stay with a neighboring sheepherder helped to settle his concern.

The weather worsened as the snow blew around and piled up against the shieling. He made a fire in the fireplace, then went out to the byre to take care of his horse. That done, he took a walk around the cottage, calling out Wynne's name in the whistling wind, just in case she had left her place and lost her way in the storm.

Still no response. He went back inside and began stripping off his fur cloak to warm himself by the fire. All he could do was pray that Wynne was staying with another family, keeping warm, and telling someone else's fortunes this blustery day when he heard movement outside the door.

He unsheathed his sword, Aðalbrandr, and rushed to the door, yanked it open, and saw the grizzled face of the woman who lived there.

Wynne scowled at him, her white hair covered in snow, her brown wool brat turned white from the flakes piled high on the woolen fabric. "What are you doing here?" she scolded, her voice high pitched and irritated, her blue eyes narrowed as she pushed him aside to enter her abode. He shut the door and blowing snow out. "Put Aðalbrandr away. 'Tis no' necessary to defend yourself against me."

He smiled at her tenacity. She had lived a hard life, had aches and pains, and yet she complained of naught. Even now, he saw her wince as she moved about her shieling, removing her cloak and hanging it on a peg.

Even as old as she must be, her face had a soft, grandmotherly look about it, the bridge of her nose dotted with freckles, and despite the narrowed eyes, they were kindly, all-seeing. "I thank you for the fire, but I was staying with the sheepherder, Rob MacNeill, and his wife, Odara. And then I knew you were here, and I had to return in this weather when you are no' supposed to be here. 'Twas a good thing I didna lose my way!"

He closed his gaping mouth and sheathed his sword. "I am glad to see you alive and well."

"Och," she said, waving a hand at him, dismissing his comment and making her way to the fire. "I will make you porridge, but then you must be on your way. I didna need rescuing. Do you think me daft? You are a warrior trained in the art of fighting. Not only that, but you are good of heart. She needs a champion, and I am no' that she."

"Who are you talking about?"

Wynne smiled a little at him, and then she scowled again. "What is the use of telling you that which you need to know if you dinna heed my words?"

Exasperated, he said, "I will return you to the sheepherder's dwelling so that you will stay warm and have company. Once the weather clears, I will go back to Craigly Castle to let James know you are well."

"You will do no such thing. You will do as I have said. Eat, then leave straight away."

"To where? In this storm? It would be madness."

She shook her head. "You are a Norseman. You live for the cold." She motioned to the storm raging outside. "This is naught to you."

True. He didn't mind the cold weather. But he did mind getting lost in it. "So I am... to rescue some woman?" He had learned long ago that even though he might not believe all of what Wynne had to say, enough of what she predicted in her cryptic way did turn out to be true, so he wasn't going to dismiss her concern outright. "What is her name?"

"That, I dinna know. She is frantic and I canna see her face, her hood hiding it from my view. I only know that she desperately needs your assistance. But I must warn you, she willna thank you for it. Still, I will feed you while your horse rests before you must be on your way."

He prided himself in doing what was right, whether it earned him thanks or not, though he would have a time of it aiding a woman in this weather, who did not wish the help. He took a seat at the table as he watched Wynne mix oats, water, and salt over the fire, stirring it with a wooden spurtle.

"Years ago, you fought alongside your da against the Sassenach and suffered a near-fatal sword wound and your kinsmen left you for dead," Wynne said, continuing to stir the oats in the water to keep them from lumping up.

He remembered waking to the horror of learning his father and many of his kin, two uncles, an older brother, and three older cousins, had died, the field strewn with bloodied bodies. Not just bodies. Family. And to his further shock, that those of his kinsmen who had survived had left him behind, the longboats slipping away into the mist-covered ocean.

"*Ja,* but what has this to do with the woman?" he asked.

Wynne waved her wrinkled hand at him again as if to dismiss his impatience. "You would not die that day, the fierce Norseman of five and ten winters that you were. You managed to steal a dead Sassenach's horse and ride far away from the bloody battlefield, bleeding, and losing consciousness."

He'd never admitted to anyone the nightmares he'd had about that day.

"You stayed in caves and a time or two in a byre, traveling for days, alone, but determined to reach your homeland."

Wynne had to have guessed. He never told anyone of his journey.

"You finally reached the Borders. You continued to ride until you made it to the Highlands. And..." — Wynne paused as if trying to recall the details of his journey that she should never have known — "a beautiful young girl found you. You thought she was Freyja, your goddess of love, beauty, fertility, war, death, and more. But she wasna and bound your wounds. When she went to seek help, you were certain you would not be welcomed by her kinsmen and traveled north until you reached our keep."

He barely heard Wynne's next words as he envisioned the dark haired girl, her blue eyes like pools of water, her concern still touching him today. He'd always wondered what had become of the lass.

"We were celebrating a feast day in honor of James being named our new laird, though he was but six and ten winters. Do you even remember? You just suddenly rode into the inner bailey as if you belonged there, head held proud, steel blue eyes daring anyone to fight you for the right to be there, your hand clutching the reins, the other secured to your blood-soaked chest. Everyone just stared at you as if they were seeing a ghost. Then you let go of the horse's reins and your face, though dirty, was wan as ash and you started to fall. James raced across the bailey and caught you, others running to help him. You were only — we guessed five and ten winters or so — due to your small size."

Gunnolf stiffened a bit. He had never been small.

Wynne sighed. "Suffice it to say, all activities abruptly stopped — the dancing, archery competitions, the sword fighting, and the games the children were playing. Everyone came to see the wild Norseman in his bloody clothes, pale as death, riding a stolen Sassenach horse. Fortunately, the Clan MacNeill took you in. They treated you as family, despite how unruly you had been."

James, the eldest of the MacNeill brothers, had fought with him in practice battle, and Gunnolf had taught him a Norseman's trick or two. Gunnolf had greatly admired the way the Highlanders had fought the Sassenach. So he had something in common with the clansmen.

"Desperately, you had wanted to return to your native lands, but our lady of the keep, who had run of the household staff, insisted you stay with us until you fully recovered from your wounds. And then, longer. You fought alongside the MacNeill men against their enemies for years until you have lived here nearly as long as you had lived in the lands of the north."

For years, he hadn't considered living anywhere else. Not when he'd found a home with the Clan MacNeill. He'd always been treated like one of James's brothers. And James's mother, Lady Akira, had regarded him as one of her sons.

"Your grandmother was like me." Wynne served up the porridge for him and then for herself.

He stared at her in shock. How could she truly know these things?

"Helga? She warned your father that he would die, and that many of your kinsmen would too. That you would find a new way of life amongst a different people. Your da didna want you to go with them then, fearing the Sassenach would take you prisoner and turn you into a slave. But you protested, saying she didna know the future. That you would be victorious. And you were. Only mayhap no' in the way you believed. You were lost to your own people, but you found a family here with the Highlanders, a new way of life amongst a different people, aye?"

"I must have spoken of this to you." Maybe when he was sick with fever.

"You know you havena. Not once have you mentioned what happened to your own kinsmen all the years you have lived here with us. You have buried the secrets of your survival. Or the nightmares you still have."

"No one wishes to hear of another man's journey through hell and back."

"On the contrary. Everyone likes a good

warrior's tale about beating death on so many levels."

He let out his breath in frustration. "All right. Mind you, 'tis no' that I fear the weather so much as I dinna take the danger to me or my horse while traveling in a blizzard such as this lightly."

"You were a young lad who was badly wounded and left behind to die. You were clever enough to steal one of the Sassenach's horses and make your way here. You had been injured and still, you were driven to complete your mission— return to your people and let them know what had happened to your da and the rest of your kinsmen. But the others who left you behind would have told them this. Instead, you were destined to help your Highland brothers win their battles and they were yours as well because you are part of the soul of this clan as much as they are. You are a grown man this time, battle-trained, and no' in the least bit wounded. You have naught to be concerned with."

He wondered how she had returned to her shieling in this snowstorm on foot and was none the worse for wear.

Wynne grabbed his empty bowl and her own. "Go, now. Find the woman and aid her. 'Tis what you do well, Norseman. You aid those in need."

"What if I *had* returned to my homeland?"

"It wasna your destiny to do so."

He didn't care for the idea that his fate had been predetermined. He liked to believe that man made his own destiny. "Is my grandmother still alive?" He threw on his wool brat and furs.

"What do you think?" Before he could answer, she said, "Of course she is. In your heart. Where it belongs."

True, he'd often thought of Helga's words of wisdom when he was at his lowest point at times in his life, but he was saddened to think she had passed before he could see her again. "So, I will find the woman soon and return her to Craigly Castle safe and sound?"

"I have told you all I know. Do you wish for me to do all of this for you?"

"Are you certain I cannot take you back to Rob's place?"

"Nay! I am here now. 'Twill take you in the wrong direction. Rob will check on me when the storm dies down. I will have Rob take word to our laird that you are on a mission of utmost importance. Now, go!"

"Thank you, Wynne," Gunnolf said.

"You will thank me later."

He suspected it would be *much* later. And he wasn't truly sure he'd have anything to be thankful for on this journey. Stooping, he left her abode and returned to the byre. After saddling his horse, he mounted and felt a hint of excitement and trepidation. Unlike when he was a lad, he had only one thought in mind — finding his way home. Now, he was leaving his home in the middle of a snowstorm at the advice of a woman who many said was mad. Not that he felt that way about

Wynne. She was more level-headed, if not a bit cryptic at times, than many people he knew.

Well, if he rode south and found nothing of interest, he would return to Craigly Castle, at least having given the task a chance.

After several hours of plowing through the snow, he reached another MacNeill shieling and sought shelter, thinking that whoever he would have to help would have to wait until he and his horse had warmed up a bit. It would not do to sicken his horse or himself before he found the lass. And in this weather, he didn't believe he'd find anything but snow and more snow.

When he knocked on the door, a redheaded woman holding a swaddled baby answered, but she was *not* of the Clan MacNeill.

Where in the world had Gunnolf ended up?

CHAPTER 2

Brina knew, as soon as she took her seat next to Seamus to share the evening meal with him in the great hall, things would not go well. He growled low to her, "Think you to slight me by turning your back on me after we won the battle? Think I dinna know that you are no' happy with this arrangement? We will marry in the morn, and I will be chosen to lead Clan Auchinleck after that. If you dinna do as I wish, I will deal with you as harshly as necessary. Mark my word. If you think your da was demanding, you havena seen how I will deal with you." His blue eyes snapped with fury as his mouth scowled even more. He hadn't even bothered to clean up, blood spattered in his blond hair and on his tunic. At least her da always washed up after a battle and changed into fresh clothes, leaving his soiled garments for the washerwomen to clean.

She knew nothing good would come of this. On the one hand, she owed her allegiance to her clan, to maintain the keep, to run it as well as she always had. She loved her people, the difficulty not being them. They strictly obeyed, no one daring to defy either her da or Seamus. Now that her da was gone, she knew she could never fight Seamus and her life would be forfeit once he married her.

"Eat," he ordered her. "And smile. You willna look like you are a precious lamb getting ready to be sacrificed for the whole of the clan."

As soon as he spoke the words, she realized just how true the analogy was, and just how much she resented it.

Her appetite having fled the moment Seamus and the men had returned to the bailey, she forced herself to choke down her smoked fish soup. It would be the last hot meal she would have before she fled the keep.

"And smile," he repeated, his eyes narrowed as he watched her.

She hated him, never more than now. At least where her da had been concerned, he'd had the right to order her about because he had been her da. But this man...

It was worse. By far, it was worse.

When Seamus had eaten his fill of food and drink, he turned his attention to her and ordered, "Go to your chamber."

He did not dismiss anyone else from the great hall. Only her. Was it because she had refused to drink? Refused to eat anything more than half her fish soup? Refused to smile? She'd tried to eat, but she'd felt ill and was afraid she wouldn't keep what little she'd eaten down.

Everyone in the hall quieted, watching her as she rose as stoically from her chair as she could, inclined her head a little to him in parting, and strode out of the hall with as much grace as she could muster, her skin burning with mortification.

When she reached her chamber, she closed the door, then hurried to the window to see what the weather looked like now. Snow was blowing all across the bailey, piled up four feet high in places. Beyond the walls of the keep, she couldn't even see the mountains or the burn the snow was coming down so heavily.

She was certain Seamus would come and beat her for her disobedience, even though until she was married to him, he had no right to touch her. But she thought if she could slip away in the snowstorm, she just might have a chance to get away.

Someone knocked on her door and she whipped around, her heart pounding. It couldn't be Seamus. Surely now that he felt he had claimed her, he would barge right in. "'Tis me, Lynette," the maid said.

Marginally relieved, Brina let out her breath.

Had Seamus released everyone from the meal now? She listened to the revelry below stairs.

She didn't think so. Not with all the loud

talking and laughing still going on in the great hall. "Come in."

Lynette hurried into the chamber carrying a chemise with small white flowers embroidered at the neckline, sleeves, and hem of the gown.

"What is this?" Not that Brina didn't know what it was, but the reason Lynette was bringing it to her this eve had her worried beyond measure.

"From Seamus. He had commissioned the chemise a week ago for you. He wishes for you to wear it tonight, my lady." Lynette laid it on the bed. She straightened and looked at Brina, watching to see her response.

Brina wouldn't touch it as if that would save her from what she would have to face when Seamus came to her chamber.

"You would do well to agree to whatever he wishes. He near killed a man who disobeyed him a fortnight ago. I doubt he would spare you if he felt you did not take kindly to..." Lynette's cheeks reddened, and she looked down at the floor. "Beg pardon. Only I wish not to have to tend to your bruises if it should come to that. Please, do as he asks. For all of our sakes."

"Because he will turn his wrath on all of you?"

"Mayhap. We are no' certain."

Brina wanted desperately to ask if anyone would stand up to the beast, but she was certain Lynette wouldn't know, and that if anyone had wished to do so, he would have spoken up before now. Everyone was too afraid. And Seamus had his close friends, five of them, who watched his back always. So if anyone wished to kill him, they'd have to kill six men, not just him.

"I am to leave this with you, help you to dress, and return to the great hall, signaling him that I have done as he asked."

Asked? Commanded, rather.

"Thank you," Brina said.

"You… you will not disobey him in this? Will you?" Lynette asked.

"What would you do in my place?"

"I would be grateful to be the lady of the keep. I would do everything in my power to ensure he was happy with me. I would bear his bairns. And I would run the keep as you have done."

"Aye. Thank you. Go then." She was surprised Lynette had said that much to her about anything. Did she really feel in such a way? If so, Lynette must have glorified him in her mind.

"You dinna need my aid in dressing, my lady?"

Brina shook her head. "I will manage. Just…give me time before you say I am ready. You know how I feel about this?"

Lynette nodded, her expression solemn.

Brina had known her since they were both little, and she was certain Lynette wasn't expecting her next move, but she quickly closed the gap between them and gave her a hug. When she let her go, both she and Lynette had tears in their eyes.

"Move quickly." Lynette curtseyed, then left, closing the door behind her.

Did Lynette know what she had planned? Brina hurried to pull out her pack, bow, and quiver of arrows.

Was she mistaken in feeling the way she did? Trapped, fearing for her life? For her people's existence? Was she making more of an issue of Seamus's role here? Maybe she was wrong, and he would be a dutiful, loving husband.

But she knew it would not be so.

He would force himself on her this very eve. Force himself, because she could not willingly allow him to have his way with her when they weren't married. And that would rile him even more. She would do anything to avoid such a condition tonight, tomorrow, and the next day, if she had the power to do so.

She paced across the chamber, and then decided, whether it would be the death of her or not. This was her choice. And no one could take that away from her.

She finished packing the small bag, dressed in her warmest wool gown, not white to blend in with the snow as she didn't have any such thing, but the lightest color she owned — a pale green kirtle and a wool brat that was as light colored as that. Beneath these, she wore a bright red gown, her best one, and the warmest. The layering would help to keep her warm. She changed into boots, slipped the brat over her head to form a hood, grabbed her quiver of arrows and bow, and hurried down the backstairs where she saw Lynette standing at the foot of the stairs, watching her. Brina's heart nearly leapt from her chest.

She'd been caught and she hadn't even managed to leave the keep yet!

The two women studied each other for a moment, but Brina saw no condemnation in Lynette's expression, nothing that said she would shout an alarm that Brina intended to escape her fate. And since Lynette was here, that meant she had not yet gone to the great hall to let Seamus know that Brina was ready for him. Lynette only bowed her head slightly, looking worried. She had told her to move quickly. She must have known what Brina planned to do.

Her heart in her throat, Brina continued on her way.

Her skin prickled with unease and her stomach was doing somersaults as she made her way to the servants' door that led outside. She hastened to the postern gate that should have been guarded, but all the revelry inside had the guards outside partaking in a bit of the ale too, and not as vigilant as they should be. Two men were still hunkered down near the stables and she assumed they were guarding the horses just in case she intended to try and leave on horseback and immediately stop her. Not to mention they would take her to see Seamus for making the attempt.

Her bow and quiver of arrows secure, she headed out. The snow helped to disguise her also as it collected on her clothes, cloaking her in the wet, white snowflakes. Snowflakes even caught on her eyelashes. The chilly wind whipped her brat about, and she so wished she could take her horse.

As soon as she was outside the massive, stone curtain walls, she ran, not stopping, the frigid air burning her lungs with every breath she took, the cold seeping into her bones. She wasn't certain she could find her da's body as much as the snow had already piled up in some areas, but she looked for him just the same. When she reached the battleground, she couldn't tell. She saw a couple of men mostly buried, all the blood covered in white as if nothing terrible had gone on here just hours earlier. They were two of her da's soldiers, dead. She continued to look, worried every minute she stayed here Seamus would realize she was gone and begin to search for her. But she hoped he'd be too much into his cups to want to leave the great hall early on, and that would give her a chance to run.

Hot tears cascaded down her cheeks as she surveyed the grounds one last time. Then she assumed that if her da had been severely injured, he was now dead, succumbing to his injuries and the cold. She would not survive herself if she didn't leave at once. She ran through the forest, the pine trees sheltering her and the ground somewhat from the snow so that it was easier to move. She ran as fast as she could far away from the castle, her home, and the only family she'd ever known.

***

Gunnolf hoped he would be invited into the shieling to warm himself, though he didn't want to impose on the poor woman. He wanted to ask which clan the woman and her husband belonged to. But he was reluctant to, certain they'd want to know which clan he was affiliated with and if they were enemies, it would not bode well. He couldn't believe he'd gone so far in the snow and gotten so disoriented when he had thought he was still on MacNeill lands.

"I am Gunnolf, and beg that you allow me a chance to warm myself at your fire for a short while before I head out again."

The woman looked at her husband, sound asleep on a plat, not stirring. Her baby was sleeping in her arms, and she turned her attention again to Gunnolf. "If you are quiet." She looked like she wasn't happy about the situation, but Gunnolf was wearing a sword, and he assumed he looked fearsome and like he wouldn't be dissuaded.

"Is he ill?" Gunnolf asked, concerned. If he had been sleeping there, Gunnolf would have immediately risen from the plat with sword in hand to ensure his wife and bairn were safe from the intruder.

"Nay," she said softly. "He walked miles from here in this weather and finally managed to make it home. I thought I had lost him."

"'Tis good he made his way here in this blizzard."

"What about you? Sit." She motioned with her

head to the hearth.

Gunnolf pulled off his furs, laying them on the floor, then took a stool and sat beside the fire. "I was traveling when the storm hit with full force. I am not sure where I am now."

"Where were you headed?"

"South. I was told to go south. That a woman would need my help."

"What woman?" She poured Gunnolf some ale.

He shrugged. "A *taibhsear* only told me the direction to head and that a woman needed my aid. She did not have a name for her. Or where she was located exactly."

The woman's brown eyes widened. "This woman you spoke with has the *taibhs*?"

"*Ja.*"

"Do you believe in such a thing?"

"Enough to venture in this direction to find the woman, if I had headed the correct way. You... would not perchance know of such a woman, would you?"

She shook her head.

Then they heard a man shout outside the shieling, "Dinna kill her! Or Seamus will kill you!"

Instantly, Gunnolf was on his feet, his blood pounding. He grabbed his furs and fastened them over his shoulders, unsheathed his sword, and rushed outside into the blinding snow to see what was going on. He couldn't see anything, only heard the whistle of an arrow flying toward him. And then felt a soft body slamming into him, knocking him back against the powdery, chilling snow.

The arrow hit a distant tree with a thwack!

For a moment, he didn't move, and the woman didn't either, her body pressed against his, warming him, tendrils of dark brown curls tickling his cheek. The horses ran past them, the riders unable to see them in the snow. Once they had ridden past, the woman tried to get off Gunnolf. She was all softness and curves, except for her sharp knee digging into his groin.

He groaned and grabbed her leg to pull it away, forcing her to straddle him. Not exactly what he had in mind, but it was better than getting kneed to death.

With renewed gusto, she struggled to get free of him.

"Nay, lassie, be still," he said, his voice gruff and a command, but low, for her ears only. He didn't want the riders to come back this way prematurely.

"Nay, you devil," she said. "Let me go!"

He noted the woman in the shieling had closed the door, either to keep out the cold, or avoid being in this fight.

"You saved my life. I wouldna harm you," Gunnolf said, trying to get past her defenses.

"'Tis my life I was attempting to save, you beast. No' yours. Let me go."

He smiled darkly at her, despite the circumstances and rolled her onto her back, pinning her down. Blood spotted the snow from her upper sleeve. He narrowed his eyes. "You have been wounded."

"A nick, naught more. I barely feel it. I wouldna have suffered even that much if you hadna been in my way. Now, let me go," she growled.

Men shouted off in the distance, still moving away from their direction. "Over here! She had to have gone this way!"

"In this blowing snow, how can you tell!" another man replied.

"They are after you?" Gunnolf asked. This couldn't be the woman he was bound to aid, could it be? Well, even if it wasn't, he was now tasked with the duty.

"You too, now," she said, her blue eyes hard with annoyance.

"I will save you." He lifted his sword.

She snorted. "Against six of them?"

"Aðalbrandr and I have fought against worse odds."

"That is what you call your sword? Or do you mean someone else?" She studied him a moment as if she wondered if he had spoken the truth. He *had* told the truth. Except a couple of the times that he had fought such odds, he'd ended up in a dungeon. But he didn't believe she needed to know that much information.

"*Ja*, my sword."

"What does it mean? This Aðalbrandr?"

"Noble sword." He saw a bow and quiver of arrows secured to her pack and lifted his gaze to look up at the lass.

"What? I may no' be able to wield a great sword, but I can shoot a man with an arrow if warranted."

"Seems to me you were not shooting at the men, but seeking refuge," he said.

"If I had the spare time, I would take care of the six men following me. Especially the one shooting at me!"

"All six men?" He smiled and shook his head. "Have you another plan? Do you know the lay of the land?" he asked, hopeful. Maybe she knew the direction they could go, and he could get them back to Wynne's abode without encountering these men further.

"Aye, of course. I live here." She eyed him for a moment further, then frowned. "Very well. Either I have to face those devils or *you*. There is only *one* of you. Och, I will have to try and save you too now. 'Twas only me who was in danger before, but you had to get in my way."

He smirked at the challenge in her words. She rose to a crouch and looked like she was about to bolt away from him when he seized her arm.

She turned to glower at him, her expression furious. "You will have to follow my lead or I will have no choice but to leave you behind."

Unless she lived in the woods near here and was used to this kind of weather, he didn't believe she could leave him behind and succeed at wherever she intended to go. He said quietly, "I have a horse in the byre."

"A horse?" Her eyes grew round and her expression instantly brightened. "Why didna you say so in the first place?" She shoved at him to let her up.

He pulled her to stand, then holding her wrist, not trusting she wouldn't try to slip away, he headed into the byre. After saddling his horse, he mounted and pulled her up onto the horse's back so that she was sitting behind him. "I am Gunnolf. May I know your name, lass?"

"Gunnolf..." She pondered his name for a moment. "Oh, oh, you are... you are no' a Highlander. *You* are the Viking I found wounded in the glen!" She sounded angry.

"That was *you*." He turned and observed her for a long moment, the woman now full grown, her hair dark still, her eyes still blue, her lips even more appealing. Then he said under his breath. "The goddess." He'd thought for sure the goddess had come to take him to her land. He sighed and moved his horse out of the byre. "I have lived among Highlanders nearly as long as I have lived among my own kind. But *ja*, 'tis a Norseman's name."

"What does it mean, this Gunnolf of the North?"

"Fighting wolf."

"I should have known." She did not say it in a pleasant way.

"I thank you for taking care of my wound. I thought you were interested in aiding me, but I did not think your people would feel the same way."

"They were ready to kill you. I went to my shieling to get the cart to haul you home, but when I returned, you were gone."

"You did not tell them about me?"

"Of course I did. I thought you were in need of help. But when I saw the way the chief and his men reacted with the look of murder in their eyes, I knew they would hunt you down. How did you manage to live?"

"It was not my time to die."

Many Norsemen had settled in the area for the last hundred years or so. Maybe some of them had stolen from her family's lands, cattle, sheep, or something else. So he understood the animosity she might feel. "What is your name?"

"Brina. It means strong in Irish. My mother named me such because she'd lost two male bairns in infancy. But I was strong and survived. Though in Gaelic it means, defender, and since I saved you from those brutes, you can thank me for defending you."

He stifled a chuckle. In no way had the lass protected him. It was the other way around. "And the clan you are with is?"

She wrapped her arms tightly around his waist, her body snug against his, her head resting against his back, and he suddenly felt very warm despite the chilly snow blowing in his face. Then he worried, would she be able to direct them if she couldn't see around him?

"Lass, mayhap you should sit in front of me, so you can tell me the way to go." Though he didn't wish her to suffer the full blast of the cold wind's force while riding in front of him, but he didn't want to be riding around in circles either.

"In this weather? I canna see anything. Just move away from the sounds of the men shouting."

Gunnolf shook his head and hoped he guided his horse in a northerly direction toward the MacNeill lands and not farther away from where they needed to go. If he could get the lass to Wynne's shieling, Wynne could tell him if he had aided the right woman.

Though he assumed she had to be the one. She didn't seem grateful in the least, rather that he was supposed to be grateful to her. "If I am to rescue you from those brigands, may I learn why you are running from them?"

She didn't respond, her body holding his close, her head still resting snug against his back. He had to admit he loved feeling her close. Had even dreamt about her and was glad for it when the nightmares had returned. Only now she was not a young lass, but a woman full grown.

"I believe I was dazed by your beauty the last time we met," he said, softly, remembering that part of his journey with fondness.

"More like you were nearly dead."

He smiled. She had been beautiful back then. He had not been too dazed to witness that.

She sounded sleepy, her voice muffled against

his back. He wondered how long she had been running. Was it the same castle that she thought to get help from when he was but a lad? Was she running from the same people who would have killed him?

"Brina. 'Tis a lovely name for a bonny lass." He didn't say anything more as he listened for the sounds of horses or men. He heard nothing but the whoosh of the wind blowing across the glen and the rush of a river in the distance. He hadn't crossed any rivers to get there. Several streams, but no rivers.

God's wounds, where were they now?

CHAPTER 3

Brina cherished the heat of the Norseman's warm body in front of her, and the way he blocked the frigid wind and kept the snow off her face. But she did not like that he was a Finn-Gall! Not with all the trouble they'd had with them. What if he was kin to those who had settled near them? The same ones who had killed her da?

Her own grandfather had died at the hand of Viking raiders before the Vikings settled on the lands near them and became farmers.

She wasn't certain how long she'd been running before Seamus had discovered she'd slipped out of the keep and beyond the castle walls, then gathered his men to hunt her down. But she welcomed this—the Norseman's rugged body as he protected her, and his horse that gave her hope that she might indeed manage to slip away from her lands without any trouble. Her feet and fingers were frozen though, and she didn't think she'd ever been this cold in her life.

She snuggled closer to the Viking, wanting to be wrapped up tight with him, to feel the warmth taking the chill from her blood. But she felt badly that she didn't know where they actually were. Because she never ventured very far from Anfa Castle or the shieling where she'd lived before that, she wouldn't have a clue where to go even if it was a warm, summer's day. Exhausted from running, she was relieved to have collided with the man, and learned he not only had a horse, but that he seemed intent on rescuing her.

Still, she didn't wholly trust him. He was a Finn-Gall after all, and she wasn't sure she could have complete faith in him that he would take her somewhere safe and not ask something of her in return. She had to admit that the Vikings living near her people only raided them as much as they raided the Norsemen back.

What if this Gunnolf of the North, the Fighting Wolf, lived among the Viking settlers and wished to ransom her to Seamus? Or what if Gunnolf was as wicked as Seamus? Just because Gunnolf treated her well now, didn't mean she would be safe with him if they found a place to bed down for the night later. He could want his wicked way with her just as much as Seamus had wanted. Except for now, Gunnolf had to bide his time or he was a dead man. Which had her feeling a pang of remorse that she had involved him in this deadly business. Though she was not feeling enough guilt to force him to release her. She highly doubted Gunnolf would anyway. For now, she was more afraid of Seamus getting hold of her as angry as he had to be. Not only had she shown him she wouldn't submit to him of her own freewill, she had forced him to come after her in a snowstorm to bring her home.

He'd beat her for certain if he got hold of her.

She thought back to when she'd planted her body against Gunnolf's next to the shieling, not really meaning to. But when she dove for the pile of snow to avoid being struck by an arrow, all of a sudden a mountain of a fur-covered man had loomed in her path. Just like that. What else could she do but tackle him with all her weight and shove him down so she didn't get shot? Not that she wanted him to either, but he had been in her way. Which was why the arrow had nicked her! It was his fault that he was now in this predicament with her.

She thought about how she'd tried to climb off him, and she'd made him groan in pain. He'd been hard all over, and she couldn't understand how she'd hurt him. But when he'd forced her to straddle him, she wasn't sure what his intentions had been, until she realized he was trying to protect himself from her wicked knee. She let a smile slip, but then frowned again, worried they wouldn't find shelter tonight, and if they did, what if Seamus found it also?

Gunnolf was a handsome devil of a man, for

being a Viking. Large, bearded, his hair more chestnut now and streaked with gold, his blue eyes disarming, he was a compelling figure of a warrior. She still couldn't believe he was the lad she'd bandaged so long ago and that he'd actually survived. She'd had reoccurring dreams about finding him and taking care of him, but then losing him in the mist. But she'd never envisioned him so tall or muscular. "Are you all right?" she asked.

"*Ja*, but I must rest my horse and get us out of this..."

His abrupt pause in speech concerned her. "What?" She wanted to sit up and peer around him, but decided she didn't wish to see what was ahead of them as much as she wished to remain tight against his back and continue to gather what warmth she could absorb from his body.

"An old Roman ruin, some of the outer curtain walls partially standing. A tower keep is sitting inside. Mayhap we can take refuge in it. It appears to have lost its roof, but inside the tower, we can at least take shelter from the winds."

"Aye," she said. "It would be better than being out here in all this weather." Then she sat up a bit taller, but losing his heat, she squeezed up against him again. "What if they are there?"

"We will have to take that chance. My horse needs rest, and we canna afford to lose him." He moved slower now toward the tower.

She listened for sounds of men talking, but unless Seamus and his men were huddled inside and trying to keep warm, maybe sleeping, she heard no one.

Then she felt the sudden shift in temperature, the ancient stone walls blocking the wind so effectively, she felt much warmer, not enough to release her hold on the Viking, but still, she sighed with relief. "No sign of them?" she whispered.

"Nay, lass. We are alone."

That sent a sudden chill up her spine, and it had nothing to do with the frigid weather.

"I will help you down," he said, his voice hushed, and she suspected he said so because she still hadn't released her grip on his body as if she was afraid, when it wasn't that at all! She was attracted only to the heat of his body. She would have felt the same if it had been anyone's body. Well, mayhap not if it had been Seamus or any of his men.

Reluctantly, she let go of Gunnolf and he swung down to the dirt floor, then reached up to help her dismount. "It will be dark soon." He set her on her feet. "I have enough bedding so that we can bundle up together, and my horse should be fine here."

When he mentioned bundling up together, she eyed him warily. He did not entertain any notion that she would want to satisfy some male need, did he? Though as cold as it was, she couldn't imagine anyone wanting to do such a thing. And yet, a wicked thought flickered through her mind so quickly, she couldn't believe she would think such a thing — of being naked with the Viking beneath the furs, of kissing him, and more.

A light amount of snow covered the floor, but it wasn't nearly as deep as outside the walls where it had blown into drifts, the tall stone walls of the keep blocking most of the snow and the wind. Gunnolf caught her attention as he brushed the snow away from an area of the floor with his boot.

She eyed the bedding as he spread it out over the cleared area. She shouldn't want to lie with a man she didn't know, or any man who was not her husband, for that matter, but she wouldn't have it any other way as warm as he had already kept her. She had seen what the cold could do to a body when someone had been out in it for far too long without proper clothing. Blackened toes and fingers. Not a pretty sight. So though she felt uncomfortable sleeping with the Viking to an extent, she knew that she had no other choice.

As soon as he finished spreading out the bedding, he turned to feed his horse some oats. And then he offered Brina ale and a piece of bannock. In silence, she sipped the ale, then chewed on the bannock while she sat on the makeshift bedding. After covering his horse with a spare blanket, which she thought was admirable that he took care of his mount just as much as he took care of their needs, he pulled out a length of cloth. "Let me see your arm, lass."

"'Tis naught."

"*Ja*, but I would have a look at it anyway."

She let out her breath and pulled back her brat to reveal her sleeve. He tore the brown sleeve, making her wince. He paused for a moment as he saw a red sleeve after that. He smiled. "How many layers do you have on, lass?"

"Dinna tear my red kyrtle overmuch. 'Tis my favorite and the warmest of my gowns."

He pulled out his *sgian dubh* and then made a small slice in the red sleeve. "You will be able to mend it easily."

She gave a lady-like snort. Easy for him to say since he didn't have to do the mending. But she watched in fascination the way he blotted up the blood and took great care not to hurt her. Then he tied the piece of cloth around her arm and looked up at her, frowning. "It will heal, no stitches necessary. Let me see your fingers."

She showed him her fingers, still cold, a little numb, and they were burning.

"They look good, the color is good. Now your toes."

She couldn't help but look affronted. His mouth curved up a bit, which had the effect of making her body instantly heat. "They are fine."

"I have warmed myself by a couple of fires today. Have you?" Gunnolf folded his arms across his broad chest, looking down at her like she was a stubborn child.

She shook her head.

"Then I will remove your boots and check your feet to make sure your toes are not too cold. That is if you dinna wish to lose them, lass."

Exasperated, she finally nodded and pulled her cloak tightly about her as he removed one boot, and then a damp sock, and took her cold, numb foot into his hands and began to rub it.

"It burns." She tried to pull away from him.

"'Tis good. If you had no feeling in them, then that would be worse." He removed her other boot and sock. "I know how to warm them, but you might not like what I have to say. However, your feet will thank you for it later if you allow me to offer my aid."

She narrowed her eyes at him, wondering just what he might suggest that she would not like. Both of them naked came to mind, and she scolded herself for thinking such thoughts yet again.

"As much as it will chill me, if you put your feet between my legs, my body will warm them and make them feel just as they did before you undertook this journey in the snow."

"Nay," she said, shocked to the core.

"'Tis your choice, lass. But if we dinna warm them, you could lose all feeling in them on our continued journey. The truth is it will be me who will suffer much more than you. Though for a while, your feet will burn. But this is a good thing. You wouldna want to know what happens when a man or woman loses the feeling in their toes or fingers completely."

"I have seen what happens," she said softly. "What must I do?"

"I will sit sideways in front of you and place your feet between my thighs." Gunnolf resituated himself on the blankets and waited for her to agree.

She shuddered from the cold and from the idea he would be so intimate with her. Yet the notion he would take her frozen feet and place them against his skin to help warm her when it would chill his own skin made her realize just how much he was willing to sacrifice for her — not just with warming her feet, but with attempting to keep her from Seamus's grasp.

"Why?" she asked.

"So that your feet have a chance to warm up again before we continue on our journey."

"Nay, why are you risking your life for me?" She pulled the blanket from her feet and offered them to him.

He lifted his blue and green plaid enough that she saw his bare, muscular legs, and then he maneuvered her so that they were positioned between his legs, the soles against the inner thigh on his left leg, and the tops of her feet pressed against the inner thigh of his right leg. Then he pulled down his plaid and covered himself and her with the furs.

He didn't even shiver as her cold flesh pressed up against his hot skin. "Better?" he asked.

"They are burning."

"Good. They will warm up and you will feel better."

"What about you?"

He smiled, and she thought his look was a bit — mischievous. "I will suffer silently."

So would she. She couldn't help thinking of the way her feet were situated between his legs. He was pressing with his thigh muscles, not just offering a warm place for her feet to rest, but ensuring that the contact between them provided even more heat to warm her feet. She closed her eyes and all she could envision were his naked legs when he'd pulled up his plaid, and how she'd wanted to see more. It was his fault that he had intrigued her so!

"I thank you," she finally said, looking up at him, his blue gaze on her, then held up her hands. "My fingers are cold, too."

***

Gunnolf smiled at the lass, wondering just where she wanted to place her ice cold fingers. But he would do anything to warm her up and prove to her that he only wished to aid her. It would be awkward from the way they were now situated for him to slip her hands against his bare skin. He offered his hands and she placed her chilled fingers in them. Then he closed his hands around her small ones and warmed them both up.

She was a beauty, her cheeks rosy from the cold, her dark hair falling about her shoulders in a cascade of shiny curls, her lips as red as her cheeks. Her eyes were blue and bright and worried. He couldn't believe she was the same lass who had come to his aid before. Or that she would be out in this weather, running for her life.

"What about *your* feet?" she asked.

"They will be fine." Though the thought of his feet locked between her thighs made him imagine other possibilities. And that notion heated his blood right away.

"They must be freezing," she said.

"I will tend to them when your feet are feeling nice and warm."

She said, "I will help you."

He smiled at the notion, but he would not let her do such a thing. He was afraid if he put his ice cold feet against her bare skin, she'd be chilled too much.

"You have not eaten yet," she said.

"I will eat when your fingers are sufficiently warmed. So tell me, lass," he said quietly, "who are you running from and why?" Now that he'd had a chance to consider her garments, he was certain she was a woman of some importance. Not just a sheepherder's daughter as she appeared to be when he'd first seen her so many years ago.

"What clan are you with?" she asked him first.

He wished he knew where she was from and who had harmed her. If she was from an enemy's clan, he was certain she wouldn't wish to tell him who she was. She needed his help, no matter which clan she hailed from.

He sighed. "I am with the Clan MacNeill."

Her eyes widened and her whole posture stiffened.

"I mean only to protect you and take you

somewhere safe," he said.

"To where? To the MacNeill stronghold?"

"The MacNeills will protect you. No one will harm you. It appears to me that whoever hurt you and wants you to return at once is the enemy here, not me or the clan I have grown to love."

Tears clung to her eyelashes and she stifled a sob.

"Lass," he said, just about to pull her into a hug, but she shook her head quickly.

"Nay, my feet are still cold."

"All right, lass. Why are you so distressed at the mention of my clan?"

"My mother was of the Clan MacNeill. She was a MacAffin."

Gunnolf closed his gaping mouth.

"She was sent away from the MacNeill castle before I was born. But she was carrying my brother and he didna live. This was probably before your time and you might no' have heard anything about it."

"Which clan are you with now?" He tried to keep the anger out of his voice. He couldn't imagine any woman carrying a bairn being treated in such a manner.

"Auchinleck."

"I don't recall anything about them. We must not have any trouble between us."

Brina looked down at their joined hands. "She... my mother, that is... was said to be... wild. But when the laird learned she was with bairn, he sent her away."

"Where was her husband?"

She shook her head.

"She had none?" Gunnolf considered that notion for a moment, but he would think that if anyone had mistreated the woman like that, the laird would have sent men after her and returned her home. Then he frowned, another notion coming to mind, knowing how lecherous the former laird was. "The laird himself was the father of the bairn?"

Brina let out her breath and nodded.

"Your mother…she is…no more?"

Brina shook her head. "She died a year before I met you."

"What was her name?"

"Davina."

Gunnolf stared at Brina in disbelief. He had not joined the clan until two years after the incident, but it had still been fresh on everyone's minds. The woman had worked in the kitchen and was said to have been wild and untamable and had run off three times from the castle that year. Some said it was because James's father had had his way with her; others said because he had not. But Gunnolf hadn't known the woman had been carrying a bairn. He wondered if anyone else had known, or if only the lass had. Maybe the laird.

"Then…I am taking you where you belong. To my home now. And even more your home as your mother was from the clan," Gunnolf said with some relief. "James, son of the previous laird, now rules the clan. You have nothing to fear from him. He is good of heart and would never turn away a woman in need."

Brina didn't seem eager to embrace the idea.

"Lass, what is the matter? Surely you see you belong with the MacNeills."

"In truth, I had hoped to. But what if I tell them who my mother was?" She shook her head. "I know what the people will say. That I am like my mother. Especially since I have run away from my own keep."

"The laird isn't like his father. So you have no need to be concerned there." Then Gunnolf wondered if she *was* like her mother, running off in the middle of bad weather with no goal in mind. "You are not with bairn, are you?"

She tried to pull her hands away from his.

"Nay, lass." He held her tight. "The Clan MacNeill took me in, a wild Norseman, not that you are wild like that. They showed me kindness and that I belonged when I had never thought I would feel such a thing unless I was home with my own kin. You will be safe."

"The Clan Auchinleck is my clan," she said, her words tight with anger. "They are my people. When no one from the Clan MacNeill would protect my mother, my da and his people did. But Seamus, whom my da had entrusted the clan to when my da died, will destroy the heart and soul of my clan. Aye, I could live with you and the Clan

MacNeill, and I am sure from what you say that I would be allowed to stay there, but accepted? I am no' sure about that. They are no' my…, well, my mother was a MacAffin, allied with the MacNeill, and they had pledged their loyalty to the old laird. Maybe some of the rest of the MacAffin married the MacNeill and their offspring would be related to me. But what of my da's people? They will have to live with Seamus's rule and suffer for it."

"Your father was chief of your clan? You are Lady Brina then."

"You didna know me as such before. I am the same as then." She spoke as if she really believed she could be the lass that he had met so long ago.

But she wasn't. She was vital to the clan as a means to make an alliance with another clan through marriage.

Gunnolf didn't know what to say. He wasn't sure what she wished of him. She wouldn't be able to rid the clan of Seamus on her own. Rescuing her was one thing, but fighting Seamus and all those who followed him? "You dinna wish to return there, do you? You must have escaped from there, if you were running all alone in the wilderness during the height of a snowstorm."

"It is my home." She let out her breath. "But my da also declared I would be wed to Seamus. The man wished it of me the morning following my da's death. Could he no' have at least given me time to grieve? Except Seamus had no intention of waiting for the wedding to bed me," she said bitterly, her cheeks even growing redder and this time Gunnolf thought from embarrassment.

"Then you canna return there. Unless you have had a change of heart concerning Seamus."

"I havena." She wiggled her toes and moved them against Gunnolf's thighs, making his staff tighten further. "My feet are warm."

His blood was sizzling. "Are you sure, lass?"

"Aye and you need to eat."

"All right, but only if you are certain."

She pulled free of him, and then moved around to crouch at his feet. He couldn't believe it when she untied his boots and pulled off one and then the other. Then she slipped off his wet socks and wrapped her warm hands around one of his feet.

"Your feet are ice cold. Do they burn?"

From just her hands on his foot, he felt his whole body heat. Not just his feet. "*Ja*, lass."

"I canna hold your feet between my legs as you have done for me as I am no' as strong as you. But, mayhap I could sit on them?"

He envisioned her sweet bare arse sitting on top of his feet and thinking how much he wished she was sitting on other parts of his anatomy that stirred to life even more from the words she had spoken and the way her soft, warm hands felt pressed against his foot.

He couldn't say yes or no. He wasn't the most talkative of men normally, but he really couldn't find his tongue. He thought she meant to keep her kyrtle and chemise wedged between her arse and his feet, and nodded. But when she lifted the layers of her gowns slightly and planted her sweet, naked arse on top of his feet, he was shocked.

She frowned and he started to pull his feet out from under her, thinking his icy, cold skin had chilled her too much when she placed her hands on his legs and held him down. The woman had a strength he didn't believe she could possess as petite as she was. And the pressure she exerted on him made his thoughts drift to carnal pleasures again. He couldn't help thinking of her in that way — not after she had shoved him down in the snow when they first came into contact, tightened her sweet body against his when riding together, and now this.

"Stay. The worst of the cold will go away," she said.

The cold she was feeling? Or the cold he was feeling?

"Talk to me," she said. "The way you are looking at me when you are so silent unnerves me."

He cleared his suddenly very rough throat. "My feet are burning." And so was the rest of him, but he wasn't sure she would understand about that.

She nodded. "Which is a good sign. Aye?"

"*Ja.*" He hid a small smile.

"Why are you out here in this weather?" she suddenly asked, sounding suspicious. "Surely, you are no' running away from anyone or anything, are you? Why were you at that shieling? I assume it was not your own if you are with the Clan MacNeill. And I dinna believe I ran far enough away from my castle to have reached your lands."

Would she believe in an old woman's visions? He had no reason to make up any other tale.

"A woman told me I needed to travel south of our lands to aid a woman. Now, if you are the woman, I am in luck. If you are not, I still have to find the other one."

"You are serious?" she asked. "You went where you have never been before, searching in this terrible storm for a woman you didna know at all because a *taibhsear* told you so?"

"She is like my *amma*, my grandmother. And though she can sound ambiguous and abrasive to some, she has lived a hard life and I respect her and her ways. She would not ask me to do anything that she truly didn't believe in. Not everyone understands a *taibhsear*'s ways."

"Do you?"

He shrugged and fished a bannock from his pouch. "Even if I did not, it seems to me I have rescued you." He chewed on his bannock.

"Whether or no' I am the one you were supposed to aid."

"*Ja.*"

She studied him for a moment while his thoughts returned to the way her sitting on his feet was heating him thoroughly.

"My mother was supposed to have the gift of two sights," she finally said, watching him carefully.

Gunnolf frowned at her, surprised first that her mother had the visions, but secondly, that Brina would share this with him. The way she observed him, he knew she was trying to determine how he viewed the news. So maybe Brina believed in them. "My *amma* was supposed to have as well."

"Your grandmother?" She raised her brows.

"*Ja.*" He frowned at Brina, wondering if she had the gift also. His grandmother's talent had not passed down to him though. "Do you have the ability?"

Brina lowered her gaze from his face to her lap. "Are your feet warm yet?"

Her reluctance to explain that she had the gift made him think she did. But he also knew some believed those who could see such things would think they were witches.

If she did have any visions, had she seen him in one? Maybe not, as she had seemed genuinely surprised to cross paths with him at the shieling. "If you are able to foretell some future happening and it has anything to do with running into Seamus or his men, I hope that you will feel free to warn me about it."

She studied him for a bit, then nodded.

He let out his breath. "Your secret is safe with me. I believe there are things in this world, and not of this world, that we cannot readily explain. Are you cold, lass?" He noticed then that her body trembled a little. He reached for her hand and pulled her down against him, not waiting for her reply.

She stiffened, but he kept her close to show she had nothing to be afraid of. Then he yanked the blankets and furs around them and over their heads. "We will share our body heat and naught more," he assured her, though truly, how could he not wish for more?

Thankfully, she did not stiffen or pull away from his over familiarity with her further, and she seemed to realize she was safe with him. It was good she could not know his true thoughts.

"So where do we go from here?" she whispered against his cheek.

He savored the touch of her warm breath on his cold skin as if they were lovers in a welcoming embrace on a frigid night. "We head north to see Wynne and learn if you are the right woman who needed my aid. And then, whether you are or not, I will escort you to Craigly Castle where you can meet your kin. I am certain they will be pleased to learn that something good came of your mother's disappearance so long ago."

"You are so very kind, Gunnolf, despite where you come from." She nestled closer, sharing her heat with him, and he couldn't help the way his body reacted.

She didn't say anything more, and he thought she must have fallen asleep.

He had never imagined holding a woman in his arms like this, trying to keep her warm while she warmed him in a crumbling Roman tower in the middle of nowhere during a snowstorm when all James had sent him to do was check on Wynne and ensure she was safe.

His thoughts wouldn't shut down though, and in case Brina hadn't fallen asleep, he asked, "Do you have any idea where we are?" He thought Brina must if she knew anything about her lands. She had said she did know how to get around out here. Surely she had not just blindly left the castle with no real inkling.

"I have no earthly idea," she said, so softly, he thought she must have drifted off to sleep, and he'd woken her.

He couldn't believe she didn't know where they were. Not when she had said she knew her way around. "You did not recognize the Roman tower ruin? Have you any notion where it is located?"

Her only response was a whispered warm breath against his neck as she breathed out softly. He thought about how he had to ensure she stayed with the MacNeill clan once he safely escorted her there. She would find a home with them like he had, he thought. Except in her case, she was truly one of their kin, even if her mother might have had a bit of a tarnished reputation.

He tried to sleep as he half listened to the sounds of the wind whipping the snow into a fury all around the outside of their private little tower. And he thought he'd managed to sleep for a while when he heard a whimpering and then a tiny howl sound outside the tower. His horse instantly neighed and began to move in the small confines of the tower walls.

Gunnolf jumped up to control the horse before he trampled them to death.

CHAPTER 4

Darkness cloaked the ruined tower and everything around them, including Brina, as Gunnolf had a devil of a time getting hold of his horse's reins. He hoped he and his horse didn't accidentally step on Brina while he tried to quiet him.

"Whoa, Beast." Gunnolf spoke soothingly to him, his hand stroking the frightened horse's neck.

He thought Brina was still sound asleep when she whispered from the floor of the keep, "What is wrong?"

"A wolf howled, spooking Beast."

"They willna hurt us," she said with conviction.

"*Ja.* I agree. It was a wolf pup, I should say."

"Where?" She suddenly stood, her soft body bumping into him.

His loins instantly stirred. He told himself it

was only because she was a beautiful lassie, and he hadn't been with one for a very long time. That any lassie would do. But it wasn't true. Something about her humor and her determination, not to mention she had come to his aid as a lad when she had to know he was her father's enemy, made him see her as something more. "The wolf is somewhere outside the tower."

She didn't hesitate to say, "Go get it then and bring it here."

Amused at her insistent tone as she commanded him, Gunnolf still frowned at her. He loved animals and had often cared for the weak and injured, but the pup could be real trouble. "You must be jesting. The pup most likely has a mother. And a father. And aunts and uncles. And other siblings, lass."

"Are you afraid of taking care of him?"

He wanted to laugh, but he smiled at the sweet lass. She'd obviously lived a sheltered life at her keep.

"I thought you said you could fight six men at once. That you had fought more than that before."

"'Tis different, Brina. I would not want to separate a wolf pup from his pack." And that was the truth of the matter. Though other considerations were important also. The lass's safety, most significantly. Taking a wolf pup with them could put them all in danger.

"What if he has lost his family and he needs our help? Maybe it is a she and she is the one you were sent to aid."

He chuckled, drew Brina into his arms, and held her tight. "Wynne was not talking about a wolf pup. She was talking about a woman. You, I am fairly certain. When it is light out, I will see if I can find it, but you will stay here with Beast."

"That is the name of your horse?" she asked, sounding surprised.

"*Ja.*"

"He was a wild one?"

"The wildest when he was young. You should have seen how hard it was for me to break him."

"Truly? You had to treat him cruelly to get him to yield?" She sounded genuinely upset to hear of it.

She seemed to have a kind heart as far as animals were concerned. "Nay, lass." He encouraged her to lie down with him again and then pulled her tight against him and buried them in the furs. "I have a gift when it comes to animals. They all love me, whether I wish to be loved by them or not."

"Do you have the same way with women?"

He smiled, but did not answer her. It was true the lasses all seemed to like him and vied to get his attention, several of them wishing he'd marry them. But he hadn't been interested enough in any lass to settle down.

He sighed. What was he to do about the wolf pup? They couldn't take it with them, even if he did discover the wild wolf had lost its pack. Yet, he couldn't leave the pup behind to die either.

Getting the lass safely to the MacNeill lands was the only difficulty he wished to think about right now. If Seamus and his men caught up with them, Gunnolf would have to prove he could fight six men and win the battle — this time.

***

Gunnolf was still sleeping when Brina heard the wolf pup whimpering outside the tower wall. She quickly found dry socks in her pouch and hurried to pull them on. Then she hastily yanked on her boots and tied them on. She fastened her brat about her shoulders and braced herself for the cold outside the tower. Amazed at how the thick tower walls had blocked the chilly breeze and kept their small sleeping quarters so much warmer, she walked through the doorway and out into the inner bailey where some of the curtain walls stood, some crumbling, some still resembling a protective wall. She shivered and walked as far away from the tower as she could, keeping it in sight in the low-light as the sun was attempting to ascend into the heavens.

A fog was also moving into the area, and she could not see much off in the distance but more fog.

She needed to relieve herself, but kept a watchful eye out for the wolf, when she saw the gray pup. She'd raised one until he had gone off to find a mate, never learning what had happened to the rest of his family, though she had looked, thinking she might find more pups.

She spoke softly to the pup, then pulled a bannock out of her pouch, tore off a piece, and offered it to him.

He stuck his nose at the food, sniffed it, then took it from her, and chewed on it. "Stay," she said, as if he'd know what she meant for him to do. She observed the partial stone walls standing against the snowy backdrop and considered the keep again, standing on top of a hill. She hadn't realized the horse had climbed it last night. She looked around at the fog-cloaked mountains and forests surrounding them, the river and a loch nearby. She was disappointed to realize she had no idea where they were.

She crunched through the crusty snow, sinking into it until she reached a partial outer wall, found a place by a cairn that afforded her privacy from the tower, and relieved herself. Then she turned to head back to the tower when she saw the pup had followed her.

"You were supposed to have stayed," she scolded, already loving him because she knew he had followed her as if she were his mother wolf, taking care of him until he was old enough to provide for himself. She held out her hand to him, encouraging him to come to her, talking to him like a mother would her baby, soft and high and reassuring.

He inched closer, then stuck out his nose and sniffed her hand, then licked it. She smiled. "Come." She clapped her thigh to urge him to come with her. But the pup just sat on the snow and watched her. She returned to him, gathered him up in her arms, and headed back to the tower.

She had barely reached what would have been the inner bailey when Gunnolf stalked out of the tower, his face grim, his blue eyes widening at the sight of her.

"I found the wolf pup. You didna need to." Then she wondered if he had worried she had run away from him in the middle of the night. "I am going home with you, Norseman. Dinna concern yourself. I had to take care of personal matters."

"And the wolf?" Gunnolf eyed the pup cradled in her arms.

"He is alone. We will take him with us. You are good with animals, so you say. And you have convinced me to go with you as well. You can handle him and take care of me at the same time." She gave him a wee smile.

He shook his head. "I still say he might have a pack."

"Aye, and if they chase after us, you can put the pup down, and we will be on our way. Or we can stay here to see if the pack comes for him." She knew they couldn't wait around. The pup had lost his family somehow, and he was all alone in this world. Which was the way she felt right now.

"We cannot stay. 'Tis light enough to travel and the snow is no longer falling. Though the fog is so thick I cannot make out the mountains. We must go. I will be right back." He stalked off in the direction she had walked, and she wished he'd gone another way. It was embarrassing to think he would find the place where she had relieved herself.

While he was busy, she hurried to pack up his blankets. Then she searched through his pouch and found more bannocks, smoked fish, and cheese. She took out a piece of cheese and ate some of it, then offered a bite of it to the wolf pup, hoping Gunnolf wouldn't catch her at it.

The pup sniffed at it like she was trying to poison it. She frowned, annoyed with him, but understood his reluctance too. "Hurry and eat it or we will both be in trouble."

Just as the pup grabbed it from her fingers and barely chewed it before he swallowed it, Gunnolf stormed around the partial curtain wall, and she knew he was upset with her.

"They are coming, lass."

Then she realized he was not angry with her, but worried about the men who were after her. Her heart began to pound with fear.

"My clansmen?" She hated that she sounded scared, but she knew they'd kill Gunnolf without question, and probably the wolf pup. She didn't even want to think of what would happen when Seamus got hold of her.

"Most likely." Gunnolf paused inside the tower when he saw she had packed everything already. "You ride behind me again. If we are drawn into a fight, I will set you on the ground and unsheathe my sword."

"The wolf." She knew that in their situation the pup should not have been a concern, but she couldn't help it. He was defenseless in the cold, unable to hunt for himself yet. He would need to be cared for if he were to survive.

Gunnolf hurried to get the pup, handed it to her, then climbed onto Beast. He pulled her up behind him, and then eased out of the tower.

"Will they see us?" She realized this was going to be difficult to manage as she wanted to hold onto the pup, but had to snuggle close to Gunnolf.

"Here, give me the pup."

"We canna leave him behind." Her voice was furious. She would stay, though she knew if she did, the men would catch up to her, and they'd kill the wolf anyway.

Gunnolf said, "Woman, I willna leave him behind, but we may have to ride hard, and you need to hold onto me, tight."

"How can you manage—"

He took the pup from her and slipped him inside his tunic, then seized her arm and wrapped it around him. Then he rode out of the tower and around the remnants of the castle walls. He continued to walk the horse through the snow and kept moving, though she had no idea which direction he was headed.

She should have been annoyed at his tone with her, but she knew he was worried for their safety. "Do you know where you are going?" she whispered, snuggled against his back, her arms wrapped around him, and she could feel the pup snuggled inside his tunic. She smiled to think of how others would see him, a Viking warrior, the Fighting Wolf, keeping a little wolf pup warm in his tunic. She thought the world of him for doing so.

"I am moving us away from the tower. They will see it and investigate to learn if you have been there. Hopefully, they will not see us if we can get beyond that ben. They will see that we camped in the tower last night."

"They willna know it was me. I didna have a horse the last they knew. Nor a companion."

"*Ja*, nor did you have a wolf. The wolf pup's, horse's, and my own tracks will help to confuse them. Though they will see your small foot prints. I tried to walk in as many of yours as I could to disguise your foot prints, but when I heard the men approaching, I did not have time enough to do much more. As to the pup, they will not know that it is a wolf, but most likely will think it is a dog's paw prints."

That was why he was going in the same direction as she had gone. She had been fortunate to come across him. He truly was a clever man. She let out her breath with relief. "Then rescuing the pup will be a good thing."

"Did you hear him howl any more last night?"

"Aye. Just think of this. No one would expect me to be traveling with you and a wolf pup. If he howls when we are traveling or settling down for the night, they will think he is just part of the wilderness calling to his pack."

"*Ja.* Now that 'tis dawn, can you tell me which way is north of your border? Or where we are in relation to your castle?"

"I... I have no' traveled much beyond my castle walls since my da took over the clan," she hated to admit, and disliking that she couldn't help them more.

"No wonder he was concerned about you leaving the castle. Mayhap also because of your mother running off from her own people?" he asked.

She'd never considered that. Perhaps her da had worried she would be like her mother and run off from her clan. And then Brina would be captured by some Highlander and forced to marry him like her mother had been. Although she had run off from her clan, and now was with a man she didn't know, it certainly wasn't for the same reasons her mother had left her clan. But Brina also believed her da's strictness had something to do with her finding the wounded Viking warrior lad when her da had been herding the sheep far from their shieling before they moved to the castle.

"Aye, you may be right. But remember how I found you? My da was sorely angry that a Viking would be discovered so close to the shieling, and I had planned to save him. Once my da took over as clan chief, he wouldna allow me to venture far from the castle, and I was always guarded."

For a long moment, Gunnolf didn't say anything, then finally made the comment, "Then he cared for you."

She snorted.

"Else your leaving would not have mattered."

"I was my da's pawn." She let out her breath. "He is dead now. And Seamus is taking his place. Unless someone else can challenge him."

"Will anyone?"

"Nay. He has five men at his back at all times. Someone who has a lot of men who would be willing to pursue this might be able to. Unless I could send word to my cousin to return, but Christophe hasna been much interested in clan politics and I have no idea where he is."

"Then I suspect your people would not wish your cousin to lead the clan."

"If someone like you, who could fight six men and win, were to challenge him…" She only said so because Gunnolf had bragged about his prowess. She didn't really mean it because no man could do that.

"Would I win the woman and lead the clan?"

She snuggled harder against him. "It would be the death of you, or he might lock you in the dungeon forever."

"You do not trust in my fighting skills?"

She shook her head. "No man could win against such odds." Then she sighed. "I am sorry that I misled you about knowing the way to the MacNeill lands."

"I cannot say I am not disappointed, but I understand, lass."

She appreciated that Gunnolf was understanding. Her da would have been furious with her. "So what is the plan?"

"We will continue to head away from the men on horseback. Mayhap we will run across some abode and can learn the direction to go. With any luck, the sky will clear, and I might know where I am."

No matter how long they traveled that morn, the fog continued to persist. They hadn't heard any sounds of men following, thankfully, but Brina was afraid that Gunnolf didn't know his way home any more than she did.

When they reached a croft, Gunnolf warned, "We have gone in a circle and have returned to the same croft where the man shot his arrow at me, or at you, as the case may be. We will stop and seek shelter for a short while. You and my horse need to get out of this weather."

She hadn't felt so chilled as when she'd been running on her own, not with the way Gunnolf kept her warm, though the wind still whipped the cold air about. "The pup?"

"*Ja*, I will keep him in hand."

He helped her down and moved his horse into the byre, while she knocked on the door.

A woman answered, rocking a baby in her arm, her eyes growing large. "Lady Brina. Seamus and his men were here looking for you."

Feeling sick with worry upon hearing the news, Brina realized Seamus and his men would be checking all the shielings for her. "Aye. My friend, Gunnolf, of the Clan MacNeill, is taking me home to see my mother's people. Except we got turned around in the snowstorm. Do you know the way to the MacNeill border?"

"Nay, no' me." The woman glanced at Gunnolf as he stooped to enter the shieling. "Mayhap my husband would, but he has gone out to hunt for you."

"Which direction?" Brina asked.

The woman hesitated to say and glanced again at Gunnolf, who could be intimidating. "North. He was forced to go with them, so they could find you. Seamus was angry, and though my husband didna want to leave me and the bairn behind, he had no choice. Beg pardon for my saying so, but Seamus will be a terror if you dinna return to the keep."

"I canna wed the man."

"We must all do what we can for the sake of the clan, aye? If they catch you with Gunnolf, they will kill this man of the Clan MacNeill. Even if he is family on your mother's side, Seamus will be angry that he has aided you in running away."

Brina was again faced with indecision. With doing what was right for her clan and with saving herself. Yet she couldn't reconcile the notion of returning when she knew how she would be abused for it. Her people would go on as before without her. "Thank you for your kindness," she said to the woman, not intending to tell her their plans.

With Seamus and his men hunting her down, and Gunnolf not knowing his way back to the MacNeill lands, she didn't feel real secure in the plan to go forward. If they caught him with her, they'd kill him. But she just couldn't return home either.

"I will find the way, Lady Brina. I will take you home to your mother's clan," Gunnolf assured her as if he knew her thoughts.

She smiled at him, but she was certain he could tell she wasn't feeling any happiness with that smile. "Come, let us go. The faster you return me to Castle Anfa, the faster you can be on your way, Gunnolf."

"Thank you, Lady Brina," the woman said.

"Are you certain, Lady Brina?" Gunnolf asked.

She grabbed his arm and meant to hurry him out the door, but he stood like a statue in place.

"Come, Gunnolf. We must go. Now."

When Gunnolf led her back to the byre, she remained quiet, not wanting the woman inside to hear their words.

"Are you certain you wish to do this?" Sounding worried for her, Gunnolf helped her onto the horse. "Once I get my bearing, I will take you straight away to Craigly Castle."

"When you left your home and fought against the Sassenach, then attempted to return home, you had a purpose. You were no' running away from anything."

"I did not return home though, lass. My purpose changed, and I ended up remaining with the MacNeills. No one would fault a lass for being unable to take on a man like Seamus. I do not want to take you back there."

"Just take me away from the shieling."

When they'd ridden some distance, she said, "I want you to take me to Craigly Castle. But I didna want to say so in front of the woman."

Gunnolf let out his breath as if relieved. "*Ja,* you have my word I will get you there safely."

But they hadn't traveled far when a man on horseback rode out to intercept them, his hair black, and his expression stormy.

Gunnolf knew he couldn't push his horse any faster and reached for his sword, though he would have to put the pup and the lass down on the ground before he could fight the man.

"Nay," Brina said. "He is one of my da's loyal men, Rory."

A scar slashed across the man's left cheek, red and angry, a fresh wound. His dark blue eyes were narrowed as he sized up Gunnolf. He growled, "Who are you?"

"He is Gunnolf of the Clan MacNeill and he saved my life," Brina said, defending him.

Rory studied Gunnolf further, an attempt at intimidation. Then still showing animosity for the man who was riding alone with Brina, he said, "Come with me. Seamus and his men are still searching for you. Come. I must show you something." He eyed Gunnolf with wariness then, and said to Brina, "You may ride with me, my lady."

"I promised to protect Lady Brina," Gunnolf said. "I will take her where she chooses to go."

Rory raised his brows to hear Gunnolf say as much. "You have no stake in this. And your life is forfeit if you remain here if Seamus learns you were with the lass all this time."

"I stay," Gunnolf said with conviction.

"Where are we bound?" Brina asked, not wishing Gunnolf to come to any harm, but she appreciated he felt it his role to protect her until she made it to Craigly Castle safely.

They rode toward one of the outlying farms, all of which she recognized now. Her old shieling wasn't far from there.

"Cadel's shieling. Why there? Seamus will search all the shielings in the area before long to ensure no one is giving me refuge."

"I wished to see you earlier," Rory said. "But my duty was to your da. Then Cadel learned you had run off in the snowstorm, and Seamus and five of his men were out searching for you. At that point, 'twas too late. When I saw you with this man..." Rory gave Gunnolf another disparaging look. "What business had you on our lands?"

"I came to rescue Lady Brina," Gunnolf said.

"Aye, he did. One of Seamus's men even shot me."

Rory frowned at her, as if he didn't believe she could be telling the truth.

"The arrow grazed my arm. I believe he thought if he shot in my direction, it would have frightened me into stopping. I dinna believe he actually thought he would hit me. But Gunnolf protected me. As to why Gunnolf was here? He learned I needed rescuing."

Rory didn't question them further of how that could have come about.

As they approached the stone shieling half buried in snow, a red-bearded man rushed outside and Gunnolf assumed this was Cadel, his green eyes wide as he saw the lass with him. "God's knees, beg your pardon, Lady Brina." Then he said to Rory, "You found the lass." He quickly turned his attention to Gunnolf. "Who is he?"

"Gunnolf of the Clan MacNeill," Brina said as Cadel helped her down. "And my protector."

Rory and Cadel exchanged looks. Gunnolf and Rory dismounted and Cadel offered to take the reins of both horses. "Hurry inside. I will take care of the horses for you. My wife will prepare something for you to eat. Your da is awake now."

"My da?" Her knees buckled, but Gunnolf quickly seized her arm to keep her from collapsing.

"Are you going to be all right, lass?" He held her for a minute until she nodded, tears in her eyes. He helped her toward the door, his heart going out to her. He wished Rory had told her the news beforehand, but maybe he was afraid she would have fainted on the horse.

"They said my da was dead." Her voice was barely audible, her whole body shaking. Her face had lost all its color as Rory opened the door to the shieling.

"That is what Seamus believed after a man struck your da such a blow he nearly killed him. I reached your da's attacker before he could deal the final blow and killed the man. Seamus had watched the man attack him, and he did naught to come to his aid. Seamus didna realize your da still lived. I managed to spirit your da away to Cadel's shieling before anyone was aware of it as the snow barreled in and the dead men were to be taken care of when they could. It was supposed to be this morn, but everyone who died on the field was buried in snow. When the snow melts, we will be out there to bury the dead, and Seamus could very well learn your da lives. Unless he believes wolves carried his body off."

Gunnolf helped Brina into the shieling, her legs shaky. "Thank you," she managed to say.

Inside a woman said, "Oh, my, Lady Brina, your da is in the next room. He will be so pleased to see you." The golden-haired woman frowned at Gunnolf and eyed the waking pup as he squirmed to see all the new people.

"Mara, this is Gunnolf. And Gunnolf, Mara is Cadel's lovely wife." Then Brina said, "But...but Seamus will be searching all the shielings for me. He will find my da instead."

"Nay, he has already come here. We hid him in the root cellar," Rory said. "'Tis concealed. Seamus didna find it. Go, lass, see your da."

Brina didn't make a move toward the room.

"Brina?" Gunnolf asked, his hand still on her arm, steadying her.

Brina knew she should see to her da, though she felt as though she'd be seeing a ghost. But she couldn't move her legs in that direction no matter how much she tried.

Cadel joined them, and everyone watched her as she battled with herself over the realization her da was still alive. And it was not a good thing, but still better than Seamus taking over the clan and having to wed him right away. Yet if her da was badly wounded, Seamus would still end up leading the clan.

She wanted to ask Gunnolf to come with her because her legs felt like they could barely hold her up. Gunnolf was still holding onto her arm and then she looked up at him, his concerned expression endearing.

"Thank you, Gunnolf. I… will see my da now." She swallowed a lump in her throat and headed for the small room. Her heart was thumping wildly. As quiet as everyone was, she assumed they all watched her as she approached the room. She paused before she entered, steeled her back, and walked inside.

Her da's eyes were closed, furs tucked up under his chin. A large gash across his forehead had been stitched and black and blue bruising surrounded it, his skin sickly pale. Had he been wounded somewhere else on his body also? His hair as dark as hers sported a dusting of gray strands, and she thought there were more of them now than the last time she had seen him.

She drew close. He was not a man who cared for pity or comforting and so she feared if she spoke to him or touched him, he would growl at her, and she would be angry right back. But she couldn't see him looking so poorly and not do something.

"You have a wolf pup. Not just a pup," suddenly Cadel's wife exclaimed to Gunnolf in the other room.

"*Ja*, Brina insisted we take him with us," Gunnolf said.

"She raised one once," Cadel said.

"I did not know that." Gunnolf sounded both surprised and amused.

"Here is some water for him," Mara said.

Brina steadied her breathing and took her da's cold hand in hers. From being out in the snow, she felt hers were still colder. "Da, 'tis me."

His eyes fluttered open. For a moment, he just stared at her as if he didn't know who she was and that worried her even more. "Da, 'tis me, Brina."

"Aye, I know very well who you are," he said crossly.

She relaxed her hand on his and meant to pull away, but he held onto her hand, despite looking so feeble. She knew then he was angry with her. Not that she hadn't expected it. She was certain Rory had told him all the news from the castle. Or Cadel had.

"You ran away," he said, his voice just as hard.

"Aye."

"In this weather."

"I dinna wish to wed Seamus." She knew her da would disapprove of her going against his wishes. But then if Seamus had left her da to die, maybe he'd had a change of heart concerning her marrying him.

"You left after the battle. Where have you been that Seamus was unable to locate you all this time?"

"A friend aided me. He is Gunnolf of the—"

"Clan MacNeill." Her da's eyes were again narrowed.

So Gunnolf had a reputation. Good or bad? He had been nothing but good to her, so she had every intention of defending him to her da.

She lifted her chin. "Aye. Rory said Seamus had not aided you in battle and a man nearly killed you. Seamus said you had died. I tried to find you, to see for myself."

"To know the devil was dead, aye, daughter?"

She scowled at him. "Nay. If I had found you had been injured on the battlefield, I would have sought help for you. I would have cared for you." She tried to yank her hand away from his, but he wouldn't release her as if it had to be his idea, not hers. "Seamus wouldna let me go to you. When I managed to leave the castle, I didna run off to save myself. I first went looking for you. Putting my own safety at risk. I couldna find you. The snowstorm had covered the bodies of the fallen, and a couple of the men I managed to find were no' you."

"Cadel and Rory brought me here to take care of me. I had been led to believe Seamus was the right man to take over the clan when I died, but it seems he wants that to happen sooner than later." Her da let out his breath in a heavy sigh. "No' that I blame him. Had I been in his place, I might have done the same."

She should have known her da would feel that way. "We must stop Seamus. He doesna deserve to lead the clan." She realized her da still wasn't letting go of her hand, and then she wondered if nearly dying had made him see things differently.

"If the clan votes him in, I have naught to say about it."

"You are their chief."

"I am wounded and unable to lead our clan into battle for now." Then he frowned at Brina. "How long were you alone with the Finn-Gall?"

"He saved my life, da. He should be rewarded not punished." She changed the subject abruptly before her da wanted Gunnolf killed for having been alone with her. "What are we to do? Seamus willna attempt to have you murdered if you return to the keep, will he? I canna see him giving you a warm welcome. Unless he runs things while you are recovering and proves that he is more capable than you and can sway the people to vote him in as chief."

"I canna travel for a couple of more days. Send Gunnolf into the room so that I may speak with him."

"How do you know him?"

"Everyone knows of the Viking lad who was severely injured by the Sassenach and found his way to the Highlands. He is the one you tried to save. Aye?"

"Aye." And she had been whipped for it.

"He has proven his worth as far as the MacNeill clan is concerned."

So her da didn't disapprove of him. "He is a good fighter. He can take on six men at once." She thought if Gunnolf was agreeable and had her da's backing, maybe he could kill Seamus and things would change.

"Six men? And you witnessed this?" her da asked skeptically. "Or did he tell you this tale?"

She felt her cheeks flame. "He didna fight anyone while we were traveling. But he did keep me safe while we evaded Seamus and his men."

"Send him in to speak with me. I will talk to him alone."

Her da released her hand finally, but she hesitated to go.

"Go, daughter. Warm yourself by the fire. And get something to eat."

She bowed her head a little, worried what he would say to Gunnolf. Then she did what she'd never done before and leaned over and kissed his cheek. "Get well, da."

Her eyes blurred with tears, but she wasn't surprised to see him stare at her in surprise and not acknowledge her gesture in any way. She couldn't explain her sudden empathy for him, except that she was glad he was not dead and that perhaps what had happened to him had changed his mind about her marrying Seamus.

She turned and hurried out of the room, praying her da would recover so that the elders would not decide he could no longer lead and allow Seamus to rule in his place. Though if he did, she was hatching another plan. She and her da would go to the MacNeill holdings and ask to be taken in. She didn't think her da would be agreeable, but she would ask Gunnolf to force the issue, if it meant saving her da's life. She was afraid that if her da did return to power and told Seamus he couldn't marry her, Seamus would force him to recant due to her da's weakened condition.

She sniffled and hastily wiped away the tears on her cheeks, then returned to the main room. "He wishes to see you," she said to Gunnolf, then took the wolf pup from his arms.

"Are you all right, lass?" Gunnolf asked, frowning.

She appreciated just how much he worried about her. "Aye."

He nodded, then strode into the other room.

She worried her da would be angry with

Gunnolf for having been alone with her for so long. She was rethinking staying here all together.

CHAPTER 5

"Chief," Gunnolf said in greeting, observing the older man, his dark hair streaked with gray strands, his face pale, and his expression pained.

The older man looked him up and down, sizing him up, not like a man who was on his deathbed, but his expression calculating, like he had a plan in mind and was deciding if Gunnolf could assist in accomplishing his goal. "You told my daughter that you could fight six men at once and come out the victor?"

Gunnolf did not think the chief would truly believe he could manage those odds *and* come out victorious. "Nay, I told her I had fought six men at once. I didna mention the outcome."

The chief smiled just a hint. "I am Robard." Then he narrowed his eyes, his expression turning hard. "You were with my daughter for all of the night and most of the day alone?"

"*Ja.*" Gunnolf wasn't worried that the chief would want him to marry his daughter. Not if he wished her to wed the man who would be chief of the clan. And being that Gunnolf was not even from the Highlands, he really didn't see that as an issue. "She is still a maid, if you are worried about that. I only saw to her safety. Naught more than that."

Gunnolf didn't offer any further in explanation, assuming that no matter what he said, if Brina's father had been concerned that Gunnolf had taken advantage of the lass, Gunnolf wouldn't be able to change his mind. He also suspected if word got out that he'd been with her all that time, alone, others might speak ill of her. Which he didn't wish. So he hoped the chief planned to make up some story to explain her absence and that in no way had she been compromised.

"You dinna desire her as a man wants a woman?"

Gunnolf didn't know what to say in response to that. Of course he desired her. He didn't believe he could lie about it either and convince the chief that he didn't. "She is a bonny lass." Gunnolf didn't want to admit to anything more than that.

The chief observed him for what seemed like forever, judging him. "I *didna* ask that. I *asked* if *you* desired her."

Gunnolf straightened. "Lady Brina is desirable. I would be lying if I said she was not. But I am not seeking a wife."

Robard nodded as if finally satisfied with Gunnolf's reply. "Many have spoken of the Finn-Gall who rides with the MacNeills. How he survived a clash with Cian Murray's men when he was wounded and greatly outnumbered. How he helped to rescue a French countess, who is now married to Niall MacNeill."

"*Ja*. 'Tis all true."

"I have heard of some of your other exploits. And even something of your miraculous survival when you fought against the Sassenach when you were but a lad."

"I would not say it was miraculous. More that I was pig-headed enough to fight to survive."

Another small smile from the chief and then a deeper frown. "Tell me, did you bring any of them down? As young as you were?"

"I did. Five men, if you must know, before I was wounded."

Again Robard nodded. "Despite not wishing a wife, you seem to have garnered my daughter's affections."

Gunnolf opened his mouth to speak, to tell him in no way had the lass shown any affection toward him in the least.

The chief motioned for him to say nothing. "She doesna give her affections to anyone lightly."

"I am not sure what you mean by affections. I did not kiss the lass or do anything other than give her a ride upon my horse, offer my food, and protect her." And warm her.

"I mean that she spoke kindly of you. I have never heard her speak thus about a man before."

Had the lass misinterpreted Gunnolf's intentions toward her? He wished only to ensure she stayed warm. Yes, he desired her, would have loved nothing more than to bed the sweet lass, as any man who was half a man would desire. If he had wished a wife and she had been so inclined to marry him, Brina might have been the one for him. But he wasn't ready to settle down. Maybe never.

He said nothing, afraid that he could have misread the situation. Gunnolf truly wasn't interested in marrying her. Or any lass for that matter. Nor was he interested in being a guardsman in her father's employ — if that's what he had in mind — just because he survived his wounds as a lad when most men would have succumbed. Or because he'd fought so many men and had come out of the fighting victorious. He was at home with the MacNeills, and someday maybe he would find a lass to wed. But certainly not one who didn't like his heritage or who required him to fight a mountain of men to have her. He was perfectly content with taking Brina to Craigly Castle and letting her get to know what was left of her family there.

He wasn't certain where the chief was going with this discussion. How did fighting men figure into the business with showing a kindness to Brina?

"Explain to me how you came upon my daughter and everything that happened until you arrived here."

Gunnolf explained everything, including how one of Seamus's men had shot her.

The chief's face reddened in anger. "She didna tell me this. I will kill the man who shot her myself."

"*Ja*. I would do it for you."

The chief nodded, looking pleased that Gunnolf would say so. "Do… do you know about her mother?"

"*Ja*. She worked for the laird of Craigly Castle. Though he died before I arrived there, and she left before James took over."

"My daughter must never know of this."

"She is the one who told me. But I remember hearing about Davina."

The chief's eyes widened. "I see. Brina was never to know. Why were you here on my lands?"

"A *taibhsear* said I had to help a woman." What else could Gunnolf say? Some didn't believe in them and would think him daft. But he had no other way to explain why he had been on their lands in a snowstorm unless he had lost his way. Which, he had, but he wasn't about to explain that to the chief. After sounding so brave and heroic, if he'd let on he had been terribly lost, how would that look to Robard? "I wasna sure I believed her, but she had revealed things that have come to pass before. So I took the chance that she was correct. Brina needed my protection, so I assume then that what Wynne had told me was accurate."

Robard said nothing for a time, and Gunnolf wondered if during the prolonged silenced, the chief was just tired from being wounded, or pondering what Gunnolf had said.

"A vision." The chief nodded. "Anything else?"

"Naught that made any sense. Could you use my help before I leave?"

"Aye. I want you to take my daughter to the Clan MacNeill holdings. You were right in wanting to escort her there to see her mother's people."

Gunnolf was glad her father felt that way. "What about you?"

"When I can travel, I will return to my keep. Seamus willna attempt to kill me as I will let on that I know naught of his treachery. He will run the day-to-day affairs while I am recovering. But I will continue to lead. I am certain he will try to keep the power he will have in the interim after I am well. I havena lived and ruled for this long without having dealt with men like him before."

Gunnolf respected the chief for his beliefs, though he knew how things could change in a heartbeat if another battle broke out between his people and another clan's and Robard couldn't lead his men. "How are you injured?"

"A slice across my belly. But I havena taken a fever. 'Tis a good sign."

"*Ja*. What if the lass wishes to stay with you?"

"She has no say in this. If she stays, Seamus will attempt to marry her, and I canna let on that I dinna wish it now, can I? No' when I am trying to show I still trust the man. After what Rory and Cadel told me about his action in battle, though I was too busy fighting to see it, I dinna want my daughter wed to the man. A man must be strong, but he must also be loyal to the chief. I can see where he is tired of waiting to be in charge of the clan and to have my daughter for his wife. I know she doesna wish this. You will take her with you."

"*Ja.*" Gunnolf had to bring up the situation with traveling alone with the lass though. Before, he was trying to protect her from Seamus and his men. He would still be doing that, but they hadn't had a choice as far as having someone chaperone the lass. "Will others cause problems for the lass if they know we have traveled together alone further?"

"You tell me that you have only honorable intentions with regard to my daughter."

"*Ja.* But what will others believe?"

"They will think what I tell them to think," Robard growled. "Cadel said you must have been turned around in the snowstorm. Do you believe you can find your way now?"

"*Ja,* if someone points me in the right direction. Do you have anyone who could ride with us?"

The chief smiled at him a wee bit. "You dinna worry you will become saddled with a wife, do you, Gunnolf? 'Tis said no lassie has managed to capture your interest for very long."

"Nay, 'tis only that if we come across Seamus and his men—"

The chief motioned with his hand in a wave of dismissal. "You fought six men. There are six of them, including Seamus, so Cadel has informed me."

"I ended up in a dungeon the last time I fought those odds," Gunnolf explained, not wanting the chief to believe he could handle that many men at once — successfully.

The chief shook his head. "I canna send Cadel or Rory with you. They are seeing to my needs, ensuring I know what is going on at the castle and if anyone has learned of Seamus's whereabouts. They may have backtracked to Jamie's shieling and learned from his wife that Brina is traveling with you and you were taking her back to the castle."

"Then when he discovers she isna there, he will look for her at the shielings in the area and discover you." Gunnolf worried about the chief, thinking he might need to move him to the castle first.

"Cadel will let the elders know I am alive and well. Seamus willna want to kill me after the Viking's attempt failed and Seamus didna ensure I was no' dead or return me to the keep to have my injuries taken care of. Otherwise, he will have to face the consequences of his actions. In the meantime, you must take Brina to her mother's family. We will prepare something for you to eat and give you more blankets and food for the journey. And when you see the *taibhsear*, tell her I thank her for sending you to save my daughter's life. Eat and then you must leave. Tell my daughter

I must speak with her one last time."

"*Ja.*" Gunnolf was glad that Brina's father wanted him to take Brina away from here as he was certain she would be better off for now with the MacNeills. But he worried about her father's plan and his notion that Seamus would not attempt to end his life once he learned Robard lived. Gunnolf was also troubled about riding alone with Brina and getting caught by Seamus and his men. He could kill a few of them, but not that many all at once. He would be a dead man, and Brina would be forced to marry the rogue.

It didn't matter that Gunnolf had no interest in a wife. He didn't want her to have to wed a man who stood by and wouldn't protect her father when he had fallen so he could take power.

Beyond that, being alone with Brina again could cause other difficulties for Gunnolf, despite what her father had said. Gunnolf didn't think the old man had any notion that he would marry Brina and then take over the clan. But what if Robard did?

Gunnolf returned to the main room to see that Brina was eating a steaming bowl of porridge. "Your father wishes to speak with you again, lass."

Brina's eyes widened. "Is he…is he going to be all right?"

As tough as the old man was, Gunnolf thought he might just very well pull through. "*Ja.*"

"Is he…angry with you?"

"Nay. We must leave as soon as we eat though."

"I wish to stay with my da."

"I am to take you to Craigly Castle."

Her lips parted. "He told you this? My da?"

"*Ja,* lass. 'Tis what he wishes." Gunnolf was glad too. He wouldn't have returned her to her castle if her father had wished it, though he was glad to have his permission to take her to Craigly Castle.

Then she frowned. "What of my da?"

"Speak to him and then we must be on our way."

Brina quickly finished her porridge, then left the room, and while she spoke with her father, Gunnolf explained to the others what her father wished of him.

"I will give you some food to take with you." Mara wrapped up some bannocks, dried fish, and cheese.

"I can travel with you for a few miles to get you started on the right path," Cadel said.

"I would go with you as well," Rory said, "but my place is with the chief."

"I understand. Is there anyone else who could go with us?" Gunnolf was still concerned about Seamus and his men and the fight he'd have if they came across them, and about the lass being seen alone with him. Before, they'd had no choice. A man had shot an arrow at her. And Gunnolf had to protect her at all costs. Now, it was a different story.

"Nay," Rory said. "If we fetch her maid to help chaperone her, the word would spread that we have found Brina. For what reason would she would need her maid then? To run away again? Not only that, but another lass would slow you down."

"Another fighting man?" If Gunnolf had another man at his back, he could fight three or four men much better than six. He hadn't planned to take another lass under his wing.

"We have no idea who is still loyal to the chief. In the past, we would have known. Seamus is so ruthless, many are more afraid of disobeying him than they are of our chief. And with him injured so... they know that Seamus would be the more dangerous man to cross. If you are worried that Robard will wish you to wed his daughter, you have every right to be concerned." Rory cast him a small smile.

Gunnolf didn't think the man was jesting.

"You have already been alone with the lass, though it appears you have only had her best interests at heart. The chief will want naught less concerning the matter," Cadel agreed. "He does what he believes is in the clan's best interest."

"I do not understand," Gunnolf said.

"Marriage, man. He will want you to wed his daughter."

"He said naught of this to me," Gunnolf said, annoyed. He hadn't saved the lass to be forced into a marriage with her. Not that he didn't enjoy sleeping with her, a necessity to keep each other warm. But he knew she wouldn't want to be married to him without having some choice in the matter either. Though often a lass married whom her father chose for her, so it wasn't usually a matter of love. Especially in the case of a woman who had some position in the clan.

"He wants you to take her to safety. You were escorting her to Craigly Castle, aye?" Cadel asked.

"*Ja.*"

"Well, you will have earned the right to marry her, if you keep her out of Seamus's grasp, and you manage to stay alive."

"I have no intention of marrying the lass," Gunnolf said, then paused as Brina came out of the room where her father was and shut the door, wiping fresh tears away.

"Have you eaten enough? We must go," she said.

"Is he...?"

"Alive, tired. He needs to rest and you and I must leave at once."

Cadel grabbed his cloak off a peg on the wall. "I will go with you. Hopefully with three of us traveling on horseback, Seamus willna realize Brina is with us since she left on foot." They bundled up and Cadel warned, "Remember what I said, Gunnolf. You have no choice. Dinna believe that you do."

Gunnolf and Brina did have a choice. That was why he was taking her to Craigly Castle because it was the right thing to do. Her father might still not survive, and then she could choose whom she wished to wed, and she would be safe with her own family. Though he wondered who was left of her mother's family.

"You canna take the pup," Mara said. "He will be too much trouble for you."

"He will warn us if we have unwanted company, and I willna leave him behind." Brina was fiercely protective of the pup, holding onto him even tighter.

Cadel led Brina and Gunnolf outside his cottage.

"The horse is Rory's. The chief said he would gift Brina's horse to him because she borrowed his without his knowledge." Cadel went to help her into the saddle, but Gunnolf did the honors instead.

Gunnolf took the pup from her and tucked him into his tunic. He regretted the lass would not be riding with him like before. He'd enjoyed how they'd warmed each other, but he was certain she hadn't had a wicked thought on her mind. He hadn't been able to help himself, thinking how warm and soft and sweet she would be beneath him in the throes of passion. But it would be better this way because two riders on one horse would tire it faster.

He knew when they bedded down for the night, his holding her close was only to keep them both alive and well. Which was the mission her father had given him.

So why was he even thinking of bedding down with her again?

They rode for several miles, and when Gunnolf saw the remnants of the Roman tower up ahead, he frowned. "We stayed here last night." As they drew closer, he could see several horses' tracks all around the area now.

"Aye, just go that way. Follow the river east, then when you come to a shieling, cross the river, and head north. By tomorrow you should be on MacNeill lands. Dinna think that will stop Seamus or his men though. If he tracks you onto MacNeill lands and finds you before you can get the lass to safety, he will attempt to kill you and take the lass back. Just dinna let them catch you," Rory said.

Gunnolf had no intention of it, but sometimes a situation like this was completely out of his hands.

For a second time, Brina and Gunnolf stopped at the Roman ruins. Cadel bid them good luck and left for his shieling. Gunnolf hoped Cadel didn't run into Seamus's men and have to explain what he was doing out here all alone. But then he saw Cadel headed away from them in a different direction, probably to disguise the fact that he had been traveling with two other riders for a time.

They rested the horses and Gunnolf and Brina drank ale and ate bannocks, while letting the wolf pup explore a bit.

"You were upset when you came out of the room after speaking with your da the second time. Do you wish to talk about it?" Gunnolf asked.

"I fear for his health and that if Seamus learns

he is still abed, he may kill him. Especially if he learns my da sent me away with you. You do know why he did it, do you no'?"

"To protect you from Seamus. Your father wants to take over the rule of the clan again and exile Seamus. But he fears the man would try to take you to wife before Robard is strong enough to prevent him."

"Nay. My da does it to punish Seamus for not coming to his aid when the enemy warrior tried to kill him. My da never does anything out of the kindness of his heart. Because of Seamus's betrayal, my da hopes to ensure I dinna marry him as a way of punishing him."

Not knowing her father, except for this one brief encounter, Gunnolf could see Brina's point. "No matter the reason, leaving as you did is the right thing to do, dinna you agree?"

She looked up at Gunnolf and nodded. But he thought she appeared unsure of the road ahead. Which was understandable. Until they reached the safety of the MacNeill lands, their success could be hard won if not impossible to manage.

***

In truth, Brina prayed her da would survive and eliminate the traitor in his midst. She fervently hoped she and Gunnolf would make it to the MacNeill holdings and safely, because she knew Seamus and his men would kill Gunnolf if they caught up to them for daring to take her anywhere. Even if he'd returned her to the castle, Seamus would have had Gunnolf executed. He would be angry that Gunnolf had been alone with her for any length of time no matter how innocent their encounter.

If her da returned to rule the clan and managed to destroy Seamus and his followers, she would be torn between returning home, or staying with the MacNeills — if she was even tolerated there. She might not like the people, despite how Gunnolf believed she would be accepted. At her da's home, she was the chief's daughter. At her mother's? Possibly, she could be a kitchen maid like her mother with a tarnished reputation. Even though she wouldn't be carrying a child, she could imagine people watching her, seeing if she had a bairn growing in her belly. The Viking's bairn. Her mother's actions would reflect on her as well. She wasn't sure that the MacNeills would welcome her with open arms.

If her da returned to power, she knew he would insist Gunnolf marry her. He needed a strong right hand. And if he couldn't get him to agree any other way, he'd force the issue by saying Gunnolf had taken her for his wife and must return her home. She was certain of it. As honorable as Gunnolf seemed to be, she suspected he would feel obligated to do so. Not willingly though. She had overheard his claim that he didn't want a wife.

They again mounted and rode off. She was glad she had her own horse to ride. Not hers, exactly, but a good horse named Baldur. She thought it odd that

Rory had named him after a Norse god of peace and goodness. But there had been rumors that Rory had ancestors who had been Vikings too.

She and Gunnolf were quiet, not speaking as they walked alongside a creek through a narrow gorge. All she saw was a white hawk flying high overhead, a cold gray sky, misty clouds moving lower and headed in their direction again, though earlier the fog had lifted into the sky for a time. Now, it was again swallowing everything up until she and Gunnolf were surrounded by thick mist. Snow draped the pine branches and the ground, though the temperature was warming up a bit and the snow was dripping, the top layer glistening. But everything from the ground up was now white.

The water gurgled in the creek as their horses clip-clopped on the snowy bank, and she heard a hawk screeching way above, hidden in the blanket of mist.

She listened to the stiff breeze blowing through the trees, trying to make out any other sounds, like that of voices carried in the wind, or of hoof beats clomping in the frozen snow anywhere nearby.

She followed behind Gunnolf, wondering how the wolf pup was doing. They'd fed him scraps of bread and cheese and he'd washed it down with cold water from the stream. But would the MacNeill clansmen take him in? She was afraid they'd kill the pup, fearful of what he would do to their sheep. But if he was raised around the sheep, she thought he would learn that they were friends, not food. Then again, what did she know? She'd raised a wolf pup along with the hunting dogs, so they had all gotten along as if the wolf was part of the hunting pack. She wanted to raise this one too.

It made her think of her mother's plight, fleeing Craigly Castle and losing her baby. That she had been all alone in the world. Then she frowned. Why had her family not stood up for her? Protected her better? Maybe they couldn't have stood up to the laird at the time.

She sighed. What if she didn't have any family left there? That her mother had not had brothers or sisters. That her own parents were dead. She wanted to talk to Gunnolf and discuss her concerns, but she knew it was safer to ride in silence.

When they stopped again, he pulled his horse into the woods, but the mist still clung heavily to the ground and the heavens above as if protecting them from anyone's view.

"Do you know who your family is? The MacAffins, but what their relation would be to you?" Gunnolf asked quietly as he pulled the pup out of his tunic and placed him on the ground to explore and do his business.

She shook her head. "Would one of my mother's family members, a sister, mayhap, be working with the kitchen staff like my mother?"

"I do not recall anyone by that name. Your mother might have had a brother or sister even. What about her da? Her mother?"

Brina shrugged. "I dinna know. My da didna

want to hear about her past. He fell in love with her the moment he saw her, from what others have told me. I heard rumors he believed she was bearing a son, and he desperately wanted one. He'd been married before, but his wife died in childbirth. My mother lost the bairn, a son. And then she lost another two. Both males also." Brina sighed. "And then I came along and my da believed I wouldna make it. Not when I was a wee lass." She straightened her shoulders, looked the brooding Viking in the eyes, and said, "But I survived." Then she looked at the ground. "My mother died when trying to give him another son. He also died."

"Was your father angry with you that you lived when your brothers did not survive?"

"Nay, he intended to make the most of it. He would marry me off to someone of his choosing. But then everyone he knew that he wished clan alliances with had wives. Seamus came along, a warrior like you, and he had a proud bearing. My da believed he would have what it took to run the clan when my da could no longer manage. So instead of me marrying outside of the clan, my da wanted me to marry Seamus. My da couldna see what I could see in the man. He is cruel, power hungry, and he will do whatever it takes to crush those who stand in his way. My da thinks that means Seamus is looking out for his best interests, but a man like that thinks only of how his actions will benefit himself."

"I agree. At least with regard to you, it seems

your da wishes something else now."

"Still, I worry about what will become of my da. If Seamus has any idea that my da knows of his treachery, he will have him killed. I am certain of it. He will make sure he dies in what appears to be an accidental death. As much as I havena been happy with my da over him wanting me to marry Seamus, I knew it would be his choice, no' mine, and I would have to live with it."

Gunnolf gave her a dark smile. "And that is why I found you running through the woods, trying to avoid being shot?"

"When I believed my da was dead, I realized my da wouldna decide that for me, no' from the grave." She gave Gunnolf just as dark a smile back.

***

Gunnolf had been pondering whether or not James would want to intercede on Brina's father's behalf and send men to rid Robard of Seamus and his men. Her father had not asked for help from them, and Gunnolf wasn't certain James would be willing to commit his men to such a mission. In any event, he would ask. First, he had to reach Wynne's home. He hoped the lass was the one Wynne had seen in her visions. He couldn't imagine she wasn't.

Still, what if the lass was not? That the one he was to aid was still out there needing his help? Then he would be on his way again. At least, the snow had subsided and the air was a wee bit warmer, enough to begin to melt the snow. The thick mist was welcome though. It cloaked them from their enemies. Yet, it also cloaked their enemies from them. He'd been listening intently from the sounds all around them, watching the wolf pup lap up water from the creek. Then the pup lifted its head and twitched its ears back and forth, his amber eyes watching the area from whence they'd traveled.

Gunnolf's skin crawled, his muscles bunching in anticipation of meeting up with Seamus and his men. Gunnolf held his finger to his lips, telling Brina to remain silent, then helped her onto her saddle.

She looked worriedly at the pup standing by the water's edge, not close to where they'd tethered the horses in the woods.

Gunnolf knew it could be a fatal mistake if he ran to grab the pup and Seamus or his men appeared behind them, swords or arrows readied. He knew it, but he couldn't leave the pup out there alone, defenseless, orphaned.

"Stay," Gunnolf said to the lass, only mouthing the word. He was afraid Brina would ride to the creek, dismount, and grab the pup. She wouldn't be able to manage him and mount again on her own. If she could have, he would have watched her back and urged her to ride on.

Then he heard the sound of hooves walking along the beach, the mist and distance not allowing him to see any riders. But he heard two of them.

Gunnolf crouched and motioned to the puppy to come to him. If he and the wolf lived through this, they had to give it a name. He wanted to snap his fingers to get the pup's attention, but he didn't want the riders to hear him. Any sound could carry a distance. Though with the flow of the river, the sound of the horse's hooves clomping on the ground, and the distance they still were, the riders might not be able to hear anything else.

The pup was staring off in the same direction, watching for the riders, ignoring Gunnolf.

Gunnolf headed for the beach. Damn his need to protect the wolf pup. He knew better, yet he couldn't leave him behind. Gunnolf moved as silently as he could across the crunchy snow to grab him. As soon as Gunnolf was close, the pup ran to him, wagging his tail as if he knew he was supposed to come then.

Out of the mist, two men galloped like dark demons. Both were black haired, the one wearing a red plaid, the other's hair pulled back, a braid hanging over his eyes as the wind whipped it about.

On foot by the side of the creek, Gunnolf was at a strong disadvantage as the two warriors bore down on him. Instead of making a stand for it, which would probably lead to his death, he seized the pup and dashed back to where the horses were. He shoved the puppy into Brina's waiting arms, her expression full of angst.

"Seamus's men?" Gunnolf quickly asked Brina.

"Aye. Both would kill you without giving it a second thought. Dinna listen to them if they say they willna harm you."

"Aye." Gunnolf knew they would kill him given half the chance just because he was with the lass. He would have told her to ride ahead, but he couldn't in all good conscience do so. Not when she had no protector to watch over her. If he were to die here, the men would catch up to her anyway, and he would be able to do nothing about it.

"I will return." He leapt onto his horse and rode at a gallop toward the men, knowing that even at these odds he could be a dead man, but he would do all he could to keep the lass safe from Seamus and his men.

"We draw no weapons against you!" the one man said, but the other man must not have heard the plan correctly because he had unsheathed his sword.

"I am here under peaceful means." Gunnolf spoke the words for Seamus's men's benefit in the event the warriors broke off the fight. But he was ready to use Aðalbrandr if necessary. He couldn't hesitate. Since they were Seamus's men, they were at cross-purposes. If these men indicated that they'd leave him and Brina be, they might attempt to ambush them later when they were trying to sleep, or return to Seamus to let him know where they were. Then Gunnolf would have to face all his men at one time. He knew from their hard expressions, they meant to kill him.

Fighting two men was much better odds than six. Gunnolf turned his horse sharply to the outside of the rightmost rider and swung his sword at him since he was the one armed. At this angle, Gunnolf had the advantage. His and the black-eyed man's swords hit hard, the vibration jarring Gunnolf's arm as he rode past, the clanging of metal ringing across the mist. Gunnolf hoped the other men were far away and wouldn't hear the sound of the swordfight.

He whipped around to fight the man again and saw the other galloping after Brina, who had taken off in the direction they had to go. The man he'd fought was anticipating taking Gunnolf down, but now the odds were only one against one, and Gunnolf smiled with dark satisfaction.

Though he had to end this quickly, ride after the other man, and take him down before he absconded with Brina.

CHAPTER 6

Her heart pounding wildly, Brina galloped along the beach away from the man pursuing her. Then deciding she couldn't outrun Lann, she guided her horse into the woods, stopped, and readied the bow. He was the same man who had shot her, when he was supposed to be bringing her in alive, not killing or injuring her! He unsheathed his sword from its scabbard.

Holding her breath, she pulled the string taut and released. The arrow struck him in the chest, but he kept coming, murder in his black expression. He would kill her, not bring her to Seamus, she assumed, and she hurried to nock another arrow. She couldn't see Gunnolf for the fog, but she heard him fighting the other man, swords clashing, a few curses in Gaelic, and some shouts in a language she didn't recognize. She prayed Gunnolf would be victorious.

She released the second arrow and it struck her attacker's chest, lodging next to the other arrow. He was so near her now, she was afraid she had only one last shot before he was too close to effectively use the bow. She readied another arrow, hoping she could hit him before he swung at her with his sword. If he killed her, how would he explain her death to Seamus? Maybe he thought to hide her body and pretend he'd never found her.

The wolf pup squirmed to get out of the plaid she'd wrapped him in against her waist, making her shot go higher than she'd planned. To her surprise, the arrow struck the brigand in the center of his forehead. Upon impact, Lann grunted, lost his sword and it sank into the snow. He fell from his horse and landed on the ground with a dull thud. His horse ran on past her. Relieved that she had taken him down, she still worried about Gunnolf, and Seamus and the rest of his men should they hear the fighting.

Her heart was pounding hard, as she considered her options. Should she ride off and hope Gunnolf was successful and catch up to her? Or wait for him?

If Gunnolf had killed Kear but was wounded, she'd have to take care of Gunnolf. She couldn't leave him behind to save herself.

She waited, watching the man she had shot full of arrows for signs of life. Lann lay lifeless on the ground for which she was grateful. She'd only killed one other man before when she'd had to defend herself. She thought she should be upset by the sight, but he would have killed her, had injured her already, and she could feel nothing but relief that he had not wounded her or ended her life. Then she glanced back in the direction of the fighting. The sounds of battle were no more, the snorting of horses, the only sound she heard. Her heart was still racing, cold chills crawling all over her as she watched for any sign of a victor. Had both men been wounded and were lying in the snow suffering from their injuries?

She was about to ride forth to check on Gunnolf, when a horse galloped in her direction, and she readied her bow. If it was the man who had been fighting Gunnolf, she prayed he had not killed her rescuer and that she could take Seamus's man down, then go to Gunnolf's aid.

The horse continued galloping toward her, the rider intent on catching up to her. The rider and black horse suddenly materialized out of the mist like a dark avenging angel, Gunnolf, a scowl on his face. His furs flying in the wind, the bearded Viking looked straight ahead at the man on the ground. Gunnolf was a welcome sight. Tears filled her eyes when she saw him well, her nerves on edge, and her body shaking from the ordeal. He only slowed down when he saw the dead man on the beach, then looked up at the woods, searching for signs of her.

"Gunnolf," she said, her voice whispered, tear-laden, thanking God he had survived.

He joined her, leapt down from his horse, and pulled her from her horse and into his arms. "Lass, I feared the other man had spirited you away."

She hugged Gunnolf lightly as the wolf pup squirmed between them. Gunnolf took the pup and set him down on the ground, then pulled Brina tighter against his hard body. "Are you all right?"

"Aye. He never reached me, but he is the one who shot me. I was afraid you hadna survived."

"Against only one man?" Gunnolf shook his head, his blue eyes sparkling with jollity. "It would take many more men than that to stop me."

"It took you long enough to rejoin me."

He smiled, tilted her chin up, and kissed her.

She melted under his kiss, even though his mouth was warm and sweet on hers, not plundering her like she had seen other men kissing women in the throes of passion. Even so, his kiss kindled a fire deep inside her. As warm as she felt, she believed the snow beneath her feet had to be melting, her body heating as he cupped her face and kissed her further.

Then he pressed his forehead against hers, as if trying to regain his senses.

She'd been kissed before—by lads when she was a younger lass, though if her da had known about it, he would have had them beaten for it. But she'd never been kissed like this. By a man full grown. A kiss full of compassion. Was it because Gunnolf was a Viking? Was he a seducer of women?

"We need to move." His voice was gruff, not angry, and just deeper than she'd heard him speak before.

"What about the men's bodies?"

"I'll move them into the woods, bury them in the snow, and we can take their horses with us. Without anyone to care for them, they might not survive. But we need to get going."

Brina helped him hide the bodies in the snow in the woods, then he lifted her onto her horse, secured the pup in his tunic, mounted his horse, and then took the reins of the dead man's horse.

They continued on their way, knowing that it would be just a matter of time before more of Seamus's men headed this way, looking for these two men. Hopefully, they wouldn't find them right away, giving her and Gunnolf a chance to reach the MacNeill lands before that. They spied the other rider-less horse up ahead, and she rode past Gunnolf to take the horse's reins. They continued on as before, Brina following Gunnolf's lead. He was riding a little faster now, and she suspected he recognized his surroundings, even though the fog continued to cling to the whole area from the ground to the heavens.

Then she saw something in the fog. Something that others could not see. A vision that came to her so vividly she thought she was seeing a ghost that suddenly appeared in the mist and was now whole, but she knew it was not so.

A white haired woman, old, yet youthful looking at

the same time, dressed in a brown kirtle and brat appeared before her at the edge of the forest. "You are no' the one he was sent to help. You know that, lass. You were no' the one who needed his aid."

The woman vanished and Brina saw Gunnolf riding ahead of her, pulling the spare horse as before. There was no woman in the mist. Gunnolf had only talked to the seer concerning coming to her aid. Was it the seer who had come to her in a vision, warning her that Gunnolf had helped the wrong woman? Would the other woman be imperiled by his mistake? Brina was afraid it was so. But she couldn't easily share her visions with others. They either did not believe her, or believed her and were afraid of her.

She couldn't help but worry about the woman Gunnolf should have aided. Would she die because Brina had sidetracked him?

When they stopped for another break, she asked Gunnolf, "Are we nearly there?"

She hoped so, but was afraid too. She envisioned an angry seer who was furious with Brina for stopping Gunnolf in what he was supposed to do.

"To Wynne's abode, *ja*," Gunnolf said. "We will stop there first, then ride another hour to the keep."

"What if I am no' the woman she sent you to fetch?"

His eyes widening, Gunnolf's expression was one of surprise. "Then I will leave you at the castle and return to seek her out."

Concerned, Brina folded her arms, trying to make sense of the vision. "No other women were out there. None that we saw, anyway."

"Ja, which is why I believe you have naught to worry about." Gunnolf drank from his flask while the puppy played in the snow.

"If I am the wrong woman, you would have to return to where Seamus's men are searching for me. What if they assumed you were the one who had brought me here?"

"I would be headed in the wrong direction, and you would not be with me. Why would I return to your da's lands after leaving you at the castle?"

She pondered that for a moment, but then frowned. "Because you have saved the wrong woman."

"I think not."

"But what if you have?" she persisted. "If you run across Seamus or his men, what excuse would you give for traveling on my da's lands?"

"I will think of something. I was turned around and so the direction I take would be different than the one we travelled. Do not worry yourself overmuch. I highly doubt there would be another woman in need of rescuing and that your circumstances did not warrant my help. Are you ready to ride?"

"You should ride one of the men's horses to rest your own, just in case." Then she let out her breath. "What if I wasna meant to be here? That I was supposed to be somewhere else?" Brina couldn't help but fret about it. It annoyed her when she had a vision like this. She was always trying to work out in her mind how to use her gift in the best way possible. Right now, she just felt anxious, like she had put the woman in danger because Gunnolf hadn't gone to her aid. That maybe she should have stayed with her da, despite his ruling her to go.

"What if the woman is injured or dying because of me?" Brina asked.

Gunnolf took hold of her hand and squeezed it. "I will find her, if such a woman exists. I do not believe this is the case. We will be at Wynne's shieling shortly." He helped Brina onto her horse, then paused. "Is there some reason why you seem so concerned over this?"

She opened her mouth to speak, but the pup woofed at something from such a distance, they both turned to see him chasing something much too far away. Gunnolf took off after him. Once he had the pup tucked securely in his tunic, Gunnolf climbed into his saddle, headed out, and didn't ask the question of her again.

Brina feared for Gunnolf and what would happen when the seer told him he had brought home the wrong woman, and he had to leave again. Would Wynne see something new in her visions? Something truly bad?

Brina prayed it was not so. She still didn't want him riding onto her da's lands with the good chance of running into Seamus and his men. She was afraid they'd kill Gunnolf just for being there, no matter the reason he might give.

As soon as she saw the stone shieling, smoke curling from the fireplace, she dreaded seeing the seer and not just in a vision this time.

CHAPTER 7

Gunnolf dismounted and raised his hand to knock on Wynne's door, knowing she would be pleased to see him and overjoyed to realize he had done as she had envisioned.

Before Gunnolf had the chance to knock on the door, Wynne yanked it open. "No, no, no." Wynne glanced in Brina's direction and frowned. "She isna the one, Gunnolf. You must head south again and search for the woman who needs your aid. 'Twas a simple task."

"She *was* in need of help." Gunnolf pulled the squirming puppy from his tunic and held him against his chest for a moment, not sure how Wynne would react to the wolf. "I will take the lass to Craigly Castle then and—"

"Nay, she is my granddaughter. You will leave her here with me. But aye, you must aid the woman in need."

"Grandmother?" Brina's eyes rounded and her lips parted in shock. "You know my name also? Brina?"

Gunnolf couldn't have been more surprised to learn of this. He couldn't believe Wynne could be correct about this.

"Aye, you knew this would come to pass. Not that this menacing Norseman would come for you, mayhap because he wasna supposed to. Or that the woman you saw in the woods was me, your grandmother. But you knew you would return to your mother's people. Give a man a task a woman should have completed and..." Wynne sighed.

"Gunnolf brought me here safely," Brina insisted, as he set the pup down on the ground and helped Brina off her horse. "Who is the other woman?" Brina asked while Gunnolf gave his horse oats before he left again.

Wynne waved her hand at her dismissively. "I know not. Only that you are no' the one Gunnolf was to have aided."

"How do you know this if you havena seen her in a vision?" Brina sounded perturbed.

Gunnolf was about to ask the very same question of Wynne.

"I dinna see her face, only that she isna wearing the same brown cloak as you. Hers is gray."

As far as Gunnolf was concerned, Brina had needed help getting here. She could not have traveled that distance on foot without Seamus or his men catching up to her or freezing to death.

"Mayhap I should leave then." Brina still sounded irked.

"Nay, you belong here with me. And I am grateful that Gunnolf brought you to me, but you must go now, Gunnolf." Then Wynne frowned at the wolf pup. "Where do you think Beowulf will be staying?"

Gunnolf wondered if Wynne had come up with her own name for the wolf or had some insight into what it should be. Being that Beowulf was a Nordic legendary hero, Gunnolf approved of the name.

"He will stay with Brina. One day, he can be her protector." He handed the pup to Brina. "Take care of Brina," he said to Wynne. Then he turned his attention to Brina. "Before long, I will come back to see how you are faring."

"Thank you for bringing me here safely." Brina took a step toward him and kissed him on the cheek, but it didn't seem enough after all they had been through.

She wrapped her arms around him and hugged him, and he embraced her warmly back, kissing her lips gently, but only because he knew Wynne was watching and Brina was her granddaughter. Otherwise the need roared through him to press his lips against hers much more passionately, hold her for longer, and breathe in her sweet scent to carry with him on the journey. He realized he had never taken his leave from a woman that he had wanted to warmly embrace or kiss before he parted company with her. Nor would he already be thinking about returning to see how she fared.

"Take care with the woman you were meant to aid. She will not be grateful," Brina warned.

A chill swept up his spine, his gaze swinging to Wynne.

Wynne had her hand on his shoulder, pushing him toward the door as if she feared he'd take more of an advantage of her granddaughter. "I told you the woman wouldna." She gave her granddaughter an annoyed look. "*This* one is *much* too grateful." Yet he knew Wynne didn't mean it with the way her eyes glinted with a bit of dark humor.

Gunnolf glanced back at Brina, knowing Wynne would take care of her, yet he felt disquieted that she might be just like Wynne. Why did Brina not tell him she knew this would come to pass? Yet he thought she had tried to warn him earlier. Had she had a vision then? It seemed to him from what Brina had said at the last, she had only known about it right before they arrived at Wynne's shieling. It didn't really matter though. Even if she'd had a vision of this earlier, he would not have risked allowing her to make her way here on her own alone.

How was he supposed to find the right woman now, if he'd found the wrong one the first time? If she was in dire straits, would he be too late now?

He had seen no one while he'd been traveling due south, but Brina. Then again, he had gotten lost and when he had returned to Wynne's dwelling, he had travelled northwest to reach her place. Without the snowstorm to hamper his direction, he would be able to head directly south.

"Someone will have to take care of the horses until one of James's men can move them to the stables," Gunnolf said.

Wynne was shaking her head. "You brought me a byre full of horses, a wolf, and didna aid the right lass."

Gunnolf smiled, winked at Brina, hoping she would be all right with her grandmother — he was still shocked over that — then mounted his own horse, and headed out again, praying he would find the other lass quickly.

***

"What if Seamus's men kill Gunnolf?" Brina asked Wynn, her voice angry. She didn't know her grandmother. If she was her kin, why didn't she use her visions to help save Brina's mother? Brina began to feed the rest of the horses in her grandmother's byre.

"Seamus and his men? If they run into him, they will try. Come, Brina. Bring the wolf pup."

"Did you see me in a vision?"

"Aye."

"And how I made it here?"

"With Gunnolf in a later vision."

"Then it was fate that Gunnolf and I met in the way in which we did, and we didna do what you foretold."

"The snowstorm threw him off course."

Brina set Beowulf down, and he curled up by

the fire. "Mayhap you mixed up your visions." Brina raised a brow at her grandmother.

Her grandmother frowned at her. "I dinna..." Then she bit her lip and shook her head. "Help me serve the food." Wynne removed the bread she'd been baking.

"Then 'tis true you have mixed up your visions before?" Brina persisted as she cut some cheese for both of them.

"Nay."

"No' once?"

Wynne looked sharply at her.

"Well, if you had a vision of another woman, but you also had a vision of Gunnolf bringing me here, he must have gone to help the other woman, *after* he brought me here. And you had the visions out of order."

Wynne ate a piece of the bannock, chewing slowly, eyeing Brina warily. "What vision did you have?"

"That my da had fallen from his horse after being wounded. I thought he was dead because Seamus didna return him home."

"He left him wounded in the glen to die, aye?"

"Aye. We met with Da at a shieling where some of his loyal people were caring for him. I worry that Seamus will learn he is there and have him murdered along with those who are protecting him."

"If Seamus learns of it, aye. 'Tis possible." Wynne drank honeyed mead from her tankard.

"Should I have stayed and tried to protect my da?"

"Nay. You wouldna have been able to protect him. Seamus would have beaten you for your impudence and wed you. You need to be here. You were supposed to be here. What did you see in your vision of Gunnolf?"

"He was in my way, and then…and then he wasna."

"He vanished?" Wynne looked shocked.

"Well, nay. I shoved him down. One of Seamus's men had loosed an arrow, and I was trying to avoid being hit until this mountain of a man stood in my way."

"Gunnolf." Wynne nodded sagely, as if there could be no other.

"Could you no' have saved my mother?"

"With my visions? She had them herself. She knew what was coming. We canna always change fate."

Brina closed her gaping mouth. "But we can sometimes…" She didn't say it as a question, because she'd seen visions, and then they hadn't come to pass.

"Sometimes. Aye. I am no' sure why. 'Tis as if some are warnings of what is to come unless we heed the warning."

"I was warned that one of the doors would be locked at the keep, so I didna attempt to use it when I fled Anfa Castle."

"Aye. 'Tis true I have had such visions."

"I couldna have avoided running into Gunnolf. He...he was in my path."

"Aye. And you wouldna have wanted to either, from the looks of it."

Brina's face warmed.

"Take care that you dinna fall in love with Gunnolf, Brina. Your da killed his brother Hallfred during the same battle that your da was struck down. Gunnolf doesna know his brother settled on the farmlands near your da's. 'Tis a tale too oft told. A fight over something not worth quarreling over and one man lay dead, the other the victor."

"Nay," Brina gasped. "You didna tell Gunnolf?"

"I only learned of it after he was gone. He believed his brother left him for dead and returned to the Northlands. Which he did. Gunnolf made a home for himself here. That life was his past. I didna remember it until just now."

"You had a vision of this?"

"Aye."

"Why? I thought they only came to us if we had some involvement in the situation."

"It does involve us. I have always felt a closeness to Gunnolf because his grandmother also had visions and we had...connected in that way. She prayed I would watch out for him like she had done. She died before Gunnolf's brother settled in the Highlands. I dinna know it either until I learned he was killed."

Brina felt sickened by the news. "Gunnolf will

have every reason to hate me then."

"Nay, 'tis your da who killed his brother, no' you."

Brina didn't agree with Wynne. She believed Gunnolf would wish he had never agreed to do anything her da had asked of him, including bringing her here. She felt saddened that Gunnolf's brother was dead, and he'd never even known he was living in the Highlands.

"What was the dispute over?"

Wynne sighed. "A blood feud, stolen cattle. His grandfather killed yours. 'Tis the way of men who canna stop their constant fighting."

***

Gunnolf traveled all day long, stopping for respites, the weather warming and the sun coming out, melting more of the snow. In all that time, he had not seen any sign of anyone, Seamus, his men, or any lass who needed his aid. He told himself that Wynne was never wrong, and yet he wondered if she truly was this time.

Early that night, he smelled smoke. When he finally reached a shieling, he knew he was on Brina's father's land. Gunnolf came through the woods and saw two horses tied up out front. Concerned they might belong to Seamus or his men, Gunnolf decided not to approach the place just yet.

Then a woman screamed from inside. He hid his horse in the woods, then ran toward the stone dwelling, the moonlight reflecting off the melting snow. He could only see the two horses. Maybe more were in the byre though.

He drew closer to the shieling, candles lighting the place and filtering through the shutters, a fire in the fireplace giving off additional light.

"Tell me where Lady Brina is!" a man growled.

Gunnolf's hackles rose and his blood heated with anger. Whoever this man was, he was after the lass.

"I dinna know. I swear it." The woman responding sounded tearful and scared.

Was it Seamus? Or one of his men bullying the woman? How many men were there? Gunnolf moved silently to a shuttered window and tried to see through the slats.

"Why would you leave the keep unless you had come with her, or planned to meet with her here?"

"I feared for her safety. When I learned she had slipped away, I thought I could find her and bring her home," the woman said, sniffling.

Gunnolf could only see a little bit of a woman's slight figure, a gray kirtle, her hands clutched together as if she was scared.

"A woman? On your own?" The man made a derisive sound under his breath, and Gunnolf saw him move into view, just his bulky size, his back to Gunnolf. "How do you know she came this way?"

"I dinna. She was distraught about her da's death. She wanted desperately to see where he had fallen and say a prayer over him. When I couldna find her where all the fighting had gone on, I thought she might be going home to her mother's family. 'Tis what I would do if I were in her shoes. Though I told her she…"

"She…what?" the man growled.

Gunnolf wanted to take care of the man at once, but he was trying to see if anyone else was in the shieling first so he'd be better prepared to fight several men if there were more than just this one.

"I told her that she needed to get ready for Seamus. Then the word spread that she had left the castle and…and I got worried, so I took her horse to see if I could find her myself and bring her home."

"You are lying," the man said again with a sneer. "Do you know what I believe? You had secretly planned to meet with her here. She bade you to bring her horse and clothes for her when Seamus was already gone."

So the man inside was one of his men, not Seamus. Disappointed, Gunnolf had hoped to make short work of him and be done with the rogue.

"There was so much turmoil at the castle over the lady running off, that you were able to slip away. And then you were both going to meet here and steal away."

"Nay."

Gunnolf moved quickly around the shieling to the door, careful not to spook the horses and give himself away. He'd only heard one man speaking.

Maybe the two horses tied up out front belonged to this man and Brina and there were no more armed men inside. Gunnolf carefully pulled Aðalbrandr from its sheath.

Sword in hand, Gunnolf yanked open the door. He quickly glanced around the room, saw a woman and her baby and probably her husband, sitting on the floor in one corner of the room, his arm around the woman's shoulders, the baby sleeping in her lap.

The tearful woman was standing near the hearth. He expected her to scream at the sight of the wild Norseman throwing open the door and wielding a sword ready for battle. Instead, she just stared at him wide-eyed, and he did likewise when he saw her. She appeared to be a little older than Brina, with eyes as blue, and hair nearly as dark. If he didn't know any better, he would think the women were distantly related. She was also wearing a red handprint on her face, and one eye was swollen, which enraged him.

Seamus's man unsheathed a sword and came toward him, swinging his weapon with deadly force. Gunnolf fell back, quickly moving outside the shieling. Not because he felt overwhelmed by the man's blows, but because he didn't want the brigand to hurt anyone inside.

"Who are you?" the redheaded man growled, slicing at Gunnolf with such powerful sweeps of his sword, Gunnolf was amused that he had bothered to ask the question. Just to hear himself talk? Or distract Gunnolf?

If the man truly wanted to question him, why not back off and give him the chance to answer? Gunnolf suspected the man didn't really care. Just like Gunnolf didn't care who he was. Only that the lass was safe from whatever he had planned to do to her. Gunnolf envisioned him taking her to see Seamus, and the questioning would begin all over again. He would not put it past the man to treat her ill in trying to learn the truth, certain the marks on her face had to do with this man questioning her and were not the result of her incurring them accidentally.

"If you were to live, I would tell you to inform Seamus that Brina is safe and will not have to marry the likes of him. But you will not be around to tell him anything," Gunnolf said.

The man grunted and took another swing. What Gunnolf didn't expect was for the man's eyes to widen right before Gunnolf thrust his sword, and collapse before Gunnolf managed to cut him. As the man fell, Gunnolf saw the arrow in his back. He looked up to see the tearful woman holding a bow in her hands, another arrow readied.

Gunnolf quickly sheathed Aðalbrandr.

"Is it true Brina is safe?" Her voice and hands trembled as she lowered her bow.

"*Ja.* And if you are of need of my help, I will take you to see her."

She turned to the family in the house. "Thank you for helping me."

"We are sorry we couldna do anything more for you," the man said.

"Nay, Seamus and his men are ruthless." Then she seized a gray brat and pulled it around her. "Take me to see Brina."

"You really did not intend to find her and convince her to return home, did you?" Gunnolf asked.

"Nay. Think you I want to see her beaten?"

"Nay. Did the man do that to you?"

"Aye. It could have been worse."

"We will take care of the man's body," the sheepherder said.

"And the horse?" Gunnolf asked.

"Take him with you, if you would. If Seamus or his men see the horse without a rider, they will surely look for him somewhere in the area. If the horse is not here, Seamus and his brigands will continue to look elsewhere."

"*Ja*, will do."

"Will Seamus say you are a horse thief if you take the man's horse?" the woman asked.

"Seamus's man is dead. Though Seamus, should he discover his body, might not believe it was a fair fight."

"He might have killed you, and a woman is defenseless against a man like that. He would have killed me if he hadna needed to know where Brina was."

Gunnolf didn't believe the woman was defenseless in the least. "You were Brina's companion?"

"Aye. I am Lynette."

"We will not get very far. Not as late as it is. But I wish to put some distance between this shieling and us."

"Aye, as do I. You took Lady Brina to be with her mother's people?"

"*Ja*. She is with her grandmother. I will take you there as well."

"I dinna understand why you took Brina there and came back this way. Surely you must have had some other reason for being here."

"It seems I was meant to assist you."

"Wynne sent you because of a vision?"

"You know her?"

"Aye. So she sent you to fetch me?"

"*Ja*. At least...I hope I have the right woman this time."

"You mean you aided Brina first."

"*Ja*. How do you know Wynne?"

"She is my grandmother."

***

Brina couldn't sleep, not with worrying that the woman Gunnolf was meant to aid could be dead.

"Sleep," Wynne said. "He has found Lynette and is bringing her here now. She had meant to find you and brought clothes, food, and your horse. Though they will have to endure the cold for a bit longer while they get some rest until they are able to travel again."

Brina sat up on her pallet. "Lynette? Oh, nay.

She followed me?" Brina rose from the bedding and paced across the floor.

Brina couldn't believe Lynette had left the safety of the keep to find her and try to help her. But maybe she had taken off too so that Seamus wouldn't beat her for not telling him Brina had left when she had.

"Aye."

That made Brina think of how Gunnolf had warmed her, and she couldn't help how much that bothered her. Would he warm Lynette in the same way? She ground her teeth. Yet she did not want Lynette to suffer from the cold.

Wynne said, "If you dinna sleep, I will make you work until you are too tired to stay awake. Return to bed. She is well. You are well. Gunnolf is well. Go. To. Sleep."

"She...isna too cold, is she?"

Wynne said nothing.

Brina stared at the flames in the fireplace. "Her fingers? Her toes?"

"She is riding your horse. She isna walking in the snow like you were."

Brina tried to hide a smile and settled back under her blankets. Beowulf joined her and she cuddled with him.

"This pleases you? That you will have your horse back? Or are you pleased Lynette will be here?"

"Both. I was just worried about her. About...the cold."

Wynne snorted. "You worried about her being with Gunnolf. What happened between the two of you?"

"Naught happened."

"He kept you warm, did he no'?"

"Aye. As a gentleman would."

Wynne shook her head and pulled her covers higher. "You...worry he will keep Lynette as warm."

"I hope that he does. He is a respectable man, even if he is a Viking."

"Good. Because she is your sister and it is important that you feel thus about her."

Brina sat back up and stared at her grandmother. "Why do you think so? My da never said she was my sister. He has never treated her like she was his own daughter."

Wynne let out her breath. "Lynette's father isna your own. But your mother was also her mother. I was going to share this with you on the morrow when she arrived."

Brina looked at the fire again, trying to make sense of it all. "How is that possible? My da said her bairn was male."

"Aye. She had twins. The boy died, but the girl survived."

"Lynette," Brina whispered.

"Aye, and that is why your aunt and uncle raised her. They were her aunt and uncle too."

"Da didna tell me she was my sister." Brina was overwhelmed with the news, angry at her father for treating Lynette in such a manner, and not telling Brina the truth.

"Your da wanted your mother. He didna want the child she bore. So he forbade anyone to discuss that Lynette was your sister. You know what they say about twins?"

Brina frowned at her grandmother.

"'Tis said by some that a man can only produce one child in a woman. So if a woman has two, she has lain with two different men. Which is another reason he probably kept it a secret."

"That isna true."

"Nay, but some believe so and 'tis hard to change their beliefs."

"My sister knew this all along?" Brina was outraged.

"Aye, your mother told her when she was old enough to understand. She also warned her never to tell you after you were born. She hoped that someday you would learn the truth when you were old enough to keep the secret. But that day never came. Until now."

"I will tell the world she is my sister."

"Your da will disapprove. Mayhap even send her away."

"I am no' longer living with my da. Mayhap my sister and I can work at Craigly Castle like our mother did. We will let everyone know we are sisters." Then Brina frowned. "If...my da wasna her da, who was?"

"'Tis believed that Laird James's da was. But

we dinna know for sure. Your mother would never say, and the old laird died some years ago, so we may never know."

Brina wanted to know the truth. If the old laird was indeed Lynette's da, she was the laird's daughter and should be afforded a better position with the staff because of it. But what if the laird's wife did not like that her husband had given Brina's mother a bairn and she was coming here now? Brina hadn't considered that. She didn't want to do anything that would hurt Lynette.

Brina rose from her bedding and stood by the fire, rubbing her arms. She hoped Gunnolf was keeping her sister warm. And then she hoped Lynette would be glad that Brina now knew they were sisters. They could truly *be* sisters now, and Lynette wouldn't just be her companion.

"Brina. Go. To. Sleep."

But Brina couldn't stop worrying that Gunnolf and Lynette would make it to Wynne's shieling safely. Brina was so glad to meet her grandmother and so happy to learn about her sister, but she still feared for them if Seamus should discover them. She knew Seamus would believe Lynette was coming to her aid once he learned of it, particularly since Lynette had Brina's horse.

***

"Will you no' lie with me so we may both stay warm?" Lynette asked as she made a bed for herself on the floor of the abandoned stone shieling, while Gunnolf made a fire, the thatched roof long gone, the walls still standing. "I may or may no' be James's sister."

He was still considering the lass's words about her relationship with Wynne. "You are James's sister?"

"I have heard rumors to that effect."

He made a bed for himself with enough distance from the lass, but still near the fire to stay warm for the few hours they would sleep before they were on their way again.

"Will you no' move closer to the fire? I promise I willna bite." Lynette smiled.

Her actions made her appear grateful that he had come along. Did that mean she was *not* the woman he was supposed to have found and taken home with him?

"I am warm enough where I am, just as you are. If you are James's sister, he will make a match for you."

She laughed in an annoyed way. "You think his mother, Lady Akira, will accept me in her household if she learns her husband had his way with my mother and I was the result of it?"

"You are not to blame for how you came into this world. Lady Akira is kindhearted. She even took me in and raised me with her sons and daughter."

"She has a daughter?"

Gunnolf shook his head. "She died a couple of years ago."

"I am sorry to hear that. Do you think Lady

Akira willna wish me to be around then, if I remind her that her own daughter is dead?"

"As I said before, Lady Akira is goodhearted. She took me in when I imagine not too many would have wished me to be around. I often fought with James, even though he was six and ten summers at the time and the laird of his clan. I was angry with the world back then, having lost those I loved, but too wounded to journey any further. I slept in the stables for quite a time when I was healed up enough before Lady Akira convinced me to stay with her sons." Gunnolf sighed. "'Tis a wonder James and his kin did not toss me beyond the curtain wall and let me fend for myself. But they kept me there until I was well enough to truly fight, teaching James and others some of my skills, while they taught me much more." He shrugged. "After a while, I had become a brother to James and his brothers and cousin, and to his sister for the time that she lived, and realized that I had found a home. If you wish it, you will also."

He knew it of a certainty. He usually wouldn't have told anyone so much about himself, but he wanted her to know that she had nothing to fear from the MacNeills.

"Are you afraid of me?" Lynette smiled at him, the light of the flames flickering across her face, her eyes bright and sparkling.

"Nay. Not of you, but of how James would react."

"Do you think he would wish you to marry

me?" She sounded surprised.

"The thought had briefly crossed my mind."

She smiled wickedly then and laughed a little. "I would tell James you had also slept with my sister, so which lass should you truly wed? Brina's da would most likely wish you were wed to her and no' to me."

"Get some rest, lass. It will not be long before we are on our way again." But it bothered him that not only did the men working for Robard believe he would insist on Gunnolf marrying his daughter, but that her sister believed the same. He knew James well enough that if he thought Gunnolf and Lynette agreeable, he would have them wed.

Gunnolf had no intention of marrying anyone. How could he help a couple of women in need and suddenly be faced with the prospect of marrying not just one, but either of them, depending on which clan wanted the deed done the most.

If Seamus didn't take over Brina's clan first, *if* Robard was no longer chief, then Seamus would most likely want Brina back. Or maybe not if he believed she was no longer a maid.

Gunnolf finally fell asleep and slept for a few hours, but woke to the sound of horses galloping in the distance. He quickly woke Lynette, put out the fire, helped her onto Brina's horse, and mounted his own. Then they traveled north again in the early morning hours as the sun began to appear behind the forest and mist again cloaked the whole area.

They didn't dare speak to each other as they quickly moved out of the area. They still had a few more hours to ride before they reached Wynne's shieling. Gunnolf was alert as to what was going on all around them and already thinking ahead. He wondered how Brina would take the news when she learned Lynette was her sister. For that matter, how Lady Akira and James would feel when James learned Lynette might be his father's daughter.

By the time they had reached the MacNeill lands, the horses they'd heard had been left far behind, when Gunnolf spied a middle-aged, portly woman making her way across the glen. She was waving frantically at him, her gray brat fluttering in the breeze, catching his eye. Gunnolf galloped off toward her and when he reached her, he saw she was Olga, one of the midwives for the clan. He knew then from her frantic expression, she was needed at once at one of the shielings.

He pulled her up onto his horse, and she directed him to the right one. "I shoulda been there long before this," she groused. "But that worthless husband of mine has been off to who knows where and left me without a way to get their quickly."

"I will have you to the widow's cottage in no time," he said, as he heard Lynette ride up beside him. At least he hoped they were in time.

Olga eyed Lynette. "Who be you? Dinna tell me Gunnolf is taking a wife now."

Lynette smiled. "Nay. No' me. He may take someone else as his wife though."

Olga snorted. "You are riding alone with one unmarried maid, but interested in another?"

"Nay," Gunnolf said. He didn't need the word to spread through the clan that he was suddenly marrying a lass. It wouldn't take long before they knew which one that might be when they learned another had joined their clan.

Olga laughed. But then she said, "Hurry, Gunnolf. I dinna have all day. She has been in labor for four days, and I had to see to another mother because she was taking so long. But then I knew I had to return to her and that useless husband of mine…" She continued to rant until they reached the shieling.

He helped Olga off the horse, and she dashed for the door of the shieling, hollering at Lynette to come help her.

Gunnolf helped her down, and then he was about to enter the abode, but Olga said, "Nay, you. Attend to the horses, or something."

Delivering a bairn could take hours, days, weeks, and so he wasna expecting a baby's cry so all of a sudden. He'd fed the horses and then paced, and Lynette came out of the dwelling smiling. "It's a baby boy."

The midwife poked her head out the door. "I dinna need your help any further, Gunnolf."

He helped Lynette onto her horse and the two of them rode off.

"She was the one, it seemed, that needed your help," Lynette said smiling. "She wasna grateful, aye?"

Gunnolf shook his head. "*Ja.* I am just glad it all worked out."

"Will you marry Brina?" Lynette suddenly asked.

"Nay. The lass wouldna be interested."

"Olga said it was past time that you did."

A few lasses he knew also felt the same way. Each would bring trouble to a marriage, he suspected. Brina more than most with the unresolved situation with her father and Seamus.

They hadn't ridden very much farther when they saw James with several of his men headed their way. Had he worried about Gunnolf's safe return? Maybe that he had never returned to the castle to tell him Wynne was all right.

As soon as he reached him, James scolded, "I canna believe you took off in a snowstorm to help a woman and didna send word." He inclined his head a little to Lynette in greeting.

"How was I to send word when I was in a hurry to aid the woman? Besides, I am a Norseman. What is a little snow to me?"

James snorted. "Wynne said you got lost and brought home the wrong woman. And now you will have to marry her."

"I spoke with Brina's da. He was wounded and in his condition, he might not even live. In any case, he only wanted me to bring her here safely, and he had no intention of me marrying the lass."

"He is alive?" Lynette asked, looking suddenly very pale.

"*Ja*, I am sorry, lass. I should have known you would not have had word." He told her that Robard was in hiding at the moment but would take over the clan again as soon as he could.

"Against Seamus and his men?"

"There are fewer of his men now. We took care of three of them."

"More will follow him, out of fear, if naught else," Lynette said.

"As to Brina, that isna the word her da sent to me, Gunnolf," James said.

Gunnolf glanced at Lynette, thinking that this conversation should be private. "Mayhap we should speak of this after I escort Lynette to her grandmother's cottage."

James looked at Lynette. "You are Wynne's granddaughter?"

"Aye."

"Where is your mother?"

"Davina married Robard, Brina's da, but Brina's mother died in childbirth. Brina's mother and mine were the same."

"And your da is..."

"No' sure."

"I'll have one of my men take Lynette to Wynne's place," James said.

"Nay. I need to learn if I have aided the correct woman this time." Though Gunnolf suspected the midwife had been the right woman all along.

"We will go with you and then we will return to Craigly Castle. My mother had been worried about you when you didna return from seeing to Wynne and making sure she was all right during the snowstorm. I had to go there myself and learn what had happened to you both. And what do I find? A lass who had been stolen from her home."

"What?" Gunnolf said, dumbfounded.

Lynette smiled, but didn't say a word in his

defense.

Had Brina lied to James about what had happened? Or had her father said Gunnolf had stolen her away? He couldn't believe it.

When they arrived at the shieling, Brina rushed out to greet Lynette, all teary-eyed and smiling. "We are sisters," she exclaimed, sounding thrilled, then she frowned to see the bruising around her eye. "Who did this to you?"

"One of Seamus's men, Kemble. But he is dead."

Gunnolf helped Lynette down from Brina's horse and the two women embraced. He was glad they were delighted to learn the news, and that Brina was treating her like her long lost family.

"I was afraid you would be upset to learn the truth," Lynette said.

"Nay. I am so happy." Brina glanced at Gunnolf. "Thank you for bringing Lynette here."

Wynne poked her head out the door. "Aye, you got it right, though she is no' the right lass either."

"I picked up the midwife and she delivered Tia's baby."

"A male. Aye. She was the one. She had a gray cloak, aye?" Then Wynne went back inside.

"She had her visions out of order," Brina whispered. "You did what you were supposed to do...in the correct order. But I dinna believe she wants to admit it."

Gunnolf was glad that was settled. "Good. James tells me there is some concern that I stole you from your home." Gunnolf wanted her to clarify to James that he had done no such thing.

"How could that be?" Brina frowned. "When I was alone as I escaped the castle? If Seamus thinks to spread such a lie to explain why I ran away—"

"Your da sent the missive to me," James clarified.

Brina's jaw dropped. Frowning, she said to Gunnolf, "I told you he didna have my best interest at heart. Now it seems he doesna have yours either."

"Come, Gunnolf. We must talk," James said. "We will leave the spare horses here so the ladies can use them when they come to the castle. Ladies, will you be needing anything?"

They shook their heads.

"Lady Akira will want to meet with you both. If your grandmother wishes to come, she will be welcome. I will return for you in a few hours. Several of my men will stay here for your protection."

Then he and Gunnolf inclined their heads a bit to the ladies in farewell. Gunnolf still could not believe Brina's da would make up such a lie about him and his daughter. Aye, that he might want Gunnolf to marry her because he'd been alone with her. But that he stole her away from her castle? He could understand if *Seamus* had perpetuated the lie so that he could save face.

Then again, if Brina was right in her assumption that her da was not to be trusted...

"Come." James motioned in the direction of the castle. As soon as they rode off, the rest of his escort gave them more distance so they could speak in private. "We have a problem."

"You know I did not steal the lass from her home."

"You didna even know the woman." James smiled at him. Then he frowned. "We still need to resolve this."

"How did you learn of it?"

"A farmer named Cadel came with the news. He must have ridden off right after you left Brina at Wynne's shieling."

"Directly from Robard," Gunnolf said.

"Aye."

Gunnolf snorted. "He could have ridden with us and helped to protect the lass."

"Apparently, his mission was to see that his chief's missive was brought at once to me instead."

"None of this is true. You only have to ask Wynne." Gunnolf knew she would tell the truth.

"I have, Gunnolf." James shook his head. "And I believe you, but you were with the lass all alone."

"So was I with Lynette."

James nodded. "She doesna have a da who is a powerful chief and who wishes this wrong righted. You see the predicament I am in."

"Her da is a wounded chief who might not live. And now this Seamus has taken over the clan so Robard is no longer so powerful. The lass herself would tell you the truth. Her sister even."

"Who would believe the lasses' words over the chief? Brina is a lovely lass. You could do much worse. Her da rules his own clan."

"She is promised to a man named Seamus. And need I remind you who now rules the clan while Robard lies wounded and in hiding?"

"Aye, so you stole the lass before she could wed Seamus, which is acceptable for our kind. According to Brina's da, she didna wish to be married to the man. Robard said his daughter showed real affection for you. When he questioned if she would rather marry you, she told him she would," James said. "Therefore he made a pact with you to steal her away if you would wed her and protect her from the brigand who wouldna come to his aid when he was wounded, but left him to die in the glen."

Gunnolf closed his gaping mouth. He couldn't believe how the chief had twisted things around to suit his purposes. "He lies. She...doesna even like Norsemen. She said so. One of my kind killed her grandfather." Gunnolf didn't believe that the lass had told her father that she wanted to marry Gunnolf when he spoke to her alone. But maybe she had. If so, he still didn't believe her da had made it her choice. Why else would she have been teary-eyed when she left the room after speaking with him the second time?

"Regardless of what was said, we still have a situation on our hands," James said.

Gunnolf appreciated James for including him as far as how they were going to handle the matter. The chief could have just said he wanted Gunnolf to rethink his position and make this right. Gunnolf was certain James wouldn't want either him or the lass to be forced into a marriage they didn't wish, though gaining support from other clans was always a good thing.

"What do you propose?" Gunnolf asked.

James shrugged. "We would have an alliance with Robard's clan if you wed Brina."

Gunnolf frowned. "If Seamus has not taken

over his clan and killed Robard in the meantime."

James looked thoughtful as they continued their journey to Craigly Castle. "The chief wishes something more of you. He says since you can kill six warriors at once, he wants you to marry Brina, oust Seamus, and take over the clan until he can regain his health. But he will have you serve as his second in command, and once he is no longer able to manage, he wants you to take his place. He has spoken in private with the elders through one of his loyal men and they are against it. But that is because they dinna know you like we do and they also dinna believe you can kill six men at once."

Gunnolf felt his whole way of life spinning out of control. He couldn't imagine trying to lead a clan that was against him taking power from the onset. Was the whole business all a lie? What if Robard only wanted him to help him overthrow Seamus and then Gunnolf was no longer needed and was a dead man? "Where did you get that idea? That I can?"

"From the chief. Pray tell, did you tell him thus?" James smirked at him.

"Nay. Only that I had fought six men at once a time or two and had *not* been successful."

"It seems he didna believe you or didna want to believe you."

"And since the man so easily lied about my promise to marry Brina, who is to say he is not lying about wanting me to run things until he is well? That he will not dispose of me once he is in charge again?"

"True. I see your point. Though if he is sincere, you have a couple of choices. One would be to marry the lass with my blessing and her da's, face Seamus and all the men he has recruited, and win over those who wouldna wish a Norseman to rule."

"Or?"

"Or continue on as before, fighting my battles, serving as my brother, staying far away from Robard's lands."

"And Brina?"

"She can do as she wishes. Marry whom she wishes. Stay here, return there. My wife will most likely want her to serve her as a lady's companion. She shouldna be living out so far from the castle in the event Seamus learns of it and still wants her. She would have no protection there."

"I agree. Though she may wish to live with her grandmother and help her. If Seamus should come here looking to return her to her father's castle and you do not give her up…"

"Her da has ordered that you marry the lass. So 'tis between the two of you. If Seamus thinks to convince me to turn her over to him, he wouldna be successful."

Gunnolf let out his breath, but then considered Lynette and her safety. If Seamus learned the lasses were sisters, he could see Seamus trying to use her as a bargaining tool. Especially if she turned out to be James's sister.

"What about Lynette? Do you think she may be your sister?"

"If she is, I will welcome her gladly into the family. But I want to investigate the matter further before my mother learns of it. I believe she would be happy, but no' if I say the lass is my sister, and then discover she isna. In the meantime, she and Brina are welcome to become part of our clan."

"What if Seamus thinks to steal her away to force your hand to give up Brina in her place?"

"They will visit with Wynne, and then the lasses will be staying at the castle."

"What if the lasses are anything like their grandmother?" Gunnolf was afraid some of James's kinsmen would treat the lasses like they did Wynne, friendly, but wary. Would a man want to marry either of the lasses if he feared she had second sight?

"It may be harder for them to wed if the men are superstitious, aye. I have considered this. I wonder if Seamus is aware of this."

"Mayhap not. I am certain the lasses would have kept their gift secret. I am not even sure Brina's da knows." They saw riders headed their way and Gunnolf said, "Looks like Lady Akira and an escort."

James let out his breath. "My mother must have gotten word about Lynette." He looked around. "Aye, Anwell is no longer with us. He must have informed her of the news."

They galloped toward James's mother and her escort and when they reached her, Lady Akira said, "Where are the lasses?"

"I was giving them a chance to visit with their grandmother. They have only just met her," James explained.

"Nonsense. Bring them all here straight away." Then Lady Akira frowned as if she remembered James was the laird and made such decisions. "Unless you dinna wish it."

James smiled. "For you, my lady mother, I would do anything."

"Good. Because I dinna believe it is safe for Brina to be there. Mayhap no' for Lynette either. I need to speak with you. Send Gunnolf to escort them."

James glanced at Gunnolf. He bowed his head

a little. "As you wish, my lady." Gunnolf assumed then that word had reached her that Lynette might be James's half-sister. Maybe because she was also Brina's half sister, she wanted to welcome her too. Though knowing Lady Akira, she wanted to take both the girls under her care. He just hoped the lasses would be all right with coming with him and that Wynne would also.

CHAPTER 8

James sighed as he rode beside his mother and escorted her back to the castle. "What is this really all about?" He wasn't about to assume she believed Lynette was his half sister. He had every intention of learning the truth first before he shared the news with his mother.

"Gunnolf must marry Brina."

Surprised she was thinking of Brina and Gunnolf and not of Lynette, James frowned at his mother. "I wouldna think you would wish this of either Gunnolf or the lass."

"Gunnolf's grandmother was like Wynne, having had the gift."

James lifted his brows in surprise. How had his mother known when he hadn't?

"I have talked to Wynne about it. Did you know she loves Gunnolf like a grandson? As to the abilities, he will be understanding of what the lass can do, if she does indeed have the gift. Many of our family members have married lasses who have special gifts. Gunnolf has never been unsettled by the notion."

"He isna married to a lass who has gifts like that either."

His mother waved her hand in dismissal. "He isna bothered by it. He willna mind. Mayhap, he doesna believe in all of it, but he still understands. He is a good man and he deserves a good wife."

"Aye, one who wishes to be with him in return." James really was surprised at his mother's thoughts on the subject. She had treated Gunnolf like a son. James couldn't believe she would want him to marry a lass unsuited to him if he and Brina didn't get along.

"Think you he will stop working for you long enough to find a wife? He deserves to have a loving wife and bairns of his own."

"He has shown no interest in any of the lasses, at least no more than a passing interest. If he were smitten with one, he would have done something about it. If Brina was your daughter, would you want her wed to a man she didna know?" James asked.

"If the man she wanted was Gunnolf? Aye. I have raised him since he was five and ten winters. I would be proud to have him married to my daughter, had I one. Even if I hadna raised him, women are oft married to men for clan gain and the couple wouldna know each other well beforehand, if at all. There would be no consideration to whether they were suited to one another or no'. But this goes beyond that."

"He was with her alone and this will hurt her chances to marry another. Also, if she has Wynne's gift—" James said.

"There is more than that to this matter."

James studied his mother's set jaw. He knew that look. She had always been good at doing what was best for the clan, and he suspected her notions had something to do with more than just a marriage between Gunnolf and Brina.

"You believe Gunnolf can rule Robard's clan."

Lady Akira took a deep breath. "Gunnolf is a good man. His unswerving loyalty, excellent fighting skills, and natural born leader traits—set him above all the rest. Yet, he follows orders well, and thinks for himself if he has lost contact with whomever is in charge at the time."

James didn't say anything as he mulled over the idea. "He couldna fight Seamus and his men alone. No telling how many are now siding with the man."

"That is where you and your men come in. He will need your aid. Once he helps Brina's da return to his place of power, Gunnolf can lead the clan until Robard is well again. Robard's people will see how good Gunnolf is at leading and in the future, he could lead them once again."

"They willna like seeing Gunnolf bringing a foreign force of his own back to their keep to oust

Seamus."

"No' quite foreign. Brina's grandmother and mother belonged with our clan and were kin by marriage."

"No' MacNeills by birth then," James said, much relieved.

"Nay. If you are concerned your father took Lynette and Brina's mother by force when she was his kin, dinna. They are no' blood relations. But they *are* kin by marriage. And since Lynette is your da's daughter, she is your half sister. So what say you?"

"I still want both Gunnolf and Brina to agree to the marriage. Gunnolf, because he is like a brother to me. Likewise, I would never want to force a woman to marry someone she doesna wish to have as a husband. And they both have to be agreeable about Gunnolf returning to her clan's lands to help her da. If she doesna wish to return there, there is no sense in Gunnolf going with a force to reclaim Robard's seat of power."

"Aye, agreed."

"Why do you really want to see the women now instead of waiting until later?" James asked, curious. He knew his mother could be devious when it came to matchmaking, and he highly suspected that was what this was all about even as she denied it.

"Lynette is your sister. But she has only just learned that Brina is hers. So I didna want them separated. I want them at the castle where I can get to know them. Particularly, if Brina will be leaving soon. Lynette may wish to return with her. And as I have said, I worry about their safety way out in the country should Seamus try to come for Brina."

Which seemed reasonable, but James still knew his mother well enough to recognize she had some other, more devious plan in mind. Maybe she intended to extol all of Gunnolf's strengths, while failing to speak of any of his weaknesses. Like how he couldn't say no to a lass if she wanted to bring her dog, a pup, or in this case, a wolf pup along on a dangerous mission. He was still amused how Gunnolf had done so for his cousin Niall's wife.

"Are you certain about Lynette's parentage? I was going to have the situation confirmed before I—"

"Before you shared the news with me? I knew their mother was pregnant with your da's bairn. He sent her away shortly after I had learned of it. My spies had discovered she had found refuge with Robard and wed him so I knew she would be safe. I knew she had been fighting your da's advances, and I had intervened on several occasions, rescuing her when I could. I wanted to find a place for her to work away from the castle. But I didn't succeed before it was too late. I had heard she had lost her bairn. The boy would have been your half brother had he lived. Once he died, there was no need to tell you. While Gunnolf was out searching for the lady, Wynne told me there had been another bairn. A twin girl. And she had survived."

James couldn't believe it.

"You know how superstitious some of the clansmen and women can be concerning twins. Robard hid the fact that a daughter had survived. Another woman raised her until she died and then Lynette was raised by Brina's mother's sister, Brina's aunt."

"Wynne knew all this, how?"

"Wynne saw a vision of her daughter when she was giving birth. Wynne helped to find a woman for her who would care for Lynette like she was her own."

"Yet, Wynne said naught to us all these years," James said, scowling. He would have brought the lass here years ago, had he known.

"The lass was happy while living with her aunt and uncle, and her cousin, Christophe, Wynne said. She was with family. Later, Lynette was a companion to Brina, even though she didna know she was her sister. And while Lynette and Brina's mother lived, she cherished Lynette, even though she was unable to raise her as her own daughter."

"I understand that, but…"

"She is with us now. But she may wish to return with Brina, should Brina go back home. So I want to visit with her as much as I can before that happens."

"Aye, I understand now." And James wished the same. He hoped that Gunnolf didn't feel it was necessary for him to wed the lass for the MacNeills' sake. The lass couldn't find a better man than him to be her husband though.

***

"He is returning," Wynne said, as she grabbed her brat and fastened it.

"Gunnolf?" both Brina and Lynette asked.

"Aye. I told you he would return for you."

Brina was worried that something was the matter, but thrilled too. She'd never felt that way about a man. That when he left, she worried about him, or in this case, she just wanted to see more of him, to speak to him further. To kiss him more and share his warm embraces. She swore she was addicted to his smiles when he was amused at her or happy for her. She'd even begun to think marriage to him might be possible. Not for her da's sake, but because he had come to her aid, and her sister's too, without any hope of gaining anything by it.

"Will you also come with us?" Brina asked, praying Wynne would because she wanted to get to know her better, and though she had known her for only a short time, she felt a kinship to her already. Some of it was because she had shared tales of their mother when she was a child that sounded much like Brina's misadventures. Like getting stuck in mud and losing a shoe, then being covered in mud while she had to dig out the shoe — all because she'd tried to catch a frog. And the time she'd found a nest of eggs in gorse, and caught her hair in the prickly barbs, thinking she'd never get loose.

"Aye, I will." Wynne smiled warmly at her, and gave her and Lynette an embrace. "Each of you have your mother's ways: Brina in your curiosity and kindness toward animals; Lynette in your friendliness and outgoing spirit. I would say that the best scenario would be if we were no' seen together or others will think you as odd as I am."

Both Brina and Lynette opened their mouths to object but she quickly silenced them with a raised hand. "'Tis their folly. But I fear the word will have already spread about your kinship to me. Because of that, I dinna believe there is any way to hide it now." Then Wynne turned to Brina. "Does Seamus know you have this gift?"

"No one does. No' even my da."

"Your da does, lass. And I fear Seamus might also."

"Then he shouldna want me."

"For his own dark purposes? To use your talent to know the future? He wouldna understand the process. That you canna conjure up what might happen on the battlefield or such things. Which is why 'tis so important to find a husband who either doesna know what you can do, or understands your gift and how it works and has no wish to use you for personal gains."

"Aye." Brina thought Wynne was trying to get her to see how being wed to Gunnolf could be a good thing. "If Gunnolf were of a mind to wed me...," she said slowly.

Lynette smiled a hint. Wynne looked as though

she was holding her breath.

"Well, if he were, then what?" Brina asked.

"That would be up to the two of you. Stay here, or return to help your da out."

Brina chewed her bottom lip, considering the danger Gunnolf would be in if he agreed. She grabbed her cloak and wrapped it around herself. "Were you warm enough last night while having to sleep in the cold?" she asked Lynette, still unable to shake the images from her mind of Gunnolf warming herself, and how she hoped he had not done the same with Lynette.

"Aye. We found an abandoned shieling. No roof, but Gunnolf managed to start a fire. We slept beside it and it kept us warm."

Brina wanted to know more, but her grandmother was looking at her with raised brows as Lynette grabbed her bag. Brina suspected her grandmother wanted to know if Gunnolf had kept Brina warm. Did he do the same with every lass? Kiss Lynette like he had kissed her?

Brina let out her breath in exasperation. She wanted to know if he had, or if he hadn't. She couldn't ask the question without revealing too much about what had happened between her and Gunnolf. And she really didn't want to know if Gunnolf had kept her sister warm. And yet...she did.

They heard a horse approaching, and Brina was suddenly filled with dread that it could be someone other than Gunnolf. Seamus, or one of his men. She grabbed her bow and quiver of arrows, preparing to ready an arrow, and headed outside, forgetting that James had left a force of men to protect them.

Then she smiled when she saw it was Gunnolf, who smiled back at her. "Is this the way you greet your rescuer?" he asked.

"You might have been Seamus and I would have had to defend myself." She realized Gunnolf had eyes only for her which thrilled her.

His gaze finally shifted to Lynette, who was also holding her bow and her quiver of arrows, a little behind her and off to the side. He dismounted. "If the one did not take care of me, the other would have, I see. James will be grateful you both will defend the castle as well." He hurried to saddle horses for them as he spoke to them. "I see you are ready to leave."

"Aye," Wynne said. "We will visit with Lady Akira for a time."

Brina was afraid of what Gunnolf was feeling about her da wanting him to marry her. He kept glancing at her as if he might even be considering such a thing, but he didn't say a word.

"What about Beowulf?" She gathered up the pup in her arms. She would stay here if he wasn't welcome at the castle. She had no intention of leaving him behind.

Gunnolf smiled down at the two of them. "We have already taken him into our pack. He would not be able to fend for himself out here, and if anyone came across a wild wolf pup, they might worry about what he might do to their sheep when he was old enough to hunt. So we take him with us."

Relieved, she smiled up at him. "Thank you, Gunnolf."

"Hopefully, if you raise him from a pup among other animals and feed him, he will not realize the livestock are for hunting." He helped her onto her horse.

"If I return to my home, they willna let me care for Beowulf." She was certain of it. Even if her da was in charge again, she believed her da would have the pup killed. He had been gone for nearly a year the one time she had raised a wolf pup, but knew she had to send him away before her da returned.

Gunnolf ran his hand over her horse's flank. "We will see." Then he helped Lynette onto Rory's horse and Wynne onto one of Seamus's men's horses.

Wynne led the way as she asked Lynette to ride beside her, which left Brina riding next to Gunnolf quite a distance behind them.

"I must tell you something that Wynne confided in me," Brina said, hating to have to bring this up now, but she had to. "Something that you will hate me for, but I dinna want you to even consider marrying me without knowing the truth." Brina hadn't meant it to come out that way. What if he wasn't considering such a thing?

He raised a brow.

She hated to have to tell him the news because she knew how she'd feel if she had a brother and someone had killed him. And to think Gunnolf hadn't had the chance to see him, to reunite with him before it had happened made it even worse. She hoped Gunnolf wouldn't be angry with her. Not that he *was* considering her as a bride prospect, but if it did happen, he had to know the truth.

Gunnolf was watching her now, his brow furrowing a little.

"Your...your brother Hallfred lived near my da's lands."

"He lives here?" Gunnolf asked, looking as though he was ready to search him out.

"Nay, listen. He died in battle with my da. His...your grandfather killed mine some years earlier in a Viking raid long before your brother moved here. When your brother settled near my da's lands, they had disputes over land and sheep and cattle. Then my da learned Hallfred was the grandson of the man who killed my grandfather, and my da couldna let go of the hate he had for your kin."

Gunnolf looked back toward Craigly Castle. "Your da never mentioned that to me when he wanted me to provide safe passage for you."

Would Gunnolf have changed his mind about protecting her, if he had known? "I dinna know if he realizes you and he were brothers. 'Tis worse, Gunnolf. He didna just die fighting against my kin.

My da killed him."

Gunnolf's expression was a mix of disbelief and anger. "How did Wynne know?"

"She was friends with your grandmother in her...way. She never met her in person, but they shared visions. She saw what your grandmother saw. She knew your grandmother's husband murdered my grandfather, my da's da."

"Wynne never told me. What about my brother? How long has she known he lived here?"

"She said she didna know until she sent you looking for the woman who needed help. Your brother was one of the men fighting my da in battle. One of the ones who died, Seamus said."

"But you know for certain that your da killed him?" Gunnolf was frowning at her again.

She had been afraid he would hate her for it. "Aye. Seamus said at least Robard had avenged his da's death during the battle."

Gunnolf's face was dark and angry. "How many of my people moved there? How many are left?"

"I dinna know. I am so sorry, Gunnolf. I didna know until Wynne told me after you went to find Lynette. I...I had to tell you."

He let out his breath in exasperation, but then he shook his head at her, his expression softening a wee bit. "None of this is your doing, lass."

"What are you going to do?"

"Where are they living, exactly?"

"I dinna know. Mayhap Wynne will. You are

going to see them?" If she had been Gunnolf, that's what she would do.

"*Ja*. I must know who is living there that is related to me. I should have returned home. I should have known that my brother had moved here."

"Mayhap you would be the one dead now instead of him." Brina was annoyed with men and their need to kill each other for no good reason. Land, power, livestock. Nothing was worth killing another man over it. "You willna help my da, will you?" Or even consider marrying her now.

***

Gunnolf thought of himself as a reasonable man. He remembered the last fight he'd had with his brother, four years older than him. It had occurred some months before the trip to the English coast at the time of the last raid they'd been on, which had been an attempt to rescue his brother from the Sassenach, and Gunnolf had been left for dead. His brother had always chided Gunnolf for his love of animals and took great pleasure in sacrificing them to appease the gods. Hallfred had only wanted Gunnolf to become a warrior. To accept their culture and realize Hallfred's offerings would bring plentiful crops to them or other gifts the gods could grant.

No matter how hard Gunnolf had tried to live with the notion, to justify the right in it, he had hated his brother for it. Hallfred could have just as easily offered up any other animal to appease the gods. Not Gunnolf's own orphaned animals that he had fostered. Their father had been just as adamant that Gunnolf gave up caring for animals that wouldn't have survived if he hadn't raised them as his own—a goat, a sheep, a puppy once, and a falcon.

That was one of the reasons he had decided to stay with the MacNeills. When he had first arrived at Craigly Castle, sorely wounded, he refused to sleep in the castle and instead slept in the stables. He had befriended a momma cat's kittens, though the mother was wild. Lady Akira had finally convinced Gunnolf to live in the castle and stay with her sons, but she allowed him to take the kittens with him. He had believed she would eventually insist the kittens live outside once he had become friends with her sons. But she didn't. She truly was the most good-hearted woman he had ever known. He'd had as much fun raising the kittens as did James and his younger brothers and sister. And Lady Akira saw in him something good and kind. She didn't see him as a man who was weak because he cared for those unable to care for themselves.

Though James had jested oft enough that Gunnolf was doing so to gain Lady Akira's favor.

"You are not at fault for what your father or anyone else has done, Brina," Gunnolf finally said. "Set your mind at ease concerning the matter."

"What about my da?"

"I do not know what the difficulty was between

my brother and your father. I will see my people and make a judgement then."

"But you must learn my da's side of the story also or you will only have one version."

"What do you wish me to do, Brina?" Gunnolf studied her for a moment.

"I want you to hear both sides."

He raised his brows a little. "By wanting me to hear both sides, does that mean you wish me to do what your father bids if I am in agreement?"

"Marry me?" Brina's whole body heated in mortification after speaking the words. She thought it sounded like she was asking him to marry her. And then she realized he might not even be talking about that, but about helping her da regain his position as chief.

Gunnolf looked darkly amused.

She let out her breath. "You meant to help my da become chief."

"Your da would insist I marry you, has in fact already, so that would be part of the deal. I would not wed an unwilling bride no matter how much your father tries to convince James that I stole you away and I must now make you my wife."

"I told you my da wasna to be trusted. I dinna wish to wed Seamus no matter what though."

"Nor me," Gunnolf said.

She felt her face heat. She always assumed when the time came, she wouldn't have any choice in the matter. So she didn't expect a man, any man, to ask her opinion on the subject. And she really appreciated him for it.

"I am...sorry that my grandfather killed yours," Gunnolf said finally, switching the subject when she didn't say she wished to marry Gunnolf either.

It wasn't that she didn't, she realized. But that she knew he had to find closure concerning his brother and what had happened. If he didn't first, he might change his mind about her and she wanted it to be a surer thing.

"I miss my grandfather. When most men are no' that interested in playing with a female bairn, my grandfather was the exception. He bounced me on his knee when I was little. And when he saw Lynette watching us, he bounced her on his other knee. I think now he must have known we were sisters, and had he been my da, he would have told our people to treat her as such. But he wasna in charge of our family and my da ruled over us."

Gunnolf nodded. "My grandfather was just like my father and my oldest brother. They were warriors, believing in the old ways. Family meant everything to them, and children were highly valued."

"For clan ties, aye?"

"Ja."

She sighed. "You are good of heart, but you and your people and mine have been at war with one another from the beginning, so it seems." She could see more trouble coming if they were to marry, and all parties were not agreeable. "Do you think the warring will ever end between our people?"

***

"*Ja*. I do, if the parties want it enough. 'Tis a way to end the strife in some cases." Gunnolf wasn't sure it would in this case.

In any event, until he learned why her father had killed his brother, he wasn't making any decision one way or another. Yet he couldn't help but think about what it would be like being wed to the lass. She was sweet and yet spirited. She seemed to have a penchant for taking care of orphaned animals like he had, even if it could put them in danger, though her reasoning that the pup could throw Seamus and his men off their trail had been good. She had managed the household staff at her own castle, though he wouldn't know how well unless he lived there for a time. And she had protected herself from Seamus's man, not wilting like a plucked flower, waiting for him to take her hostage, or worse. She reminded him of some of his kinswomen who served as shield maidens and fought against their enemies, except instead of using a sword and shield, Brina used a bow. She was bonny and he certainly couldn't deny he desired her like a man desired a beautiful woman.

Most of all, he believed she was interested in him in a marriageable way if he could live with the fact that their clans were fighting. He had wanted to laugh when she'd put the question to him about marrying her. What if he had said he would, even though he knew she wasn't asking him to marry her in truth.

When they reached the castle, Lady Akira greeted the three ladies and ushered them up to her chamber.

James took Gunnolf aside. "We will be having a feast and then what are your plans?"

Gunnolf told James what had happened concerning his brother.

"I am sorry to learn he was here and that you knew naught of it. And this other business..." James shook his head. "So, you have no intention of marrying Brina then."

Gunnolf wasn't sure how that would play out. If he wed the lass, would that strengthen ties between his people and hers? Or cause more trouble?

"For now? Nay."

CHAPTER 9

Everyone greeted the ladies with great cheer and welcoming, to Brina's surprise, when she and her companions arrived at Craigly Castle. She believed the people would act as though Wynne was someone to be feared. But they didn't. Brina did worry that they would treat her and Lynette ill because of their mother's situation, but again, they didn't. She thought a lot had to do with the way Lady Akira greeted them as though they were her long lost daughters, and Wynne was her best friend. James's wife, Lady Eilis, the woman often affectionately called Mikala, pearl of the sea, was just as generous with her friendship. Brina saw that she was with bairn and wondered when the baby would come. She treated Brina and Lynette like they were her sisters, and everyone fell in love with Beowulf. Eilis's cousin, Fia, was there also, and just as dark haired as Brina and a real beauty.

Brina wondered why she was not yet married.

Even a man called Eanruig, James's senior advisor, made them feel especially welcome.

The wolf pup likewise had fun playing with some of the hunting dogs and a litter of pups, the older dogs making him behave when he got too rough.

Brina wondered if the wolf pup would be allowed to play with the hunting dogs at home, if she were to return. If Seamus was to continue in her father's stead, she knew she could never go back. Yet, even though all were welcoming here, this still didn't feel like it was home. Despite the way her da had acted toward her, she knew in his heart, he thought he was doing right by the clan, making them stronger, more invincible, less likely to be overrun by another clan. So, though she'd hated the notion of marrying Seamus, she knew her father had not chosen him to spite her, but in an effort to ensure the clan remained powerful.

With all the greetings from everyone, Brina was caught up in it for a moment, but then she couldn't help herself and looked around for Gunnolf. He and James were observing them, smiling, appearing glad that the ladies had been accepted by everyone.

She smiled at Gunnolf, and his mouth curved up even more as if he was pleased she had acknowledged he was there. Then she realized not only had he been watching her, but Lady Akira, Laird James, and Lynette had. Brina wanted the floor to swallow her up.

Eilis's and James's three-year-old son, Ian, took her hand and smiled up at her. "You wanna play with me?"

She would love to. But Lady Akira motioned for all the ladies to follow her up the stairs and so Brina took Ian's small hand, glancing over her shoulder to see if Gunnolf had left, but he only winked at her, as if he knew she couldn't keep her eyes off him. Her body heated with embarrassment, the rogue.

The ladies provided Brina and Lynette sewing materials so they could work on something while they talked in Lady Akira's chamber before the meal was ready as they settled down on cushioned benches.

"You must have been shocked when Gunnolf ran into you as he did. James was quite upset with him for no' telling us what he had intended to do," Lady Akira said.

"Nonsense," Wynne said. "He's a warrior. A Norseman. A little snow would never slow him down."

"Well, we are glad both of you, Brina and Lynette, made it here safely and truly hope you will stay with us," Lady Akira said. "Now, as to this matter with Gunnolf, we all understand that your da insists he marry you, but while you stay here, your da has no say in the matter. We wouldna want you to wed anyone you dinna want to."

"Aye," Brina agreed, looking down at Eilis's

young son, his dark curls the color of James's hair, as he ran his hand over her gown in a shy way, dark brown eyes glancing up at her, dark lashes framing them beautifully. She suspected he wanted to sit on her lap. Animals and children always drifted her way.

"Ian," his mother said. Eilis sat to get comfortable on a cushioned bench, her gown covering her rounded belly, her second bairn due in the spring. "Brina may no' want you to sit on her lap." Then Eilis looked up at Brina. "He is usually shy around those he has only just met."

Lynette smiled and shook her head. "Whenever Brina isna busy with managing the household staff, the children talk her ear off or want her to hold them. Some mothers say she overindulges them. Others love her for it. Animals? The same way."

Brina laughed. "I canna help myself. If I am no' overly busy, I can carry a bairn on my hip and give a mother a break." She looked down at Ian. "Would you like to sit on my lap?"

He nodded. She smiled and lifted him up, and he settled on top of her gown.

"As to Gunnolf, he is a good man, but even the most decent of men have their faults," Lady Akira added. "Even the man I have considered marrying, Tibold, chief of the Clan Chattan, has such faults. He is my son, Angus's father-in-law. And I think I will wed him, if he ever gets up the courage to ask."

Eilis smiled at her mother-in-law. "You should

just ask him, I keep telling you."

"He would marry you in a heartbeat," Wynne agreed. "As to a man's faults, aye, you know the truth of it."

Brina knew no one was perfect, herself even, but she was dying to learn what Gunnolf's faults were so she could make a better decision with regard to marrying him or not.

"If an animal is in need of mothering, he will be right there taking the orphan in. I could just see him taking one into his chamber and staying up all night with it until he was certain it was out of danger. Even onto the pallet where the two of you are sleeping once you are wed," Lady Akira said. As if it were a foregone conclusion.

Brina's whole body warmed with embarrassment. She wasn't used to women talking about her sleeping with a man, even if she had already done so with Gunnolf, not in a carnal way, but still...

Brina wondered if Lady Akira only said so because she knew Brina had wanted to rescue the wolf pup, and not that it was Gunnolf's doing this time.

"He did in his youth. He is terribly stubborn also. If he had it in mind he wants something, he will go after it if it kills him."

"Like trying to return home when he was a lad and terribly wounded?" Brina asked.

"Aye."

"But this is a good thing, is it no'?" Lynette

asked.

Brina nodded, agreeing with her.

"For my sons and my nephew, Niall, I would agree. When Niall and Gunnolf had been ambushed and lost track of each other, Gunnolf would have done anything to locate Niall, even gotten himself killed over it. No one is more loyal to the family than he is and treats my nephew and my sons as his own brothers," Lady Akira said. "That goes for the way he cares about everyone in the clan, I might add."

"What of his own brothers?" Brina asked softly. She didn't know if they knew about what had happened to him with regard to her da. If Lady Akira was trying to convince Brina she should wed Gunnolf despite all his "faults," she thought it was important for them to know the situation.

"Gunnolf never spoke of his brothers. Mayhap that says volumes of his relationship with them right there. However, this could sway his feelings about marrying you at your da's request." Then Lady Akira turned to Lynette. "He rescued you as well. What if you were to wed him instead?"

Blushing, Lynette smiled.

Brina didn't think she'd ever seen Lynette blush that way. Had Gunnolf kissed her? Was she interested in marrying the braw warrior, even if he was a Viking and not a Highlander?

"He is a handsome man, and he did come to my aid, but I dinna think he has any interest in me." Lynette glanced at Brina. "What about his interest in you?"

"He wants to see his people and learn what had happened between my da and his brother. I asked him to talk to my da about it too. To learn both sides."

Lynette's brows rose. "What did he say to that?"

"He wanted to know if that meant I wished him to return to Anfa Castle, and he would challenge Seamus, to do as my da bids."

"Wed you, then," Lady Akira said, looking hopeful.

"Do you?" Lynette asked.

"I dinna want Gunnolf to get himself killed. Then again, I worry about his visit with his own people. What if they dinna trust him because he has been living with the MacNeill clan all these years and no' with his own kind? Even though the MacNeill clan has had no quarrel with the Norsemen settled here."

***

When they went to the great hall for the meal, Brina led Ian down with her, his small hand in hers, and she knew she'd made a best friend. She thought she would sit with him at the meal. But when she reached the great hall, a nursemaid took Ian, and she really wished he could stay with her. He looked disappointed too.

Beowulf bounded over to her and when she sat down to the meal in the great hall, he lay at her feet. Lady Akira seated Gunnolf next to Brina while

Lynette was between James's wife, Lady Eilis, and Lady Akira. Brina suspected Lynette was James's sister and they wished to keep her here as part of the family. That saddened Brina as she hoped that if she returned home, Lynette would go with her, and she would tell her people the good news. That she was her sister whether her da approved or not.

Brina was not seated at the head table as befit her rank, but she was fine with that. She was glad to be next to Gunnolf, whom she more than enjoyed being with.

"I see you made friends with Ian," Gunnolf said, his eyes twinkling with mirth.

She was surprised Gunnolf had really noticed.

"Aye, he is sweet and misses sitting on his mother's lap."

Gunnolf smiled. "No room for him there now."

"Aye." Brina took a bite of her mutton. "When are you leaving to see your kin?"

"On the morrow, first thing."

"What if...they are no' happy to see you?"

"Have you seen a vision of this?" he asked, frowning.

"Nay. I just mean, all these years you have been dead to them." She realized after she brought the subject up, she probably shouldn't have. What if his people were angry that he had stayed here and lived with the Highlanders, forsaking his own people? The welcoming from his people maybe not be forthcoming. Rather they could be wary that he showed up at all. Yet, *they* had left him for dead.

"Truth be told, I hadna considered it." Gunnolf chewed on his mutton, seemingly deep in thought.

She rested her hand on his arm in a consoling manner. "I am sorry, Gunnolf. I shouldna have brought it up."

His gaze shot to hers. There was a way he looked at her, not just as a friend, but something deeper, more…carnal, anytime she touched him. She pulled her hand away from his arm, thinking maybe she was being too forward.

"I only thought to see them, to learn from them what happened. I did not think of the consequences, truly. I am sure they would be shocked at first to see me. Mayhap, angry with me for not returning home. I had not quite considered that they would not welcome me home as a long, lost warrior."

"But if your brother lived here in the Highlands, how can they fault you for having done so?"

"Because I did not tell them I still lived. I lived, instead, with the Highlanders."

"Unless…unless your grandmother saw you in a vision and told them you lived here. Mayhap no' in this place, but in the Highlands. Mayhap that was the very reason your brother and others moved here."

Gunnolf continued to eat, but didn't say anything further as if he was pondering the whole matter.

"You willna go alone, will you?" She worried if

they didn't like it that he didn't return home that they might believe he was the enemy now.

"I will. I cannot bring a force of Highlanders with me to see my own people."

She sipped from her ale. "What if something happens to you? What if you are taken prisoner?"

"By my own kin?"

She couldn't help feeling anxious about it. He was right in not wanting to take a force of Highlanders with him. They could construe it that he was with the Highlanders and might even intend to fight his own kind. On the other hand, she could see they could very well be angry with him for not returning to his people and want to make him pay for it.

"What if they thought to try and convince you to turn me over to them? And then they could ransom me to Seamus as proof of your loyalty to your kin?"

He leaned back on the bench seat and took a long look at her. "I am loyal to the MacNeill clan, having pledged myself in word and deed forever, lass. You are a guest of the MacNeills. I would not promise to hand you over to anyone, Seamus, your da even, or my kin. Not unless you wished it."

"What if they threatened your life if you didna do so?"

"Do you oft worry about my welfare?" His stern expression had vanished and in its place, a look of amusement made her believe he wasn't taking her seriously now.

She frowned at him. This was grave, not something to jest about. "When you are putting yourself in danger, aye."

"I have never had a lass worry about me before when I was putting myself in danger."

She would have thought the lasses who had an interest in him would all be concerned for his welfare. She sipped more of her ale to cool her fevered cheeks and choked on it.

He patted her back. "Are you all right?"

Her body heated with mortification. When she finally caught her breath, tears filling her eyes, she didn't want to see if anyone was observing her. Most were still conversing at the meal. But a few *were* watching her and Gunnolf, Lady Akira, for one. She didn't seem to miss anything.

Brina finally stopped coughing, gathered her composure, and figured that subject was best left alone.

James rose from his chair. "'Tis time to begin the games and dancing. Let us move this outside."

Everyone headed out to the inner bailey where Lady Akira spirited Brina away to talk with her in private.

Gunnolf sighed, folded his arms, and watched as a couple of the men played on a lyre and flute, and men and women began to dance. A handful of men took up the sword to best each other and others were testing their skills at archery. James quickly joined Gunnolf.

"Why not join in the games? Best the men at

sword fighting or dance with one of the lasses? What ails you? You never stand off to the side and watch the others. It would not be because of the one wee lass you saved from Seamus, would it?"

"Nay. I must see my kin whose farms border her da's."

"Have you considered her da's offer?"

Gunnolf frowned at James. "Her da killed my brother."

"You told me once how cruel he was to you. That was one of the reasons you stayed with us even after you were well enough to leave."

Gunnolf snorted. "I did not know brothers could be friends." He glanced at James. "Like you and your brothers and cousin are to me. We are not of the same blood, but I could not have chosen better brothers."

James smiled. "Aye. The feeling is mutual." He sighed. "She wouldna be a bad choice, my friend."

"You would gain her clan as allies, if I were to manage to oust Seamus and take over the clan."

"Aye, my thought exactly."

Marginally smiling, Gunnolf shook his head.

"So what will you do?"

"Seek out my kin. Learn what the matter was between my brother and her father, and then make a decision."

"Aye. Will you need me to ride with you? Some other men too?"

"To see my kin? Nay. To help remove Seamus from power, mayhap. If it comes to that. Returning there may present another problem if we learn her father is dead and Seamus is deeply entrenched in his place. Will anyone care then if I had married the chief's daughter, then tried to take control of the clan? I highly suspect her father's men would side with Seamus against the Norseman."

"However, you do bring some power to the table. Not only have you proven yourself in battle numerous times, you will also be allied with me. And Seamus canna say that. He is a lone wolf, from the sounds of it. We can even ally with your people against Seamus should he remain in power. But the main point of the matter: is she even interested in a union between the two of you?"

"My family is one of her clan's enemies."

James glanced around and saw her dancing. "She doesna seem to treat you as though you were her enemy. Go dance with her. That is a command."

Gunnolf shook his head. "I do not believe you have ever commanded me to do anything. Asked, but never commanded."

"I do it for your own good. And because my mother is waiting for me to do so."

Gunnolf chuckled. "All right. I will do this, but it does not mean she will accept."

He left James and walked across the bailey to speak with Brina, now standing alone, smiling at the children dancing together. "Brina, tell me where my kin are living in relation to your da's lands."

After she explained where they were, from

what Wynne had told her, she pulled Gunnolf into the shadows of the stables. "Do you think your people will be angry with you that you did not die?"

Gunnolf smiled a little. "You mean they will be angry I did not return to my village."

"Aye. What if they feel you betrayed them by living with the Highlanders instead?"

"I have every right to feel they betrayed me by leaving me behind for dead."

"They should have checked all the bodies."

"*Ja.* You cannot know how I felt—alone, wounded, in a strange land, fighting to survive on my own."

She shook her head.

"I will leave before first light," he said.

She nodded, tears in her eyes.

"Brina, what is wrong?"

She shook her head again as if she couldn't speak.

"Brina?" Gunnolf tilted her chin and looked into her tearful eyes, hating to see her distress. "Your father cannot force us—"

She threw herself at him and hugged him tight. "I worry that your kin would rather hurt you for living with Highlanders all these years, rather than welcome you. And then what will we do? I will have to come and rescue you."

Gunnolf laughed and kissed her. Her mouth was warm and willing and sweet, and he realized she might never have been kissed before like he had kissed her. But he awakened a fierceness in her that he had not expected. She held on tight to him, pressing her breasts against his chest, her mouth against his lips as if she was afraid she'd lose him on the morrow.

He couldn't stop the desire coursing through his blood, the need to have her in his bed, and not just for some immediate fulfillment. He wanted more between them.

"If you keep kissing me like this and holding me close, I will have to insist you wed me, per your da's orders," he said, his voice already ragged with lust.

He felt her mouth curve against his, and he smiled before their tongues tangled. His raging need for her was spiraling out of control. Even now, he had to keep his hands on her hips, wanting to slide them over her breasts, to feel the pointy tips against the palms of his hands instead of just against his chest.

He was hard and wanting and he was certain she felt his steel staff pressing against her, showing just how much he craved having her. Yet it didn't frighten her but seemed to excite her. She didn't pull away from him, which was not good because he didn't seem to have any control when it came to her.

He finally ended the kiss and held her for a moment longer, not wanting to let go.

He felt more for her than he had for any other woman. A kinship, maybe because of her love of the small wolf pup that had needed their help. Maybe because she worried so about his welfare. No one had worried about him like she did. And yet he also admired the way she handled a bow, the way she had fought to protect herself and would have taken care of him also. She had not run away when she could have saved herself in case he had been wounded. She had searched for her father when he had been wounded when she could have traveled farther away from her home instead. And she had tried to take care of him when he was wounded so long ago.

He could tell she cared about her father even if they had not always gotten along. He saw it in her anxiousness when she had learned he was alive, and wanting to remain there to protect him as if one small lass could have saved her father from a man such as Seamus.

"You would not wish to ride with me on the morrow to see my kin, would you? Serve as my guard?" He only said it in jest, trying to make her feel better, though the way she had been kissing him and was still clinging to him, he thought she was feeling a little better.

"You canna be serious. Your brother's wife, Inga, would want to kill me once she learned my da mortally wounded her husband on the field of battle."

CHAPTER 10

The festivities were still going on when Gunnolf considered Brina's words about Hallfred's wife. He had forgotten all about Inga being promised to Hallfred as his wife when they were five and ten. Hallfred had been nine and ten at the time. Would she still want to wed Gunnolf like she had when they were younger? And how had Brina known about her? *Wynne.* Had to be.

Then he saw three women who regularly flirted with him and were always hoping for more than a passing comment, now watching him with Brina near the keep while others were still dancing. They were all winsome lasses, but they didn't have the allure that Brina held for him.

"Do they wish you to wed them?" Brina asked, startling him from his thoughts.

He hadn't even realized she'd taken notice of

them. He kept his arm around Brina's waist as if she belonged with him. He had never done that with a lass either, showing any display of affection for a woman in front of the clan as if wanting everyone else to know they were together. And that he wasn't interested in any other lass.

"Mayhap, but the interest would be all theirs, not mine."

"You are no' keeping me close to protect yourself from them?" Brina asked. Her tone was serious, but he believed she was teasing him.

"Nay, to protect you from any man who might show an interest in you."

"That would be foolish on their part, dinna you think? No' when you can handle six men at once."

He laughed. "You will never let me live that comment down."

She smiled up at him and he realized just how much he truly enjoyed being around her. "Dance with me," she said, and pulled him into the area where others were dancing.

He hadn't remembered a time when he'd had more fun with a woman either, just enjoyed being himself, laughing, making mistakes — dancing wasn't something he usually did — and just having a good time. Tomorrow would come soon enough and he'd have to deal with his own kin, and hoped they would be welcoming. Tonight, all he wanted to think about was Brina, and how much he treasured being with her.

When it was late and everyone was retiring to

their pallets for the night, Gunnolf took Brina to the guest chamber that she and Lynette were sharing.

"I worry about you," Brina said again. "You be careful. Dinna let your guard down."

"I will be thinking about you," he said quite seriously. He realized he was doing a lot of that lately too whenever he wasn't with her, or even when he was.

He leaned down to kiss her and ignored the people retiring to their chambers who giggled or tried to slip by as unobtrusively as they could. Lynette reached the room and brushed past them to open the door, then shut it.

Lady Akira and Lady Eilis headed up the stairs, Eilis smiling, Akira clearing her throat in a motherly way that said Gunnolf needed to let Brina get her sleep.

Brina wrapped her arms around Gunnolf's neck. "Sleep well, Gunnolf. I will pray all goes well for you."

"I will return before you know it. Enjoy this time with your sister, grandmother, and the rest of the MacNeill clan. We will have business to discuss when I return."

She raised her brows in question. He only kissed her back in response. And then with the greatest reluctance, he pulled away, heard more people on the stairs, Fia, this time, who smiled at them, and James, who slapped Gunnolf on the back. "See you in the morning," James said.

Then Gunnolf said good night to Brina,

wondering why he was really going to see what was left of his kin when he had made a new beginning here so long ago, and he was looking to start a whole new adventure with the Highland lass.

***

"My mother worries about you," James said, seeing Gunnolf off early the next morn, having broken bread with him before he left. "We will ride with you to the border of our lands."

James and five of his men went with Gunnolf, though he had expected to go alone. This was why he saw them as family.

But he also knew James had a hidden agenda. "You wouldna do badly married to the lass whether you stay here or no'. I will pledge as many men as you need to deal with the threat to her da."

They rode in silence for a bit, then Gunnolf nodded.

"How long do you intend to stay with your people?"

"I am not sure." Gunnolf supposed it depended on the welcome he received.

"If you dinna return in a sennight, I will bring a force to ensure your safety."

"They would not kill me or take me hostage."

"Still, if you dinna return, we will come, either as a force to free you, or to meet your kin."

"It will take me two days to travel there. Two days to travel back. I may stay for a few days."

"Aye."

They talked about their people, and for a very long time, James's people *had* been his people. And nothing had changed that. When they finally reached the border, James looked uneasy.

"I will be fine and I will return and tell you all that I learn." Gunnolf inclined his head to James and the others, all whom wished him well.

And then he was off, hoping that he was correct in his assumption. He still couldn't get over the notion that his brother had married, though why Gunnolf hadn't realized that, he wasn't sure. He tried to envision Inga, his childhood friend who had fought against him just as vigorously as any man would when practicing swordsmanship, and how she would look today, grown into womanhood. She had wanted to marry him, if her father hadn't wished her to wed his older brother.

She would be in mourning now. He wondered how his brother and she had fared together. Had they loved each other? Why was he even wondering such a thing? He had always known she would marry his brother, both their fathers dictating such an arrangement, and Hallfred had continually reminded Gunnolf of it. When the family thought Gunnolf dead, did Inga shed a tear for him?

Then the realization struck him like a blow to the gut. If Hallfred had been freed and really had spoken on the battlefield, telling one of his clansmen that Gunnolf had died when he knew very well Gunnolf had not...

Anger welled up in him. But then he let out his breath in irritation. Hallfred was now dead. What was past was past, and he had to think of what today and tomorrow would bring.

***

"Dinna worry about Gunnolf," Lynette said, practicing archery with Brina in the outer bailey.

Whenever Brina worried about something overmuch, she felt better practicing with her bow.

"He will see his childhood sweetheart." Brina couldn't help feeling irritated about it, when she had no business doing so. "Wynne told me so."

Brina couldn't help worrying about her da too, and she felt sure that Gunnolf would be the one to save him and get rid of Seamus. Maybe Gunnolf could take charge until her da was better, and they could contact her cousin. He could return and take over, and Gunnolf could go back home to his MacNeill family. What if instead, he decided to stay with Inga, and then fight Brina's family on his own people's behalf?

She saw the way Lady Akira treated him just as fondly as she did her firstborn son. And everyone else genuinely liked Gunnolf: slaps on the back, tankards raised to him wherever he went. Even early this morning before everyone was awake, she'd learned James and some of his men had ridden out with Gunnolf to the border as a sign of true friendship. So she really wasn't certain how this would go.

"I worry about Hallfred's wife, Inga," Brina

said.

"You think she will want to wed Gunnolf now, and he will help to rule their people?"

"'Tis a possibility, do you no' think?"

"Anything is possible. That you will even find a man here that you will fall in love with among those of the MacNeill clan."

Brina sighed. "Are you interested in anyone here?"

"I havena had the chance to meet with anyone but Gunnolf and James." Lynette glanced over her shoulder and smiled at the men who were supposed to be practicing swordsmanship but instead were watching them, smiling, eager to maybe even court one of the women, or both. "Lady Akira has been like a mother hen to both of us and keeping the men at bay, though she didna stop you from kissing Gunnolf last night."

"How do you know that?"

Lynette smiled at her. "Everyone knows that."

Brina couldn't believe the whole of the clan had seen, or at least the word had spread about the deed. "Will you stay here if I return home?"

Lynette's eyes widened.

"I mean, if someone goes home to put an end to Seamus's rule."

"You worry about your da."

"Aye."

Lynette readied another arrow and shot at the burlap figure of a man, striking him in the head. "He wouldna acknowledge that I am your sister."

"Before, aye," Brina said. "If you were to return—"

"Nay, I willna return. I am home here. Welcome. Loved."

Brina took a deep breath. "You know that I love you as a sister. I always have."

"Aye. But I would have a difficult time returning with you, no matter how your da has changed. If he ever were to change. He isna my da, but I understand your need to return home." Lynette gave her a warm hug. "No matter where we live, we will always be sisters. Aye?"

"Aye." The knowledge they were sisters and would be separated didn't appeal.

"Come, you are still trying to beat me and so far I am doing better. Put that fearsome Viking out of your thoughts and concentrate!"

***

On the second day of Gunnolf's journey, three men rode out to meet him way before he even reached the first shieling. They wore patchy lamb fleece cloaks over light-colored wool tunics, highly decorated penannular broaches holding them in place. Swathing bands, or *spjarrar*, wrapped around their trouser legs, protecting them from the cold and dense brush. One of the men was blond-haired, the other two brown-haired. All looked prepared to fight, their hair braided in part on the sides, the blond holding his sword in hand.

"*Ver heill ok sæll!*" Gunnolf called out in his native tongue, greeting them with be healthy and happy. "I am Gunnolf, brother of Hallfred, son of Gustavson!"

His words had the men stopping in place as if they were seeing a man who should be dead, who looked similarly to his older brother, Gunnolf suspected. "I survived and lived to see my kin sail away and leave me behind. My brother Hallfred had been rescued, so not all had been lost."

They still didn't move from their spot of dormant grass and grilled him about his family. Then finally, the darker-haired, older man of the three said, "Come, Gunnolf, son of Gustavson. Inga will know you when we do not."

"Fair enough." Gunnolf rode toward them and they flanked him while they galloped to the center of their village, men and women, farmers alike, watching the stranger in their midst.

Then he saw Inga riding through the village, shield and sword readied as if she were going to fight him, her blond braids flying, and her green eyes narrowed like a cat's.

"Inga," he said, "'tis me, Gunnolf. I have only now learned my kin live in this glen."

"And your brother is dead." She wielded her shield with an attempt to knock him off his horse, but instead, he moved out of her path, and grabbed her arm, yanking hard until she fell to the ground with a thump.

Gunnolf hadn't expected this and didn't want to fight her. He swore everyone was holding their breaths, anxious to see how this would play out between them. They wouldn't interfere unless a champion stepped forth to stop Gunnolf. He hadn't wanted to earn her ire. He'd only wanted to see his people and give her his condolences for his brother's death.

These people were not his own. They must have been from a different village and followed his brother here. Gunnolf didn't know any of them, all except for wild and beautiful Inga.

He leapt off his horse, shield in hand, just in case she attacked him again. Which she did. She still made the same mistakes with him as she did in their youth. Yet even so, she managed to knock him back a few paces with her brutal attacks, striking sword against sword or slashing at his targe, even striking his targe with hers.

The men and women cheered her on. Not because she was a woman, but because she was one of them, their ruler, and he was unknown to them, even if his brother had once been their leader.

She was hard to beat, slashing at his sword with all her might, proving to her people, and to him, she had what it took to lead her people. Maybe her anger had something to do with his not dying and not sending word. Or maybe that she had to wed his brother and wasn't allowed to wed him.

Except for filling out more, she was the same Inga, challenging him, passionate, in charge.

He wondered if he looked any different to her, other than his height and the whiskers he now wore. In battle, he was as fiercely determined to win and not lose his life as any of the men or women would be, but he always held back in practice fighting with her, and it seemed to make her more aggressive, maybe even angrier. She didn't want to him to hold back because she was a woman. But he had no intention of fighting her as if she had the strength of a full-grown man.

Unable to keep from comparing her to Brina, he realized the two women were as different as night and day. Brina was a fighter too, but only in a defensive way. Not as a warrior. He preferred a woman who would be his wife having babies and keeping his bed warm, and not challenging him to a fight every time he looked sideways at her. Brina's hair was nearly raven in color, whereas Inga's was pale blond. Both had blue eyes, Inga's icy when she looked at him; Brina's like the sky, wide and expressive.

He realized the interest he'd had in Inga all those years ago had something to do with the way she had aggressively pursued him. And maybe something to do with the thrill of it all, knowing if they got caught, his brother or their fathers might have had him beaten or killed.

There was something to be said about living dangerously and the pleasure that wrought, which brought him back to thinking about Brina and how worried she was that he'd be all right. Had she seen a vision of his brother's wife trying to kill him?

He finally knocked Inga down and when she tensed to jump up from where she lay, he pinned her down with his body. He was unwilling to fight her further, no matter how determined she was. So her next action surprised him. It shouldn't have.

She released her shield and sword and grabbed him around the neck and kissed him as if claiming him for her own. Her kisses bordered on barbarism, as if she was still angry and fighting with him, making him yield.

He pulled away and offered his hand to her, but she got up on her own and said to her people, "This is Gunnolf, Hallfred's brother. He will be my husband and lead us to victory against those who killed his brother!"

***

"She tried to kill him and then she kissed him!" Brina paced across the chamber where Lady Akira and several other ladies were sewing gowns.

"Who? Gunnolf? You saw this in a vision?" Lady Akira looked up from her embroidery work, her eyes wide with shock.

"Aye." Brina was completely disheartened. That the wild woman tried to kill him, one of her own kind, was bad enough, but the kissing part was worse.

"Dinna upset yourself over it." Wynne dismissed her concerns completely. "It doesna mean he has any interest in the woman."

"Did he kiss her back?" Lynette seemed to be the only one there who understood Brina's concern and was helping her to focus on what she'd seen.

"I couldna tell, but he was on top of her." Brina

stopped pacing only long enough to glance at the women whose jaws all hung agape. "He had knocked her down and then pinned her to the ground."

Gasps followed.

Brina ground her teeth. "Then she slid her arms around his neck and pulled him down to kiss him."

"Where were his hands? Was he embracing her back?" Lynette asked.

Though Brina had thought Lady Akira would ask them to change the subject, she seemed just as interested in learning how Gunnolf had reacted.

"I dinna know. I was climbing the stairs and ran into a man, which caused me to lose the vision instantly. I tried to think of what had happened, to see more of the vision, but it was gone."

"You canna force a vision," Wynne scolded her.

"Dinna you think I know that?" Brina lowered her eyes. She was so angry at both the woman and Gunnolf, she couldn't think straight. "Sorry, Grandmother."

"'Tis all right, child. If she is his brother's widow, she is most likely angry with him and the world for her loss." Wynne watched Brina, appearing to want to soothe her fears.

"I believe she wants more than that." Brina stalked over to the window and peered out of the tower in the direction Gunnolf had gone.

"She wouldna want to wed him, would she?" Lynette asked, her eyes wide with surprise. "Her own husband's brother?"

"She isna like us. She wields a sword and shield meant to kill a man. She may very well wish it. Even our people will marry a widow to take care of a sister by marriage and her bairns."

"But she tried to kill him, you said," Lynette reminded her.

Brina wheeled on her in anger. "Gunnolf is a Viking! Mayhap that is what he likes in a woman."

Lady Akira smiled, but Brina didn't think it was funny at all.

"Then next time you see him, loose an arrow at him. But do try to miss or the idea of marriage may no longer be possible," Lynette said.

Brina groaned, grabbed up her sewing, and sat down next to Lynette again. "I could never fight that kind of a woman for his affections."

Lynette smiled at her.

"If I wanted to," Brina quickly said.

"You dinna need to fight any woman for his affections," Wynne said. "Be yourself. I am to understand that during the dancing, he kissed you in the shadows by the stables. Who says he would not prefer a nice Highland lass who just kisses him back instead of fighting him for the honor?"

Brina opened her mouth, her skin burning with mortification, then closed her mouth, not knowing what to say to that. If anyone had not seen them kissing, the word had to have spread to every soul by now.

***

Gunnolf had only been with his brother's

widow a day when he realized he didn't want to stay any longer. He would leave on the morrow. The young girl who had fascinated him when he was five and ten winters and she the same age only born in the summer, was a warrior, a leader of her people, and completely bitter toward the Highlanders. Not that he didn't understand the situation, but she didn't like learning that he'd lived with some of them and been friends and called them family. He would never feel any differently about her, and he could never view all Highlanders in the same manner as she did.

"I still cannot believe what Hallfred had said about you. That he saw you dead. You must have passed out and he thought you were dead," Inga said, eating mutton beside Gunnolf at a long table, several others seated at more tables in the long house.

"He knew damn well that I was not dead."

Inga frowned at him. "You must have been badly injured. How would you know?"

"When Hallfred and my gazes met, he told another of our clansmen I was dead. I was breathing, alive, feeling half dead, *ja*, unable to speak, but I was not in Valhalla, and he knew it. He did not like that you and I had feelings for each other back then. Mayhap still would have, had I returned with those who had lived."

Inga growled her displeasure. "Too bad he did not die back then. So what are you going to do?" She speared a piece of cheese with her *knifr*, a small, single-edged knife, plain and not ornately decorated like the longer ones his people used as weapons. "We will never be at peace with the Auchinleck Clan."

"What if I were to manage to oust Seamus who rules there now and when Robard no longer can rule, I step in to take his place? Then I could make peace with you. Even before that, really, as a bargaining tool. I will not aid him unless he agrees to peace between your people and his."

Inga's eyes rounded and she didn't speak for a second. "*My* people?" She scowled. "You are no longer one of us?" She shook her head. "You would never be able to lay siege to the castle and take over. With us at your side? There are too few of us."

"Nay. I rescued the chief's daughter and escorted her to see her kin at the MacNeill castle. He believes I might be able to unseat Seamus so that when Robard is well, he may take his place as chief again. In the meantime, I would rule."

"A Norseman? Do not delude yourself."

"Robard knew of my loyal support to James and his clan. He seems to believe I would be a good choice to aid him."

Inga stiffened her back. "This child of his that you rescued. How old is she?"

Gunnolf knew before he said anything, Inga was going to be angry that Brina was not a wee bairn. "Full grown. Her da promised her to Seamus in marriage, but Seamus betrayed him. Now Robard does not wish her to marry him."

Inga scowled again. "He wants *you* to marry her? Think you this Robard would honor his commitment to you? You go in, kill this Seamus, restore power to the chief, and he has you murdered."

Gunnolf hated to agree that Inga could be right. He didn't know Robard, only that he was ruthless, and even his daughter had said the man was untrustworthy. But what if Gunnolf married Brina? Wouldn't her father honor his word then? For her sake?

Maybe not. Maybe Robard would still conveniently eliminate Gunnolf so that he could rule and then give Brina to some other man, who was a true Highlander and loyal to him and elected by their clan.

"Did you kiss her?" Inga suddenly asked, her voice raised shrilly.

Gunnolf didn't believe his business with the lass was any of Inga's concern, but he knew if he said no, she'd know he had lied. And if he said yes, who knew how the shield maiden would react.

"I am considering marrying her." Gunnolf watched as Inga's face turned red with anger.

"You would marry one of them over one of us?" she screeched. "They killed your brother!"

She didn't mean just that he would marry one of the Highlanders over one of their own people. If he had said he preferred another woman living in Inga's village, he knew Inga would be just as incensed. She had it in mind he would marry *her*, no one else.

"Go!" she shouted at him.

He inclined his head and rose from the table. "The best thing I can do for our people is to end this war between us, in any way that I can."

"By marrying that daughter of his? Brina? Take care, Gunnolf. You may have survived the battle when you were five and ten and all these years living here and fighting the Highlanders' battles, but all it takes is one person's treachery that could be your undoing when you think them a friend."

"Thank you for your advice." Gunnolf headed out of the longhouse, though he noted Inga speaking to one of the men, who watched Gunnolf go. He didn't like the dark expression on either Inga's or the man's face.

Did she think to have Gunnolf murdered so that he couldn't wed Brina and try to end the war between the Norsemen and the Highland clan when Robard's people had killed her husband? Did she still want revenge?

He wouldn't put it past her. She might have had it in mind that Robard could be the enemy, saying one thing, but meaning another, but Inga could very well be the same way.

He realized then as he mounted Beast and left the village, that he trusted only the MacNeill clan and Brina, despite having just met her. She only worried about his well-being and about her father's. She didn't seem to have any hidden plan.

He still wanted to give Inga's people a chance

to live in peace. He didn't know if he would be able to manage ousting Seamus, or if Brina's father would actually reward him or attempt to kill him once he returned Robard to power. The more he thought about it, the more he believed it was the only way to possibly reconcile things between Inga, her people, and Robard and his, then return Brina to her home, if that's what she wished.

Gunnolf thought about how he usually was doing some task for James or his brothers, saving someone or another, but he had never actually made plans to take care of a situation that James or his kin, in most cases, had not asked him to do.

The bigger question was whether Gunnolf could settle down with Brina. Would she be happy with him, the Norseman that he was? Would he be happy with her?

All he had to do was think of the way she had reacted to the wolf pup, risking her freedom and even endangering herself for the life of the pup should Seamus have gotten hold of her. She had worried about him during their journey, and then when he was off to see his kinsmen, something no other woman had done. He smiled fondly, thinking back to the way Ian had taken to her, the boy shy around strangers. Yet there the lad had been holding her hand as they'd entered the great hall, and she was speaking to him while he was smiling up at her. Gunnolf could envision her walking with their own son like that, when he'd never given it much thought before. He thought about Lady Eilis and the way her gown tented over her expanding belly and considered what it would be like to know Brina was carrying his bairn.

He knew what he had to do. Convince Brina he was the right man for her as he knew she was the right lass for him. He never believed, as many times as James said he would, that he'd find a lass he truly wanted to marry.

He was heading toward the MacNeill lands at a trot, but it would take him a day and a half to reach them and half a day to arrive at the castle. He intended to leave in the morning, not when the sun was beginning to set. He heard two horses following him, and he was trying to decide what to do. Continue on his way until it was too dark to travel. Or stop now, and fight the men he assumed Inga had sent to track him down. He didn't want to fight her people. He didn't want to fight anyone. Though he had no intention of being beaten, either, if he could help it.

Gunnolf stopped his horse, and faced the two men, both burly fighters—the blond and darker haired man from before. He should have already unsheathed Aðalbrandr, but wanting to show he didn't intend to start a fight, he waited. They began walking their horses, drawing closer, and then stopping, waiting to see what he would do.

"Inga wishes you to have words with me?" Gunnolf asked, certain she wanted them to do more than that.

"I have a chance to be with Inga as her husband

if I kill you," the blond said, his hair braided on one side, his hand on the hilt of his sword. "I could see she has a fondness for you that she did not share with your brother. What if you return and want to take her for your wife?"

"I have no wish to fight you. I hope to bring peace between Robard and Inga. *Ja* at one time I had feelings for Inga when I was much younger. Many years have passed since then. We are different people now, both of us. If you wish to wed Inga, you have my blessing."

"I do not ask for it."

"Then what? We fight? You kill me or I kill you and then Inga can continue to fight Robard, or I should say Seamus and his men? To what end? You have settled here to farm. Then farm and leave the fighting for another time. For something truly worth fighting for."

"Tell that to Robard."

"Robard needs my help. If I can aid him, I will ask for peace between his people and yours in return."

"And his daughter?"

"I will marry her if she so wishes it."

"Inga wants you dead. Here and now. She does not want peace. And she does not want you to marry the Highland lass. But I am willing to give one of our fellow countrymen the chance to infiltrate the keep and bring peace to the region, or bring them down. If you return here with the notion of taking Inga for your wife, I will kill you."

Gunnolf inclined his head a little, turned his horse, and continued on his way, listening for the sounds of horses' hoof beats. There were none but his own and finally the other men turned around and headed back to their village, crisis averted, at least for a brief moment in time.

But Gunnolf now knew the direction he was headed, and that meant he was bound for a fight.

CHAPTER 11

When Gunnolf finally arrived at Wynne's shieling, he saw smoke curling above the chimney and thought maybe Brina and Lynette were there with Wynne. He hoped that they had not done something to upset the MacNeill clan and the women had all been asked to the castle. Though he couldn't imagine anything so absurd. They'd be alone here and unprotected.

Gunnolf dismounted and hurried to the door, raising his hand to knock.

Wynne opened it before he could. "They are no' here. They are still at the castle. I couldna stay any longer. Too many people were asking me what their futures hold. How can I know that?"

"And mine? What vision have you for me this time?" He hoped Wynne would say that Brina would accept his proposal of marriage.

"I have had no visions concerning you. But

Brina had one of you kissing the woman from your village. I dinna believe she will be speaking to you when you see her next. What are your plans now? Are you returning to her lands to help her da?"

Gunnolf couldn't believe Brina had seen what had happened between him and Inga in one of her visions. Would she now truly be angry with him over the whole matter? Hopefully, she would realize he had not wanted to fight the woman, nor pin her to the ground. What if she had not seen the fight? He stifled a groan. He could imagine her seeing only him shoving Inga down, lying on top of her, and Inga kissing him next. It would be much harder to explain his actions then.

He took the honeyed mead Wynne offered him, and feeling parched, he drank all of it. "I will return to her da's lands and aid him. James said he would spare some men to assist me in taking Seamus down. I will help to ensure Brina's father is restored to power."

"What about Brina?"

"I will wed Brina if she will have me. Depending on the reception I receive from her kin and how Brina feels about it, we will either stay at her brother's castle or we will return here. What about Lynette? What does she wish to do?"

"For now, she will stay here. She is happy here and is enjoying the attentions of Lady Akira, Laird James, and his wife."

"I am pleased to hear it." Gunnolf had known Lady Akira would accept her, as well as James and the rest of the clan. He was glad for the lass.

"We didna expect you to return so soon. Did you make peace with your fellow countrymen?"

"Of a sort." If convincing Inga's henchmen not to battle with him to the death was making peace. "I must continue on my way to Craigly. Thank you for the mead."

"Aye. I am sure most will be pleased to see you return."

"Most." Gunnolf remounted his horse.

"All but Brina. Did you kiss the woman back? Brina couldna tell. She said you were on top of the woman and that blocked her view."

Hating that Brina had witnessed all of that when he had assumed she'd never know, Gunnolf frowned. "Who else knows of this?"

"Lady Akira and James's wife, several other ladies, and well, you know how the word will spread."

Knowing just how fast the gossip would carry, Gunnolf groaned. "Take care, Wynne. We will see you again soon." He thought the ladies' visions could be helpful. Now he saw how much trouble they could be.

When Gunnolf finally arrived at Craigly Castle, James met him at the stable. "You are back sooner than I had expected."

Rather than pretend he didn't know what he suspected most of the clan would have heard by now, Gunnolf said, "I understand Brina had a vision."

James smiled. "Aye. Pray tell, did you kiss the lass back?"

"My brother's widow? Nay. And I want naught to do with the lass. She and I are at cross purposes."

"What of Brina?"

"That remains to be seen."

James slapped him on the back with good cheer. "Come, 'tis time to eat."

Though Gunnolf was famished, the prospect of not eating with Brina, if she was angry with him, disappointed him. He hoped he could speak with her in any event.

When they arrived at the great hall filled with clansmen and women, he saw Brina, the wolf pup sitting at her feet, and Lynette standing beside her, talking near the high table. He knew with having so many people around, he should wait to speak with Brina alone about the matter with Inga. But he couldn't. He headed straight for her through the crush of clansmen. Lynette saw him first, folded her arms, and smiled at him in a way that said she knew he had some explaining to do and it amused her. Beowulf saw him next and ran to greet him.

Brina turned her attention in his direction and scowled. The pup jumped all over him in excitement as if he had missed him terribly. At least the pup was glad to see him. Gunnolf lifted Beowulf into his arms. "I believe you have grown in the short time I was gone. Have you been eating all the hunting dogs' food?"

Beowulf's wet tongue tried to lick his face, his

tail wagging wildly. Gunnolf chuckled and joined Brina, then set the pup down on the rushes on the floor. Beowulf bounced between the two of them for attention. Gunnolf nodded a quick greeting to Lynette.

"We need to talk." Gunnolf took Brina's arm and led her to a bench, wanting to at least speak to her in a semi-private way, Beowulf tagging along behind them.

"About the kiss?" Brina asked, raising a brow.

"If you mean Inga…" He had to clarify that she wasn't talking about his kissing Brina.

"Aye, the very one." Brina looked crossly at him as if it perturbed her that he wouldn't already know just who she meant.

"Seems it is the topic of conversation. I am glad to know it means naught to you as much as it meant the same to me." Because it didn't. He wasn't making light of the issue, but only trying to say that he hoped she didn't put any stock in what had happened.

Brina yanked her arm free from his grasp. "You are saying that kissing her meant naught to you?"

"I did not kiss her. And for your information, lass, I was attempting to keep her from fighting me further, which, if you had seen any more of the vision, was the reason for my being on top of her."

"Was it her plan then? To fight you until she could kiss you?"

"I do not think she wanted to kiss me more than she wanted to kill me for not telling her I yet lived.

But Inga wed my brother. I still have no interest in her as a prospective wife. I cannot emphasize my feelings on the matter more." He didn't know what else to say to prove to Brina that Inga meant naught to him except to tell her so. At least for now. He meant to show Brina just how much she meant to him when they didn't have quite so many witnesses.

Brina sat next to Gunnolf at the table as Lynette joined James and his family at the high table. She knew she should be so annoyed with him over Inga. But just seeing him lying atop the woman and not jumping off her or something to show he truly wasn't interested in the shield maiden irked Brina. "Was she angry that my da had killed her husband?"

"I think not as much as she was angry that your father wants me to marry you. Another man wishes to wed the shield maiden. He said she never loved my brother."

"But she loved you? Why else would she have kissed you?" Brina assumed she sounded like a shrew and didn't like feeling that way. But she couldn't help it. The image of the woman kissing him was still clear in Brina's mind.

"She may have thought she did. But we are not the same people as in our youth." Gunnolf waited patiently to answer all Brina's questions, which she thought was a good sign. Not once had he glanced in the direction of the venison sitting before him, nor had he lifted his tankard to drink of his ale. He was proving to her that what she had to say was more important than satisfying his own needs when she was certain he was thirsty and starving after all the traveling he had done.

"But you loved her once?" Brina asked, to be clear on the matter.

"I loved that she was wild and crazy and wanted to kiss me when other maidens were not in the least bit interested."

Brina couldn't believe any lass wouldn't be interested in a kiss from Gunnolf's lips. Even now she wished he'd kiss her, to prove to her he had no feelings for the Viking woman. Though she finally moved on to more important subjects. "How did the rest of your people treat you?"

"Naturally, they were supportive of Inga. She sent two of her men to kill me and I am certain they were willing to do so."

Brina's jaw dropped. She wanted to kill the woman herself! "Why would she do such a thing if she loved you?"

"I had no interest in marrying her. And she knew I intended to wed you. If you would have me." Gunnolf took Brina's hand in his and stroked her gently.

Brina's body heated with embarrassment to think he would tell the Viking woman he was marrying a Highland lass—not any Highland lass, but her! The daughter of the man who had killed Inga's husband. No wonder the woman wanted to eliminate Gunnolf. Brina knew then that he had to care for her more than he did Inga. She blinked back tears. No man had ever wanted her like that, who would be willing to risk his life like he had.

"Is this a proposal?" she blurted, finally realizing he had given her one in an offhanded way, when he should have asked her before he told Inga the news!

"I am not well-versed in asking a lass to marry me. I have not had any experience at it. Should I get down on bended knee?"

She smiled, loving him, thinking to say yes because he had told Inga first of his proposal. "If I tell you that you should and you did, Beowulf would jump all over you and ruin the whole effect."

Gunnolf chuckled.

"Aye, aye, I will. With all my heart, I wish this union between us," she said, her stomach fluttering with excitement and trepidation.

"You have made me the happiest man alive." Then he kissed her on the mouth, slowly, surely, and reluctantly pulled away. "We still need to discuss more before we make the announcement, *ja*?"

She wanted to kiss him more, not talk more, but she knew this was important. She sighed and nodded. "What happened concerning the men Inga sent to kill you?"

"I convinced them I would not fight and that I had no interest in marrying Inga, but that I would try to bring peace between our people."

"You would do this for my da?" she asked, still

shocked at the shield maiden's actions, but knowing Gunnolf was the one she needed most in her life, no matter what the outcome — staying here, going there. She still wanted to help her da though.

Gunnolf shook his head and leaned over and kissed her cheek. "I would do this for you."

"After seeing how Inga reacted, do you think you could still end hostilities between our people?" She was afraid the woman would retaliate further, not wish peace.

"'Twould remain to be seen. I would do my best to secure a peace treaty with them. What if your elders do not want me to be in charge? No matter what though, Seamus is still a problem."

"Which you can handle without any difficulty. Three of his loyal men are dead, aye? So you could easily manage the rest." After seeing the way he handled others with diplomacy, dispatched Seamus's man, and had dealt with so many others over the years in battle, she was certain he could deal with Seamus satisfactorily.

"What if others have rallied to his cause? Or if not, what if they do so in response to a Norseman attempting to run your castle until your father has healed enough to take over?"

"We would be married. My da would back you. And you are a braw warrior. Believe me, my da would never have asked you to marry me if he didna believe you could rule until he was well, and rule once he no longer can. I think this could be a good thing between your people and mine." She truly believed it would work.

"You said your father only chose me because he was angry with Seamus."

Which she still thought was true, knowing the way her da was. "Aye, but even so, he wouldna have picked just anyone to wed me. He would have chosen someone he thought could successfully beat Seamus and lead the clan. Do you no' agree this could be a way of healing the wounds suffered by both parties?"

"*Ja*, lass, I do, if all goes according to plan." Leaning close to her ear and whispering against the soft lobe, Gunnolf agreed, thrilled beyond measure that she wanted to marry him. "I could not stop thinking about you."

"And I you," she whispered back.

"Then we shall wed, not because your da wishes it but because—"

"We were meant to be together. From the first time I saw you in the glen when you called me a goddess."

He laughed. "You are still a goddess to me."

"And you are the braw Viking who wouldna die that I so wished to care for and worried about for years."

"You did not tell me that. This day was meant to be. I love you, Brina. I will make you proud to be my wife."

"I couldna love your any more than I do."

"Good, because the love I have for you is mutual. Eat and drink because once I make the announcement, I fear Lady Akira will want us wed right away."

Brina laughed and started to eat of her venison.

Gunnolf downed some of his ale and looked at the hall filled with friends who were his family. He'd never thought he'd leave this place and live among people who fought his own kin. Even if he led her clan, would that change his people's mind about fighting Brina's people?

Being chief of his own clan, allying with the MacNeills, which would be a way to pay back all their kindness to him in an immense way, making amends with his own people, all of that had appeal. Brina was bonny, sweet and innocent, intelligent, but willful. She didn't ply her womanly charms on him like other lasses did. Yet, she did make him yearn for something more. She'd stirred his loins like no other woman had done, when she hadn't even been trying. He couldn't deny he wanted to bed her. But he wanted a wife who wanted him just as much, not as a bargaining tool in some play for power. She deserved better, and he was glad she loved him too.

"We wed on the morrow," he said, slicing off a chunk of venison. "Whether I return to help your father or not. We will wed and I will protect you from Seamus. He will never hurt you."

"If he kills my da, he will have hurt me."

Gunnolf kissed her cheek. "I will return with some of James's men and will do what I can. I cannot promise I will be completely successful."

"I want to go with you."

He was surprised to hear her say it. He suspected she was worried about her da's health. In no way did Gunnolf want her in any danger. "You must know how I feel about that."

"I need to see to my da's care. I can stay with Cadel and his wife until we see how this goes. What if you need my help in gaining access to the castle though? We could say that James was having me returned, but he has to see my da and speak to him about Lynette. Seamus would be a fool to earn James's ire. James has too many brothers who are in charge of clans or can call on other clans to come to his aid. Seamus wouldna realize that James perceives you as his brother and would most likely believe that if Lynette wed someone in the MacNeill clan, Seamus could benefit from the arrangement."

"I do not like the idea. Too risky. What if Seamus believes you will marry him?"

"Unless you lay siege to the castle for months, what other choice have you? My excuse for returning would be to see my da, that Cadel had sent word he still lives, and I beseeched James to bring me home. You will tell Seamus I am your wife and James will verify 'tis true."

"If Seamus even allows James and his men into the castle, he will have us disarmed."

"Aye, but any man loyal to my da will aid us, arming us as soon as we are inside the castle."

Gunnolf took her hand and squeezed gently.

"What if your father did not survive his wounds?"

Brina knew that could very well be the case. She didn't want to believe it, yet she knew it was important to think of worst-case situations. "We will learn what has happened from Cadel before we approach the castle. If he tells us my da has died, then we will return here. Inga and her people will have to make peace with Seamus on her own."

"I still do not like the notion of you coming with us."

"We have to learn if my da is dead or alive, and aid him if we can. I strongly believe I can help us to gain access to the castle when James might no'."

"I worry what Seamus will attempt to do to you once he has you in sight."

She lifted her chin and pulled Gunnolf down for a kiss and whispered against his lips. "I will have my Viking warrior to protect me." Then she wrapped her arms around Gunnolf's neck and kissed him fully on the mouth, loving this, loving him.

The hall filled with conversation suddenly grew very quiet, and when she and Gunnolf broke free of the kiss, cheers resounded.

Gunnolf raised his tankard of ale. "The lass has agreed to wed me!"

Woots and whistles and more cheers filled the air.

"Tonight," Lady Akira said smiling, though she appeared serious about it.

"Tonight," James agreed, and Eilis kissed her

husband's cheek with approval.

As soon as the meal was done, Lady Akira, Lady Eilis, Fia, and Lynette quickly ushered Brina out of the great hall and up the stairs to Eilis's chamber.

"I have a gown you may wear for the wedding," Eilis said.

"I do also," Fia, Eilis's cousin, said.

"I will wear my red one." Brina loved that gown above all others, which was why she had worn it beneath the rest, protecting it on her journey. Not to mention it was so bright in color, she knew she would have been spotted a mile away across a glen. And it was her warmest.

"'Tis a lovely gown," Lady Akira said, holding the red one up and admiring the embroidery work. "Even prettier than the red one Matilda wore when she married King Henry."

"You were there?" Brina asked, surprised.

"My sons have been to the English court a number of times, and I went with them on that most festive of occasions. Aye."

"Must have been wondrous." Brina had stitched for weeks embellishing the details on the hems of her sleeves, neckline, and skirt. She never imagined she would be wearing the gown to her own wedding. "Will you wed Tibold?" Brina asked, thinking that if Lady Akira loved the man, she should not let another day pass without making her feelings known, as the ladies helped her out of her blue one and on with the red.

Lady Akira attached an embroidered circlet to a veil over Brina's hair. "I have to be asked."

"Ask *him*," Eilis said.

"Aye, ask him." Lynette's eyes were bright with amusement.

Fia just beamed. "I will go with you when you do."

Eilis laughed. "You only wish to see Tibold's sons, the ones who are no' wed."

Fia blushed.

Brina wished she could meet this man whom Lady Akira thought so fondly of.

"With your dark hair, the red looks astounding," Lady Akira said.

"Did you believe this was where we were headed?" Brina asked.

"Aye. And we are glad. I wouldna wish Gunnolf to marry a woman no' suited to him. You are perfect for him," Lady Akira said.

"But I have my faults too."

"He will love you just the same." Lady Akira sighed. "You are beautiful, Brina. Come, let us no' keep Gunnolf waiting any longer as I am certain he is concerned that you might change your mind as James worried about Eilis when it was her turn to walk down the aisle."

All the ladies laughed.

***

"What bargain have you struck with the lass?" James asked Gunnolf as they waited for Brina and the other ladies to meet with them in the stone chapel.

Appearing to have found a home here, Beowulf was chasing several deerhound pups through the building, yipping and growling.

Gunnolf explained what Brina wanted to do. He knew at once James didn't like the idea the way he frowned, just as Gunnolf didn't, but he knew her notions were valid also.

"I dinna like it," James said honestly. "But her plans have merit."

"Anything could happen though. I still do not trust her father or that his people would still be loyal to him."

James rubbed his chin thoughtfully, then folded his arms. "What if none of his men provide us with weapons?"

"'Tis a possibility. We have never let that stop us from waging war in the past. A few aggressive men, tactics that can force a man to lose a dirk, and the next thing we know, our men are armed and theirs are not."

James smiled. "Aye. You dinna feel pushed into this marriage, do you?"

"Nay. The time is right. She is the right woman for me." Gunnolf knew why Lady Akira was in a rush to have this done. She was good at thinking up battle strategies and ensuring that their people benefited from clan politics and often advised James on matters, whether he wished it or not. They had to do something now, and not wait any longer, if they were to learn if Robard still lived. Not only that, but Lady Akira was an excellent judge of character. She knew that Brina and Gunnolf would be good together, and once she decided something, she hurried to make it happen. Just as she did when Eilis came into their lives, and James had fully intended to marry another lass.

Even so, Gunnolf wasn't certain how Lady Akira would react regarding Brina going with them. He hoped that Brina would convince her how sound the plan was, and somehow they would manage to pull it off with little blood spilled. Only Seamus and his men's, if they decided to stay and fight.

Eilis entered the chapel and motioned to her husband that it was time to do his part.

"This is the best part," James said to Gunnolf before he left to escort Brina there.

"For *you*? Or for *me*?" Gunnolf grinned.

James laughed. "I knew someday I would see you tied down to a lass. You will find being married to Brina is well worth it."

Gunnolf agreed and waited while James left the chapel and the other ladies accompanying Brina hurried to take their seats. After attending so many weddings in the MacNeill chapel over the years, Gunnolf couldn't believe he was now the groom eager to see his bride and waiting for his own wedding to commence.

When Brina entered the chapel wearing the red gown she'd worn underneath the others when he'd first met her, her arm on James's arm, Gunnolf's heartbeat quickened. He couldn't wait to say the vows, celebrate, and slip away to his chamber with her, then make love to his beautiful wife.

CHAPTER 12

This was happening so fast, Brina couldn't believe she was truly marrying Gunnolf. Never had she imagined she would be wed to a Viking, not with the trouble they'd had with them. Yet she recalled the day so long ago when she'd found him bleeding in the tall grasses and had wanted to get help for him, wanted to help him herself, and then he had vanished. Who would have ever thought their paths would cross again? And this would be the result?

When she saw him standing at the altar, waiting for her to join him while James escorted her down the aisle, she felt her knees weaken. Gunnolf stood so tall, his eyes dark, a warm smile in place. Like most women she'd known who had suddenly found themselves marrying, she was excited about the prospect of the bedding later this eve, but also worried. Would she please him?

She hoped they'd be successful in helping her da, but she wasn't marrying Gunnolf for that reason. Yes, her da wished it of her. And yes, it meant she couldn't wed Seamus. But more than anything, she wanted this. She wanted Gunnolf.

Before she knew it, she was standing beside him, saying her vows, looking up at him, his blue eyes steady on hers until he lifted her face gently so that he could kiss her. She closed her eyes, blocking out everyone else as if she and he were standing in the shadows beside the stable, supposedly out of everyone's sight. She parted her lips, beckoning him to kiss her like he had kissed her before. Her hands settled on his waist to give her balance, because when they were kissing, she felt her world spin out of control. Like now, his mouth pressed against hers, sweetly at first until somehow tongues came into play. He pulled back and looked down at her as if she were the most beautiful woman in the world

She smiled up at him, still nervous about tonight, but wishing they could finish what they started right now.

Among cheers and well-wishes, he led her out of the chapel and back to the great hall where they had yet another feast—more spirits, music, laughter, and celebrating.

"You told Lady Akira about what we were doing on the morrow?" Gunnolf asked Brina.

"Nay. I knew she wouldna like it and try to convince me no' to go." Brina glanced at where

Lady Akira and James were speaking. Lady Akira's jaw dropped. Her gaze shot toward Brina. "I believe James just told her."

Lynette was frowning, then speaking, and both James and Lady Akira were listening to her. Lady Akira shook her head, but Lynette raised her hands in a way that said what else could she do about it. Lady Akira shook her head again.

James began to speak, and Eilis put her hand on James's arm, then spoke.

Brina had a bad feeling about this. "Is she saying I shouldna go?"

"Not sure, lass. But everyone looks distressed over it."

Brina sighed. "I am going. I have to."

"Just as we planned. We will be leaving before first light so I thought we would retire sooner than is usual for a couple newly wed. You do not think we will appear too eager, do you?"

Brina laughed. But it was more nervous laughter than anything.

He reached over and squeezed her hand as if to reassure her and she loved him for it. "I will make the announcement that we are retiring to the bedchamber because we have such an early start in the morn," he said.

Brina's whole body warmed with awkwardness at the thought. She knew this would be the way. Everyone would know about it, but it still didn't make it any easier. "Lady Akira said they would help me get ready for you."

"I would help you, but I know they feel they must." Gunnolf smiled, then frowned. "As long as it does not take too long." He rose from the bench and raised his tankard. "We must leave before dawn and so—"

Cheers and whistles filled the hall and Lady Akira, Fia, Eilis, and Lynette rose from their benches, then headed toward Brina and Gunnolf's table.

"They dinna appear happy that we are leaving so early," Brina said.

"The celebrating will go on for much longer and no one will miss us." Gunnolf pulled Brina into his arms and kissed her soundly before the ladies reached them. "If they do not come for me soon, I will meet you in my chamber anyway."

Brina smiled at him. "I love you, Norseman."

He chuckled and kissed her mouth again. "I was getting used to you calling me Viking. I love you just as much, Brina." He glanced in the ladies' direction as they approached and bowed his head a little.

Brina saw the strain in Lady Akira's expression, and the other ladies looked just as upset. Brina thought it was a good thing to retire early to bed since they had to get up so early on the morrow. Clearly, they'd breached some kind of protocol.

As soon as they'd escorted her to the chamber, Lynette and Fia began to remove her gown, and then her chemise. They helped her into a new one embroidered around the hem.

"What is wrong?" Brina didn't want them to be upset with her.

"I am traveling with you on the morrow," Lynette said. "Laird James says you are going with Gunnolf. You canna go alone. I have been your companion for years. I know all there is to know about you. And I can help to protect you if need be."

"Nay." Brina didn't want her sister to come and chance being hurt. "You canna. The risk is all mine. You said yourself you would stay here if I were to return home."

"Aye. But I meant if you returned for good. If everything was settled with your da. My mind is made up. I am going with you and we will watch each other's backs. When your castle is free of vermin, I will return here with Laird James and his men, and we can see each other whenever we are able."

"I dinna wish either of you to go," Lady Akira said.

Though Brina had only just met Lady Akira, she was like the mother she had lost, and she knew Akira wasn't just saying it to include her because she didn't want Lynette to go.

Eilis nodded. "'Tis too dangerous. Anything could go wrong."

"What if this Seamus has taken complete control over the clan? What if they dinna want Gunnolf to lead in the interim? Or Robard to return to power?" Lady Akira asked.

"Anything is possible." Brina let out her breath in exasperation. She didn't think she was going to have this discussion with the ladies on her wedding night or on the eve of what could turn out to be a major disaster for them. She also had no idea Lynette would want to go with her. She would love it if her sister was with her under other circumstances, but she didn't want her to share the risk.

"Lynette, I appreciate your concern, and I value our friendship so much so that I canna let you go with me."

"You said yourself that I was the reason for James going there to see Robard as a pretense he doesna realize Seamus has taken over. James is going concerning me. That I am his half sister and he wishes to make it known that not only was he grateful that the clan took care of me for all these years, but that he wishes an alliance. What better way to prove he is sincere than to take me with him? It willna appear as though he intends to do battle with Seamus then."

Brina hated that Lynette's words made sense. She really didn't want her half sister in harm's way, but it appeared she was going anyway.

"I am coming and that is all there is to it." Lynette did have her stubborn streak, but Brina knew it was because she worried just as much about Brina.

Lady Akira looked on the verge of tears. Brina

was afraid she had only just gained a daughter and didn't want to chance losing her as she had lost her only daughter already.

Eilis took her arm. "Come, my lady mother. All will be well. Did you see Lynette and Brina plying their skills at archery earlier today and the day before? I wouldna wish to be in their line of sight when they loose an arrow."

Brina was surprised Eilis had seen them practicing.

Lady Akira didn't seem relieved to hear it. "We must leave the chamber before the eager groom comes and throws us out." She gave Brina a small smile and hugged her soundly. "Gunnolf is so much like a son to me. He will love you well. I want us to get to know each other better. I dinna want the two of us to be strangers."

Brina gave her a hug back. "You are like the mother I lost, my lady. And I hope that when Tibold and you are wed, you will invite us."

Lady Akira laughed. "I will, if it comes to pass." She turned to Lynette. "I would like to speak further with you before you leave."

"Aye, of course."

"Eilis?" Lady Akira said.

"Aye."

Lady Akira patted Fia on the shoulder. "You as well."

Everyone gave Brina smiles and hugs, left, then Fia winked at her and closed the door.

Brina paced across the room, the large bed

taking up much of the chamber, a chest in one corner, and pegs on the wall above that where tunics and a belt were hanging. Her gaze drifted again to the bed, the furs piled up on it, the curtains draped around it, open for now. She rubbed her arms from the chill in the chamber and the nervousness she was suddenly feeling now that the ladies had left her alone. She wasn't thinking about tomorrow but tonight—and making love with Gunnolf in his bed.

Now, more than ever, she thought of the women back home telling a maid what to expect when she made love to a man for her first time. "Spread your legs wide, relax, and let him push his staff inside," she'd overheard the one say, the other agreeing.

Brina shivered and rubbed her arms, thinking how it would feel to spread her legs wide for Gunnolf. Titillating and wanton.

In her thin chemise, she was cold and though she had thought to kiss Gunnolf and help him to disrobe before they retired to bed, she felt too chilled to wait. The furs looked so warm and inviting. She hoped he wouldn't think her afraid of making love to him and hoped he'd be here soon.

She slipped underneath the covers and began to warm up. She breathed in his spicy male scent from the bed clothes, never imagining she'd be in the warrior's bed, waiting in anticipation of making love to him when the door opened. She barely breathed.

Gunnolf entered the chamber, shutting the door behind him. "I met the ladies on the stairs. I could not wait any longer for them to send me word that you were ready."

She smiled, glad he couldn't wait to be with her. "I was cold and climbed under the covers to get warm."

He began to strip off his clothes in the candlelight. "I am glad you did. I would not want my bride to catch a chill." He frowned then as he sat on the bed next to her, the mattress sinking with his weight, and removed his boots, then socks. "What were Lady Akira and the other ladies so concerned about?" He stood and removed his belt.

She eyed his plaid, looking for any sign that he was eager to make love to her. She thought she saw a small rise, but she might be mistaken. Didn't he have to kiss her first to make it happen? "Lynette wants to go with us tomorrow."

Gunnolf's brow furrowed even more deeply.

Brina explained why, waiting expectantly for Gunnolf to pull off his tunic next. Once he dropped his plaid to the floor, he pulled the covers aside and climbed into bed. But he was still wearing his tunic! "I am in agreement with Lady Akira, but I understand Lynette's reasoning, and it could aid us." He touched her cheek in a heartwarming way. "No more talk for now about tomorrow or anything else. 'Tis time to make love to my bonny wife."

Still partially clothed, he began kissing Brina's

lips. Maybe for their first time, he believed they should be wearing garments when she thought they would both be naked. Maybe it wasn't done that way. She was glad she had not removed her chemise or he would have thought her truly bold. Once his kisses turned from sweet to passionate, she forgot all about it. All her senses were heightened as she breathed in his masculine scent, felt his tongue teasing hers in a wickedly, wonderful way, and his body pressed against hers, hard with desire. She tasted the ale he had been drinking—robust and spicy.

His hand cupped a breast and he rubbed her nipple until the sensitive tip peaked. Unexpectedly, he licked it through her thin chemise, the wetness making it all the more sensitive as his warm breath caressed it. The sensation was nothing like she'd ever felt before. Wondrous and wickedly enticing. His hand slid down her thigh, and he slipped her chemise up until he was touching her bare flesh.

She gasped at the thrill of the sensation his warm hand had on her naked skin.

Their gazes met, his eyes like the dark blue sky of night. Then he bent his head and kissed her again. His fingers played with her nipple, and she kissed him back with a fervor that shocked her.

She never imagined the joy she would feel with his touching her like this, even though his kissing her and lying with her before had filled her with a craving she'd never expected either. But this was so much more.

Now, desire stirred longings deep inside her, her breath and his labored, their kisses more insistent. His hand swept down her belly and lower until he snagged her chemise again. This time he pulled it up higher, until he was able to slip it over her head.

She didn't want him to believe she was squeamish about seeing him completely naked, and in truth, she was eager to see all of him, so she tugged at his tunic to help him remove it. Once it joined her chemise on the rushes on the floor, he looked down at her, his expression one of admiration. She took her fill of him at the same time, the light golden hair on his chest that trailed down to that most wondrous of male parts, his thickened staff stretching out to her. His nipples were hard pebbles. She was wet for him already, wanting him to join her. But she noticed the old wounds on his side and a couple more on his other. She wished he had never been wounded. She was grateful he was alive and well and ready to make love to her.

When Gunnolf began to stroke his fingers between her legs, she dug her fingers into his side and clung to a thread of sanity. Every stroke lifted her higher, to what end, she didn't know, but she loved the feelings he was stirring deep inside her. The primal need to couple with him. The raw animal instinct that told her she needed him inside thrusting and filling her with his progeny.

His mouth was kissing hers again, his actions

seemed near desperate before she felt her world collide and break apart. She cried out in wonderment, her whole being wrapped in a state of bliss. No one had ever mentioned that part of the lovemaking. It was truly wondrous.

"Are you ready, Brina?" Gunnolf whispered against her ear, his voice husky, barely able to rasp out the words.

Oh, aye, she was ready to do that again.

"Aye." She knew this part of their lovemaking would hurt the first time. Cook's helpers had mentioned it to the maid. That if the woman relaxed, she would be through it in no time. And then it would all be good after that.

"Breathe, Brina."

She'd forgotten to breathe as Gunnolf pushed the tip of his manhood barely inside her, and she tightened her body against the intrusion. Relax, she told herself and then she felt the tinge of pain. Slowly he filled every inch of her deep inside. Then he began to thrust, but the kissing started again and she loved the way his mouth claimed hers as she claimed his back. Her hands explored his back, her body accepting him. She relished the feel of him deep inside her, the heat of him pressing against her.

His kisses grew more urgent, and then he stopped pumping into her and held still. She waited with baited breath, worried something was wrong as she looked up into his strained face.

Then he began thrusting again as if driven until

he groaned, and she felt his hot seed fill her. It was an incredible feeling of joy. Gunnolf continued to thrust, then stopped and collapsed on his side, pulling her close, kissing her jaw and throat, then her mouth again.

"Are you all right?" he whispered.

"Aye. It was beautiful."

In that moment, she thought of how he could have given her a bairn and for the first time she worried—would she be able to bear a healthy son who would live and grow up to manhood when her mother had been unable to?

Gunnolf smiled, leaned down, and suckled a nipple, then kissed Brina's lips again. "If this had not been your first time, I would make love to you again tonight. But we must wait."

"I love you, Gunnolf. I canna wait until we can do this again." Once they removed Seamus from Anfa Castle, she imagined how she and Gunnolf could make love in her own bedchamber. The thought gave her wicked pleasure.

"As soon as you feel ready. Sleep, lass. We will be on our way in the morn before we know it."

She prayed the journey ahead would be safe for all. Though she knew it was foolish to wish for it, she hoped with all her heart that her people had rallied together and thrown Seamus beyond Anfa Castle's walls. Seamus would return with fewer men than he had left with, all because of the trouble she and Gunnolf had caused, well, and Lynette who told her about the man who threatened her at the shieling when Gunnolf came to rescue her and she had shot the brigand. Would her people believe Seamus was incapable of fighting his battles alone?

She fervently hoped they would think so. Then she wondered what he had told them concerning losing three of his men. That the lass he intended to make his wife and tried to locate had managed to kill them?

She snuggled against Gunnolf and let out her breath. He stroked her back, but then he must have felt the scars across her back.

"What is this?" he asked, concerned.

"Naught." She stiffened, not wishing to discuss this with Gunnolf, now or ever.

"You have scars on your back." He pulled a candle closer to inspect her back.

She didn't want to tell him her da had lashed her for disobeying him. What if Gunnolf wouldn't come to his aid then?

"Brina, tell me."

In exasperation, she let out her breath in an annoyed way. "My da didna like that I had run off a couple of times, exploring on my own. This was before we moved to the castle. He had come home with the sheep and I was still out exploring."

"Bastard."

"It was his right as my da. Though I dinna think I deserved the punishment." Not when she had been trying to protect the wounded Viking lad in the glen so many years ago. But her da had felt differently and she hadn't spoken to him for a fortnight after he had lashed her. Even after that, the resentment had lingered on.

"Never. A child needs guidance. But not to be lashed where the marks leaves permanent scarring."

"Dinna be angry with him over this. You have suffered wounds—"

"Wounds in battle, lass. This is not the same. He is a bastard." Gunnolf blew out the candle and settled back down with her and stroked her back.

"And your wounds?"

"The one I had when you found me lying on my back in the tall grass was battle-related. And the others as I grew older and fought many more battles, the same."

"Did no one teach you to stay out of the path of a warrior's sword?"

He laughed. "I must remember that for the future."

"Good, because I love you for all that you are, and dinna want to see you suffer any more injuries. After seeing you so terribly wounded, I had nightmares about you for years."

"Oh? I had the same about you—only they were not nightmares—of the beautiful girl who bound my wound and left me to get help, your raven hair flying behind you. I thought for certain you were a goddess who had come to take me with you. I kept thinking I would be with you in that other place, but then I came to my senses and realized I was in too much pain to be dead. I believed your kin might hunt me down should you reach them. I do not believe I have ever had such a time climbing onto a horse."

"I am so sorry, Gunnolf. If I could have, I would have nursed you back to health myself. I did fetch a cart first. So I hadna gone for help yet."

"Which probably was the reason I successfully made my escape."

"You didna come back to tell me you were alive and well." She knew he wouldn't have. Why would he?

"Ahh, but I did, Brina. When I was well healed, I returned and learned the shieling where you probably stayed was occupied by some other sheepherder and his family. He did not know of a lass who had lived there. I thanked the family and returned home."

"Were you alone? 'Tis a wonder the sheepherder didna come for my da and tell him a Vi—Norseman had come into his territory."

"I was with James and some of his men. The sheepherder knew of James and that he was laird of the MacNeill clan."

"But if you were with James, why didna you come to the castle?"

"And what? I did not know you lived there. And if I had, what would I have said? That you saved my life? I was still a Norseman and didna know as much of your language back then." He stroked her hair and kissed her forehead. "It was best we met like we did much later instead."

"Me plowing into you and taking you into the snowbank?" She thought about how one day, they would tell their bairns of how they first met.

He touched her arm around where the arrow had nicked her. "The wound is but a tiny pink line."

"It wasna much." She was surprised he'd even noticed it when the candle was lit. She ran her hand over the scar on his side. "No' like yours."

He smiled. "If you keep touching me, I will not want to sleep."

She snuggled against him. "For fear of falling asleep in the saddle, I bid you good night."

"Was it…good for you?"

She smiled at him, loving that he was concerned how she felt about him. "Beautiful. More than beautiful. Truly astonishing." She sighed and then he sighed too, as if he was finally satisfied that everything was right between them.

She knew that they should be together the moment he had asked her to marry him. But tomorrow was the beginning of an ordeal she really didn't want to face. She listened to Gunnolf's heartbeat, and she'd never felt as protected as she did in his arms tonight.

CHAPTER 13

Knowing where he was going and with no blinding snowstorm hampering his way, Gunnolf found it amazingly easy to navigate through the mountains, around lochs, and across streams. The sun was chasing away the mist, a few clouds lingering high above. With James and his men escorting them, Gunnolf felt the women were at less of a risk, yet anything could befall them, and he wished they had remained safely behind at Craigly Castle.

He hadn't thought Brina would quit hugging Beowulf before they left either, reassuring him over and over again that she would return for him. Gunnolf wondered how that would go over with her father, should they restore him to power. Gunnolf loved her for the way she treated the pup and admittedly he had also given him a hug and rubbed his head before they left. Beowulf was having so much fun with the deerhound pups, Gunnolf suspected he wouldn't miss him or Brina anytime soon.

Gunnolf had it in mind that he could even help her father return to his position, stay around for a time until everyone felt secure that he could manage, and then Gunnolf and Brina would leave again for the MacNeill lands and stay there.

When they finally reached the old Roman ruins, they set up camp there.

"I hope we dinna find Beowulf's family here when he isna with us," Brina said, laying out their bedrolls.

The snow had all melted off and it was a little warmer than it had been when they'd come through here before. This time, his horse and hers remained with the others while men guarded them. But Gunnolf was staying with both the ladies in this part of the keep's remains to ensure their protection. That meant he really couldn't make love to his bonny wife. Though most likely she needed to heal some more from their first bout of lovemaking.

James brought Lynette's bedding into the keep, and Lynette sighed and said to James, "I really feel I should stay with you." She made a pointed look in Gunnolf and Brina's direction as if to say they needed their privacy.

"Nay," James said. "You wanted to come and part of the deal is that the two of you ladies stay together while Gunnolf watches over you. I know I can trust him to keep you safe. As to other matters, I have sent two of our men ahead to speak with Cadel to learn what we can about your da, Brina."

"What if they think your men are really Seamus's hired mercenaries, and they are looking for my da to kill him?" Brina asked, alarmed.

"The two men met Cadel first when he came to Craigly Castle to tell me your da demanded Gunnolf wed you," James said.

"All right, but what if Cadel isna at home?" Brina asked.

"The men are being careful. You have naught to worry about," James said. "Be sure and get your rest. We should have some word in a few hours. I will let you know what we learn."

"Thank you."

Lynette took hold of James's arm and pulled him toward one of the openings to the outside of the area of the keep they were settling in. "I am going to talk to my brother for a while."

James seemed surprised, but then she tilted her head to the side as if trying to tell him that she wanted to give Brina and Gunnolf some privacy. He finally seemed to realize what she was attempting to do.

"Oh, certainly. We should go over the plans concerning what we are going to do exactly. We will be a while, but I will ensure my sister's safety in the meantime." James smiled at Gunnolf and Brina, then escorted Lynette out of the ruined keep.

Brina closed her gaping mouth. Gunnolf

chuckled and pulled her into his arms. "We have been riding all day. You are probably sore."

"Can...can we try it?"

"*Ja*. It would my pleasure, but if you feel uncomfortable in the least, we will stop. I want this to be as pleasurable for you as it is for me."

"Oh, aye, but we must hurry."

This time, they didn't remove their clothes though. It was too cold in the ruins of the keep. Instead, she lay down on the bedding, and he joined her. He lifted her gown and began to pleasure her as he had done last night, kissing her, making her hot and wet for him, his fingers stroking her. She wasn't hurting at all. Just feeling exquisitely uplifted as if she were climbing the highest mountain. Then she was soaring, her hands in Gunnolf's hair, his mouth on hers, muffling her cry of ecstasy as she fell off the edge of the world in bliss.

He continued to kiss her, but didn't make a move to lift his tunic to take his pleasure.

"We can do it," she assured him, wanting this intimacy between them, eager to have it, insistent.

"On the morrow, mayhap when we bed down for the night."

She clung to his shoulders then. "Nay, now." What if something bad happened and they couldn't make love ever again. She wanted this intimacy between them, his loving her like she loved him. They could be separated tomorrow night by circumstances beyond their control. "Nay, this night." She insisted because he was only kissing her and massaging her breast, and not fulfilling his own need. She felt his manhood pressed against her, and knew he was ready for her, knew he wanted her.

He still didn't enter her. "Brina," he said softly, his voice ragged with desire.

She reached down and lifted his tunic until she felt his flesh against hers, warm and hard and wanting.

"I dinna want to hurt you. If I do, you might fear it the next time, worried it will always hurt. You must have time to heal."

She frowned at him. "Think you I am a delicate flower?"

He smiled then. "You are delicate and strong and beautiful and stubborn."

She smiled back at him. "Then you know I willna take no for an answer. Make love to me unless you dinna wish it."

"I wish it."

She grinned. "I can tell."

He chuckled, and then he sighed. "If you are too uncomfortable, stop me. I mean it, Brina. I want this only to bring you pleasure."

"You bring me joy. Now hurry before Lynette tires and returns to the keep."

Gunnolf loved his bonnie wife, and though he craved having her this eve, he really didn't want her to hurt. But he suspected she worried they might not be able to make love tomorrow eve. That they may be separated by some unforeseen predicament. Maybe for more than the night. Maybe for an eternity. Knowing she might still be sore, he tried to enter her as slowly as he could, restraining his need to thrust, to conquer, to claim her for his own. He loved her dearly, the Highland lass who called him Viking, who had shoved him down in the snow, and berated him for being in her way, blaming him for the arrow nicking her.

She was wild and loving and all his. He felt her tense, whispered against her ear to relax, and began to rock inside her, slowly at first, allowing her to stretch her tight sheath around him until he felt her ease up. She was beautiful and eager to please when she didn't have to do anything to please him at all. He loved everything about her, the way she widened her eyes when she saw his ready shaft, the way she thrust her hips slightly, as if learning how to enjoy the act of consummation even more, the way she moaned so softly when he was kissing her throat or her breasts, making him harder even faster.

Since she had to be somewhat uncomfortable from their first bout of lovemaking, he thrust, wanting to prolong the pleasure, but knowing he needed to let her heal no matter how much she had wanted him inside her again.

His blood on fire, he continued to kiss her, hoping to get her mind off any pain she might be feeling, pushing deeper inside, and felt the end coming. He thrust again, her hands on his naked arse warming his skin that was exposed now to the cold, and he loved her touching him, making his blood even hotter. Then he groaned with the release, their hearts pounding in unison, her fingers stroking his hips now. He continued to pump into her until he was completely done, feeling both the pleasure and a sense of real gratitude that she had chosen him to be her husband. No one else.

He pulled out and kissed her mouth slowly and warmly, wanting to connect in this way too, praying he had not hurt her too much again. She wrapped her arms around his neck and kissed him just as thoroughly back as if proving she was fine. He tugged her gown down and pulled her into his arms, and loved how she snuggled against him.

"Are you all right?" Gunnolf kissed the top of her head and caressed her arm, hoping she would be feeling better soon.

"You make me feel desirable and loved, and I love you." She sounded sleepy and content, and he was glad she was well.

He pulled the furs over them, and they heard Lynette enter the ruined keep. She slipped into her bedding and settled down.

He wondered just what kind of a fight they could be in on the morrow. He didn't even want to think of Brina or her sister being in the middle of it.

***

It didn't seem as though they had slept long when James shook Gunnolf awake. Though he could tell it was later than he first had thought from the hint of light in the sky. He carefully disentangled himself from Brina so as not to disturb her and joined James outside.

"What word have you?" Gunnolf knew the men who had sought to have word with Cadel must have returned with news.

"He wasna there. No one was. The family was gone. Her da was gone. Some bloodied rags were left behind on the bed. It appeared they had been eating porridge and rushed out of there."

"By force? Or had they fled?"

"No' sure."

"How long ago?"

"Mayhap last eve. No' long."

Brina bumped up against Gunnolf, and he wrapped his arm around her. "Did you hear?"

"Aye. When do we leave?" Her voice was strained, and he couldn't blame her.

"As soon as everyone is ready," James said.

Brina hurried back into the keep and Gunnolf lit a torch from one of the campfires and set it up on top of one of the walls so they could see to pack.

Lynette groaned. "Next time, I am going to bed earlier." Then she glanced at Brina. "Oh, Brina, what is wrong?"

Gunnolf had grabbed their bedrolls, saw Brina was tearful, but when he went to comfort her, Lynette said, "I will take care of her.

"I will ready the horses." He pulled Brina into a warm embrace first though.

She hugged him heartily back.

He kissed her on the cheek. "Will you be all right?"

"Aye. We must leave at once."

"*Ja.*" He wiped away her tears, kissed her lips, then he grabbed the bedrolls and left.

"My da was no longer at Cadel's shieling. They left in a rush or were found and..." Brina couldn't finish her words. "My da could be the worst of tyrants at times, but I have seen his tenderness too. A time when a boy had lost his mother and was crying his heart out and Da lifted him onto his lap and told him that I had lost my mother much the same way. But that my mother and his were in a place where they were loved and couldna hurt any longer. I canna say how much that touched me. I think he dearly wanted a son. He loved my mother and he was bitter about losing both her and his son. Then my cousin, whom he treated like a son, didna want to stay there with him. He wanted adventure, excitement, and not to be told what to do. He refused to take on any responsibilities, though my da attempted to groom him to be the next clan chief." Brina helped Lynette on with her brat.

"And that is why Seamus came to be."

"Aye."

Lynette hugged Brina. "We canna know what has happened to your da. Mayhap he is well and being cared for at the castle. We canna give into our anxieties about it. We will know soon enough."

"Aye, I know, though I canna help but worry about him."

"Your da is a fighter. Look how he managed to survive on the battlefield when everyone thought him dead."

"True." Brina gave her a hug back. "Be careful this day."

"Aye, you too."

After the ladies and the rest of their party mounted their horses, they headed for Cadel's shieling. When they arrived, Brina, Lynette, and Gunnolf searched the shieling for any clues as to what had happened while others searched the surrounding area.

"We could spend the next couple of days looking for your father, or we can go the castle and see if we can learn if he has been taken there," Gunnolf said, grasping Brina's hands in his own.

"We take our chances and travel now to the castle." They would spend too much time searching for her da, if Cadel and others had moved him to another location. Best to do what they came here to do. See Seamus and learn if her da was there, and deal with the traitor.

"Once we have Anfa Castle in sight, you will stay in the glen, far from the castle and out of the archers' range," Gunnolf said to both Brina and Lynette. "I will approach first and speak on James's behalf."

"You willna," James said. "I will speak for myself and for Lynette."

James's senior advisor said, "Mayhap I should do the speaking. Does Seamus even know either of you?"

"Nay. I have never met the man. As I doubt you have," James said.

Eanruig shook his head.

"Have you met Robard?" Gunnolf asked James.

"Once, when I was a lad. I dinna know that he would recognize me now."

"We go together," Gunnolf finally said.

"I need you to plan the next course of action if anything happens to me, Gunnolf. I need you to see the women home safely if this doesna work out the way we had planned."

Gunnolf didn't like the idea one whit. But James was still the laird and Gunnolf, brother that he might be, had to follow his direction.

"*Ja*. But I still do not like the strategy."

"Noted."

"What do you wish for me to do?" Eanruig asked.

"You will come with me when the time is right," James said.

They traveled in the clearing next to piney woods in silence after that, but before the force was even in sight of the castle, Gunnolf thought he heard a hushed voice in the woods nearby. He motioned to speak to James and apprised him of it in case he had not heard. But he was worried about the women with them if they should be drawn into a fight out here.

"Cadel and his wife, mayhap?" James asked.

"*Ja*, could be. Unless 'tis a trap."

The woods had grown quiet.

"If 'tis Cadel and they have Robard with them, they will not be able to move quickly with him," Gunnolf said.

"Unless 'tis no' Robard and his loyal subjects."

"We have to search the woods," Brina whispered.

"*Ja*, that would be my advice. If Brina's father is out here, we need to take him back to the shieling."

"Agreed." James organized his men to search with him, while Gunnolf stayed behind with Brina, Lynette, and five more men at the edge of the pine forest.

It didn't take long before they heard swords clashing and the yelling of men.

"An ambush!" Brina said, readying her bow.

The other men with them looked anxious to join the fight.

But Gunnolf didn't want to release them to fight when the women needed their protection. Yet if James was overwhelmed, he could use the extra men to battle on his behalf.

If James and his men fell to the sword, Gunnolf couldn't keep a force of enemies from taking the ladies hostage.

"Go, Gunnolf. Help him," Brina pleaded.

Gunnolf motioned to three of the men to join in on the fight. But then the fight came to them, four men riding out of the woods, a golden-haired man in the lead.

"Seamus," Brina called out in surprise.

Now Gunnolf knew who the devil himself was, and targeted the man, his hair shaggy around his shoulders, his brown eyes narrowed in contempt.

"I take it that you didna bring Brina back to me if you are fighting us," Seamus said, slashing his sword at Gunnolf.

"We came here in peace." Gunnolf didn't truly believe his words would sway the man intent on killing him. "You and your men are fighting Laird James MacNeill of Craigly Castle. He comes here to tell your people that Lynette—" Gunnolf slashed back at the brigand when Seamus struck at him again "—is his half sister."

Seamus paused only for a moment before he raised his sword to swing it. "Why is my bride-to-be with you?"

"To see her da. Where is he? James wishes to work out an agreement between our clans. But no' if you are trying to kill him."

Gunnolf saw the other men who had been protecting the ladies engaged in combat now. Brina and Lynette were poised with bows stretched taut, attempting to hit one of the men if they could get a clear shot.

"Her da is dead," Seamus said, his face hard, his tone of voice unconcerned.

"Because you killed him?"

Seamus's face reddened in anger. Seamus thrust his sword at him, but Gunnolf angled his horse backward and came again at the man, only to slice against his targe. "A Viking killed him! He sounded like...*you*," Seamus said.

"When Robard was struck down, you did not go to his aid. After that, you did not check him over to ensure he lived or had truly died." Gunnolf realized how similar his situation was to Robard's now when his own brother left him to die on the field of battle, only in this case, Seamus had left Robard to die when he had treated him like a son.

"Whoever is telling you these lies? Brina? She was so distraught, she would make up any tale so that she wouldna feel so bad. She wouldna believe her mother or her newborn brother had died either when it happened. 'Tis sad, but true."

Gunnolf shook his head. "I met Robard myself. He had been wounded and was being cared for."

"Then he lied that he was the chief. We have buried him along with all the others that died that day. 'Twas a shame that his only daughter wasna there to pray over his grave."

"If he has died since I saw him last, Seamus, 'tis because you killed him when you didna have him taken to the castle the day of the battle and have his wounds treated," Brina said and ended her words with the release of an arrow.

Seamus jerked his targe upward to block the arrow, but Gunnolf charged in and struck him across the chest with a slice of his sword.

The padded leather Seamus was wearing helped to deflect some of the blow, but he still jerked back in his saddle and before he could retaliate, Gunnolf saw a trail of blood across his chest where the cut was made. Seamus's targe was also sporting one of Brina's arrows. She was shooting at someone else now.

"Why has Brina returned? To what end?" Seamus growled.

"To bring forces to ensure her da's safe from the likes of you."

"She need no' worry about me. 'Tis her cousin that she should be concerned about."

"Her cousin? He no longer resides here," Gunnolf said, surprised. He struck at Seamus again, connecting with his sword. "Do not tell me he has returned and taken over." Strange irony that. If her cousin had taken over while Seamus was out searching for Brina, then had he sealed off the castle so Seamus couldn't return? If that was the case, Brina had brought Seamus down as much as her cousin had.

"I was loyal to Robard all along when his nephew abandoned the clan and him," Seamus growled.

"Just think if you had not left the chief to die, Brina would not have run away, you would not have left the castle in search of her, and her cousin would not have taken over in your absence. Oh, and I would not have had the chance to save the lass and wed her."

Seamus's jaw hung agape before he attacked Gunnolf with such viciousness, there could be no more talking, only a fight to the end.

They struck back and forth, the woods quieting where the rest of the fighting had been taking place. Gunnolf prayed James and his men had been victorious while he concentrated on trying to take Seamus down.

"Her da told me how she had cared for a wounded Viking warrior when she was young. He should have done more than whipped her for it."

Gunnolf glanced in Brina's direction, shocked to hear the truth. Her father had beaten her for aiding him so long ago, and she hadn't told him? Why? Because she feared he would not save her father's hide?

Gunnolf felt pure loathing for the man. Had he known...

He let out his breath and struck at Seamus, slicing again across his belly, splitting open his leather vest and revealing a deep sword wound, blood spilling out of the cut.

Seamus faltered in the saddle and Gunnolf struck the final blow. "You should have been loyal to your chief as he would have given you everything a man desired, a beautiful woman who should have been cherished, most of all."

Seamus fell from his horse and lay on his back on the grass, looking up at Gunnolf still seated on his horse. "You should have died in battle alongside Robard. What will James think when he learns you have wounded his half brother?"

"In no way are you related to James. And I was

not there at the battle between Robard's men and Hallfred's. I have served James for years and have fought many Highland battles alongside him."

"You are...a traitor to your...own people then," Seamus gritted out.

Gunnolf dismounted and stood over the man. "Nay. They left me for dead. See you the similarity here? You say you are James's half brother. How is that so?"

Seamus's red face was turning gray. "I am Lynette's...brother, so some...would say."

"And Brina's half brother if what you say is true. But her twin brother died. Only Lynette survived."

"Nay. Why do you...think Robard...took me in? He thought...to punish the...MacNeill clan...for throwing the lass out of the keep..." Seamus coughed up blood. "...when she was carrying twins."

"But you were not raised by him. You only came to the castle when you were grown."

"The midwife...gave me to another family to raise."

"If you are my half brother, why would you want to wed me?" Brina asked, sounding horrified.

"I didna learn the truth... until your cousin enlightened me, shouting it...from curtain wall, afraid to fight me face-to-face once he had locked me out. He said...I was the bastard son of James's da...and should return there."

"Did...did my da know?"

Seamus shut his eyes and didn't respond. Gunnolf knelt beside him, but saw the dirk in Seamus's hand before the man opened his eyes and struck at him with it. Gunnolf tore it from his grasp and stood.

"Answer me!" Brina demanded.

"You would have to ask him... if he is still alive."

James joined him and Gunnolf was glad to see he was unharmed, but he felt badly that Brina and Lynette were distressed about this new revelation. "Our men, James?"

"Uninjured. His men are either dead or ran off. I heard what he said. Are you telling the truth that you are my half brother?" James asked Seamus.

But he had closed his eyes again. Gunnolf leaned down and put his hand on his throat, feeling for a pulse. He shook his head at James.

"A shame. I would have loved to have had another brother. Though 'tis possible he would have tried to take over my clan."

"And the bastard intended to wed Brina." Gunnolf looked to see how she was doing.

Tears had filled her eyes and Lynette's also. Hell.

He hurried to join the ladies, helping Brina down from her horse while James helped Lynette.

"He may have lied," Lynette warned.

"He may have," Brina agreed. "That would be a good way in the end to upset all of us."

"What about your cousin?" Gunnolf asked,

wondering if they would find him to be receptive to their arrival or would he see them as trouble? And would he be a good leader of Brina's clan?

"He was always a spoiled brat," Lynette said. "Robard was always bending over backwards to suit Christophe when he was a child. He was the son Robard had never had. Christophe knew Robard would do anything for him. Mayhap he learned Robard had been injured or had died and he returned to take over the castle with no one else to tell him what to do."

"Would the elders of your clan call him chief when he had abandoned the clan?" Gunnolf asked. "Unless he has the ability to lead them and fight well, I would think not."

"I dinna know. Seamus said Da was dead. Did he no' find him then? Or did he find him and kill him?" Brina asked, wiping away tears.

Gunnolf pulled her into his embrace and kissed her damp cheek, not wanting to see her so distressed. "There is no telling. We will have to go to the castle, do you not agree, James?"

"Aye. I agree."

Gunnolf said to Brina, "We will see if mayhap your cousin found your father and took him there for safekeeping." He didn't want to think that maybe even her cousin had located him and killed him. Though it was possible her father had died of his wounds. They needed to find Cadel if they couldn't discover her father. Maybe he would have the answers they sought.

"In the meantime, I will do what I had intended before, offer a tie between our clans, but only if he keeps peace with Inga's," James said.

"How many men did Seamus have with him?" Brina asked.

"Around twenty," James said.

Brina considered two dead men nearby. "I have never seen these men before."

Lynette studied them for a moment. "Neither have I. He must have hired mercenaries."

They remounted their horses and headed for the keep. Gunnolf couldn't help worrying about the ladies' safety though.

"Since we have no idea what to expect, I suggest we follow our earlier plan. The ladies stay a safe distance from the castle's archers' reach." Gunnolf still couldn't believe that Seamus had been Lynette's twin brother.

"I agree. Until we know what kind of reception we will get, we have to be wary of Brina's cousin's response to our unexpected arrival," James said.

When they saw the four stone towers of the castle, they could see movement along the wall walk. Distant shouts could be heard as the guards called out a warning to their people.

"Mayhap we should have a change of plan," Brina said. "If my cousin sees Lynette and me approaching with you, they may believe you are no' the enemy."

"Or that we are with Seamus and caught the both of you and are returning you now." Gunnolf still didn't want the ladies to draw too close to the castle.

"I am going with you," Brina said to James. "My cousin willna take action to harm me. He has no reason to. And my people would revolt against him if he did."

James agreed. Gunnolf still didn't like the plan, but he went along with it as determined as everyone was. He rode forth with Brina and James, ready to fight.

When they were close enough, Brina called out to the guards. "'Tis me, Brina, returned with the support of Laird James MacNeill of Craigly Castle to help my...our people."

Gunnolf wondered at first why she had not said to help her father, but then suspected she didn't want to sound as though she would be unwilling to accept her cousin as chief.

"Lynette is with us and she is Laird James's half sister, we just learned. His lairdship wishes to forge a clan alliance. He and his men took care of Seamus and his mercenaries. Let us in to speak with my cousin."

A swarthy guard named Ahern came down to speak to them. "Christophe welcomes you home, Lady Brina."

"Ahearn," she said, inclining her head in greeting, her expression grim.

Then they allowed the ladies and their escort into the inner bailey.

"You will have to leave your weapons with the

guards," Ahearn said, then spoke with James. "Welcome, my laird. Our chief will be eager to hear your plans for an alliance."

"What about my da? What has become of him?" Brina asked.

"I thought you knew he died on the battlefield. Everyone else did. We thought that was why you ran off. That you didna wish to do as your da had commanded. Seamus had our men help bury those who died while Seamus searched for you."

"Did anyone verify that Robard's body was discovered, proving that he was actually dead? If so, where is he buried?" Gunnolf asked.

The guard sliced him an irritated look.

Did Robard's own men not have any interest in learning the truth? Maybe they truly wished him dead.

CHAPTER 14

"Where is Cadel and his wife?" Brina asked Ahearn, the grizzled old guard, before he led them into the keep.

"I havena seen Cadel since he left the battle and returned home to his wife."

Brina exchanged glances with Gunnolf and James, but she could tell they thought it was best to keep quiet about her da's being alive. If he was still alive.

James stopped, took one of his men aside, and spoke to him in private. Then the man gathered ten of James's men and they headed back out.

"Some trouble?" Ahearn asked, wary.

"Just making sure that none of Seamus's mercenaries are about," James said, and gave the guard a dark smile.

Brina suspected James was having his men search for her father along with Cadel and his wife to provide them with protection if need be. If they found them, she knew James's men would inform them Brina had returned with help, Seamus was gone, and Christophe was now in charge.

She wondered what her da would think of that. If Gunnolf had been serving as chief, he would be on his horse, ready to do battle against Seamus no matter how many soldiers he might have recruited. Not only that, but Gunnolf would ensure her people living in outlying areas were safe from Seamus's vengeance.

She wanted to go with the men to find her da, but she knew that would look suspicious. She didn't trust that Christophe had suddenly shown up to take over. And wasn't that a cowardly way to deal with Seamus anyway? Just lock him out? Maybe that was why Seamus had solicited the aid of mercenaries. To attempt to take the castle back.

"Christophe," Brina said when she saw her cousin, his raven hair shoulder length, his blue eyes quickly shifting from her to Gunnolf and then James. He finally saw Lynette and nodded, as if the women were back where they were supposed to be.

He should have been ashamed that someone else had to bring them home instead of their own clansmen.

"I see you have finally returned," Christophe said, as if she had just taken a walk in the glen.

Brina narrowed her eyes at him, furious that he would do naught to find her da or deal with Seamus. "Aye, I returned. With help to save our people from Seamus."

"You had no need. I took care of the matter easily enough."

By locking him out! And anytime her people needed to leave the castle, Seamus and his mercenaries could have struck at them. But she bit her tongue and didn't speak her sentiments out loud like she wanted to.

"Come, we were just getting ready to sit down to a feast." Christophe beckoned to a golden-haired woman to come forth, and she stepped forward. She smiled, but not in a friendly way. "This is my cousin, Brina. Her da, my uncle, was the former chief. And this is Lynette—"

"My sister. I am Laird James MacNeill. 'Tis a pleasure to make your acquaintance."

"I see. This is my lovely bride, Guennola. We were wed this past year. You can show her how to manage the staff, Brina. Though after you show her what you used to do, you will have to find another duty. I am sure Guennola can think of something."

The woman gave her a simpering smile. Brina inclined her head a little to Guennola, but didn't comment about her "new" role. Brina had worked for years at learning everyone's personality and knowing how to motivate them the best she could with as little angst as she could manage. Though there were always those who were difficult no matter how she managed them. She didn't figure this woman would last a sennight before she was ready to give up and have someone else do all the work for her.

"The elders have decided you are their new chief, I take it." Brina tried to keep from showing her temper, though she was certain she looked annoyed as much as she was frowning. She had no intention of teaching this woman how to do anything. All she cared about now was ensuring her da was truly alive and learning what he wanted to do.

"Mayhap the two of you can serve as her companions and fetch whatever she needs when she needs it," Christophe continued as if his earlier comment hadn't gotten enough of a reaction from Brina.

She remembered then how Christophe had always tried to unsettle her in front of her da, as if to belittle her for being only a woman, his daughter, and not the son he had wanted so badly.

"You are mistaken about why we are here," James said. "Lynette is returning with me. It remains to be seen about Brina however. I am sure she will want to go wherever her husband goes."

Christophe suddenly looked in Gunnolf's direction as if he hadn't really noticed him before this, his expression unsmiling. He ground his teeth like he always did when he was attempting to keep his temper in check. "Who are you?"

"Gunnolf. And since you are the new chief of the clan, I hope you can see your way to making peace with Inga and her kin."

"I have every intention of killing every last one

of them." Christophe paused, waiting to see Gunnolf's reaction, who did not react, which Brina was glad for. "After they killed Robard, of course." Christophe motioned to the head table. "Come, sit."

Once they were seated, Christophe turned his attention to Brina. "What I want to know is who gave you permission to wed anyone other than who I decided since you did not wed Seamus?"

"My da, as was his right."

"I have never known you to lie—"

"Aye, 'tis true. My da was wounded on the field of battle. That much is true. But he didna die there."

Most everyone in the great hall was watching the head table because of Brina's return, and the special guests her cousin was entertaining. Even more so as Brina's words were heard by those closest to the high table and were spread to the rest of the clan.

"That is why Gunnolf asked if anyone from the clan had truly witnessed my da's burial." She looked at her kin sitting at the other tables and spoke louder for them all to hear. "He was your chief. Did no one think to ensure that he had died before believing everything Seamus told us?"

Everyone looked shocked to hear the news; a few looked a little guilty.

"He was alive, last we saw him and he asked if Gunnolf would consent to wed me. And so we married at Craigly Castle."

Gunnolf's expression softened a bit, his eyes

smiling. Her da never asked anything of anyone. Or rarely. He demanded obedience from those he was associated with.

"If Robard is alive, why is he no' here? Why didna you bring him here?" Christophe asked, angry, as if it were their fault that he was still beyond the castle walls.

Guennola looked just as distraught as Brina's cousin. "What does this mean, Christophe? You will no longer be chief?" She acted as though the notion was repugnant to her and nothing else mattered but the position he would hold.

"He isna alive any longer. He was terribly wounded. He would have died by now or returned to the keep." Christophe slammed his tankard on the table. "You sent men away to search for him?" he asked James, sounding furious. "You didna say this when they left."

"And to see if any more of Seamus's mercenaries were about." James was eating his roasted grouse, not in the least bothered by Christophe's temper. "About this alliance between our clans--"

"Where was he and how badly wounded?" Christophe asked, ignoring James's comment, appearing more worried about the ramifications if Robard returned and might be angry with him for taking over.

Brina wasn't sure he would be. He'd always wanted Christophe to return home and be the clan chief someday. Maybe even now, if her da couldn't manage the clan any longer. Would their people even back Robard over Christophe now?

"I am done, thank you." Even though it was Christophe's place to end the meal, Brina rose from the bench and Gunnolf immediately joined her. "I am going to search for my da." She couldn't wait a moment longer.

Several of her kin stood also and she was heartened to see their response. Unless, they had more devious intentions and wanted to ensure her da would not return to take over.

Christophe's face reddened and he stood. "I will lead a search party."

Why? To save face? To look like a man of action? Or to ensure they didn't find her da alive?

"Five of my men and I will go with you," James said. "My sister will stay here and visit with your wife."

Lynette immediately objected. "Brina will go and I will remain with her to watch her back."

"Watch her back? From whom? Her own kin?" Guennola asked, appearing highly agitated that Lynette would even insinuate that Brina was in danger from her own people.

"Mayhap you were no' listening," Lynette said, her tone caustic. "Some of Seamus's mercenaries could very well be about. One of the men with Seamus already shot Brina with an arrow, so who would say he wouldna try that again."

Guennola snapped her gaping mouth shut.

James took Lynette's hand in his. "Are you sure

you dinna want to stay behind?"

"Nay. My place is with Brina."

"All right. Some of my men will go west with you, Gunnolf, and Brina, the others will come with me."

Brina prayed they would find her da alive, and hoped all this could be resolved easily. But she feared it would not.

***

When Brina and the others were well on their way, she said to Gunnolf, "Is James staying close to Christophe to ensure if he finds him first no harm comes to my da?"

"That was the impression I had. I am sure Christophe would have had the same notion. Better to be vigilant and ensure your da remains alive, than leave it to fate."

"Do you think mayhap my da was still corresponding with my cousin and that is why he showed up so fortuitously? I canna imagine Christophe would have just happened to be in the area and took over while Seamus was searching for me."

"I was thinking the very same thing. You and Lynette know him better than I do. Do you believe him capable of killing his uncle to stay in power?"

"Aye," Lynette said without hesitation before Brina could respond. "He didna like to be told what to do so he left. He didna want to work at leading a clan. He just wanted the status. Look how he handled Seamus!"

"Aye," Brina agreed. "I wouldna have thought it possible until I saw him serving as chief of the clan."

They saw a rider approaching from the north and Brina smiled. "'Tis Rory." Then she frowned. "I hope he isna bringing us bad news."

They rode toward him and Rory greeted them. "Lady Brina, Gunnolf, Lynette. I have had word you brought men here to take Seamus and his men down."

"Aye, Laird James MacNeill and his men helped us to do so," Gunnolf said.

"Where is my da? Is he well?" Brina quickly asked.

"Aye, though he needs to be in his own chamber where he can rest and fully recover."

"Which my cousin has probably commandeered as his own. Take us to him. Can we move him to the keep?" Brina asked.

"Only if Gunnolf and the men he brought can protect him until we have assurance that he willna come to harm."

Brina looked to Gunnolf. She couldn't speak for James or his men. She didn't know if they could or would want to stay for a while longer.

"I will stay and help protect the chief," Gunnolf said, and Brina loved him for it.

"As will I," Brina said.

"As long as James doesna want to drag me off, I will help our chief recover also," Lynette said.

Rory looked like a weight had been lifted from

his shoulders. "Aye, I thank all of you. This is the best news we have had since he was struck down. Come this way then. He will be eager to see you. He will want to know if you have already married Gunnolf. If not, he insists that you do so right away at the chapel."

"Gunnolf and I are wed." Brina smiled at her husband.

"And no one had to insist on it," Gunnolf added.

"Then all we have need of is a feast to celebrate the good news."

How different Rory's greeting was from the way her cousin had reacted upon her return. She was glad they had come back to help her da. Though she knew it wouldn't be the greatest of situations. Not with Christophe wanting to hold onto the position of chief and the knowledge the elders could want Christophe to continue to lead even after her da was well. She was excited to see him though, but worried he would look as bad as he did the last time she had seen him.

When they reached the shieling, Rory quickly escorted them inside while the rest of the men with them waited outside to serve as guards. She was shocked to see her da sitting at a table, eating fish stew, the color returned to his once pale cheeks.

"You look well," she said, meaning it.

"Come here, daughter."

Unsure what he wanted from her, she did as he asked. He seized her arm and pulled her closer for a hug. He was much stronger than she thought he would be. She was glad for that, but also shocked at his unreserved show of affection for her, especially in front of others. She assumed it was because she had returned with help to save him.

"You know Christophe has returned and taken over the clan," she said.

"Are you married to Gunnolf?" he asked, ignoring her comment.

She was surprised he wanted to know that when she thought he'd respond to her comment instead. "Aye."

Gunnolf smiled at her.

"Good. Aye, I have had word concerning my nephew. What about Seamus?"

"Dead by Gunnolf's hand," Brina said, proud of him. "Many of Seamus's mercenaries are dead or gone also. But I have a question. Seamus said he was James's half brother, Lynette's twin. Lynette is my half sister. That meant Seamus was my half brother as well. Did you know this?"

"He lies. But if there is any truth in the matter, I would never have arranged for the two of you to wed. Does that ease your mind, Brina?"

"Aye."

"I have heard while Seamus searched for you, he lost some of his loyal men."

"Aye. Mayhap that is why he had to hire mercenaries. Da, what about Christophe? Gunnolf promised to protect you while you heal until you can return to power. Do you think Christophe might wish you harm because he will want to keep the power he has now?"

"He has only the power the elders gave him. Dinna worry about him. Gunnolf, help me to my horse. Rory, thanks be to you and Cadel and his wife for all your help. You will be rewarded."

Gunnolf helped her da out to his horse and assisted him in climbing into his saddle. The effort appeared to pain him, and Brina hated to see his face turn pale, his hands unsteady on the reins. But no one said a word about his difficulties, which would have made him feel helpless.

Once he was sitting on his horse, he nudged him in the direction of the castle. "You are staying with me," he said, as if he was ordering her and Gunnolf to remain with the clan, which was so typical of the way he always ordered her about.

"It depends," Gunnolf said.

"On what?" her father asked, his temper rising.

"You whipped Brina for attempting to take care of my wounds when I was a lad," Gunnolf growled. "Only a bastard would do such a thing to his child."

"I agree I was wrong. My da, Brina's grandfather, had died at the hands of a Viking. My da and I were very close. When I learned a wounded Viking lad had been found on my lands and Brina was giving comfort and aid to him, I lost my temper. But never again after that."

Brina quickly changed the subject, not wanting to dwell on the past, but glad her da had admitted he was wrong. "I have a wolf pup I am raising. Well, Gunnolf and I are raising. He is playing with James's hunting dogs for now. But if I am to return, we must be allowed to raise him at the castle."

"You dictate to me now, daughter?" She swore her da looked to be giving her the merest of smiles. "I hope that Gunnolf will be chief. If he wishes to raise a whole pack of wolves, 'tis his decision."

Gunnolf appeared just as astounded as Brina felt. "But Christophe is in charge. He says the elders agreed to his being chief," she said.

"Gunnolf is a true warrior. He can lead our people into battle, and I believe we will be victorious. Not only that, but I believe he can make peace with the other clans and create alliances too. He is already allied with the MacNeill clan and they are a powerful people."

"Aye," Brina said. "But only if we dinna go to war against the Viking settlers. And since Lynette is my half sister, whenever she visits our castle, she will be treated as my sister. She is also James's half sister, so it behooves you to be nice to her. When you are well enough to take charge again…"

"I dinna intend to. I wish to be like your grandfather was with you when you were little, and I will bounce your bairns on my knee someday. 'Tis time for someone else to fight the battles."

"But what of Christophe? Will he no' be furious? Vengeful, mayhap?"

"I am certain he will be both. I hear he has a fair-haired wife who has no idea how to manage a household. When Christophe's only solution to lead is to lock out his enemy, and his wife has no idea how to manage the household staff, do you no' think the clan will suffer?"

"Christophe would have me teach her how to manage it, and then I would fetch for her whatever she wants," Brina said, irritated at the very thought.

Robard chuckled. "I canna see that happening. You were groomed for the position from when I took over. I doubt the woman would want to work as hard as you do. But when Christophe left the clan, a lot of our kin grumbled about his neglecting his own people. When he didna fight Seamus himself, but locked him out of the castle, our men didna like it. They need a warrior who will show them how it is done." Robard eyed Gunnolf next. "With your reputation, Gunnolf, I am surprised you only took out Seamus."

Gunnolf motioned to their escort. "I had to leave a few for James and his men."

The ones with them serving as escort rallied to agree with him.

Eanruig said, "I am going to find Laird James and let him know we have found the chief and are returning him home."

"I will recommend Gunnolf is the chief," Robard said.

"Should I tell your nephew this?" Eanruig asked.

"Nay. He will learn soon enough when he returns home. I can imagine him campaigning to keep his position, telling anyone who will listen that I am unfit to lead any longer. But I believe his words will fall on deaf ears."

Eanruig nodded and took off in the direction that James had gone.

"But Gunnolf is a Norseman," Brina said.

Robard cocked a brow at her. "Norseman is it now?"

"He is my husband."

"There will be some who will object, but he has never raised a hand against us. And if he can forgive me for killing his brother, we can forgive him for being related to the man who killed my da. He had naught to do with it in any event."

"Mayhap Gunnolf doesna wish to be chief." Brina thought he would because who wouldn't want the position? But then again, he was vastly loyal to the MacNeill clan. Would he feel the same way about her people?

Gunnolf said, "We shall see. James would ally with us if I were. I am not sure if I can sway Inga and her people to be at peace with us, but I will make every effort to ensure it will work. We will have numerous allies in James's brothers and his cousin's help. As long as your people are agreeable, I would be glad to be chief."

"How would you handle Christophe?" Robard asked.

"He is a member of the clan. I am sure he can find suitable work within the clan."

Robard snorted.

"I would ask Rory to be my second in command," Gunnolf added.

Robard nodded. "He would be a good man to have at your side. And he may very well take you up on it."

"I hope he does."

Brina couldn't be more proud of Gunnolf. She was glad he had told her da off for having lashed her when she was younger, and she was glad that her da had admitted he was wrong and the reason for it. She knew her father had been close to his own da. She could see now why her behavior had angered him so.

Still, he should have controlled his temper better. She hoped when she and Gunnolf had bairns of their own, they would never resort to such cruelty.

Would the elders really approve of Gunnolf taking over? Or would they prefer Christophe? If that were the case, they could safeguard her da until he was well recovered, and then she and Gunnolf would return to Craigly Castle.

CHAPTER 15

As soon as James saw his advisor, who had been riding with Gunnolf, approaching, he hoped he had good news. His expression was serious, though as he grew closer, he smiled a wee bit.

"We have found the chief and he is still recovering from his injuries, but he is riding back to Anfa Castle," Eanruig said in private to James.

Christophe and his men were off some distance walking their horses, also searching for any sign of Robard and those who were caring for him and must not have seen Eanruig's approach.

"That is good news." James was pleased to hear it for everyone's sake.

"Robard wants Gunnolf to take charge of the clan."

"He will be a good leader for the clan in the interim until the chief fully recovers." James's friend and his brother in arms deserved the chance to prove he could lead.

"Nay, no' just for the time it takes for him to recover, but he wants him to continue to lead his clan," Eanruig said.

James was truly astonished. Though he assumed that if the clan respected Gunnolf as their interim chief, at some future date, he could be the next chief. This would be good for all those associated with Gunnolf. His own kin. James's. And Robard's. Gunnolf was fair and honest, a hard worker, a good fighter, and a leader of men. "I had Seamus's body retrieved. The other men will be buried as well, but if he was truly my brother and had been raised alongside me, his life might have been very much different."

"Aye," James's advisor said. "He would have had me to help keep him in line."

James agreed and thought again about Gunnolf and his potential role as chief. As long as the elders didn't object to a Norseman being in charge of their clan over one of their own. In this case, Christophe.

"Do you believe Christophe will fight Gunnolf for the position?" Eanruig asked.

"There is no telling with a man like that. He might. Or he might just leave again. There still may be an issue with the elders concerning Gunnolf's heritage." James watched Christophe and his men, not wanting to tell them Robard was returning to the castle just yet so that he would have time to make his way there and settle in.

Eanruig nodded. "They would do well to put aside their grievances and listen to the truth. That he would be an excellent leader."

"Aye. I agree."

"So what do we do if Christophe fights Gunnolf?" Eanruig asked.

James knew Eanruig or any of his men would stand up to fight for Gunnolf. "He must fight his own battle to win this if he so chooses."

"Will he want to, do you think?"

"Only if he feels 'tis what Robard and his people want. He wouldna take over if the majority dinna wish it." And though James knew Gunnolf would take charge and lead, he would also take into account what members of the clan wanted.

"What if others get involved?"

"Then we will help even the odds." James watched one of Christophe's men point in their direction. James suspected Eanruig had just been spotted and they must have realized he had been searching with Gunnolf.

Eanruig nodded. "Just what we wanted to hear. But if Gunnolf stays here, we will sorely miss him."

"Aye, he has been like a brother to me." James's mother was right though. Gunnolf was a born warrior and leader of men. If he could have this opportunity, James gave him his blessings. "I believe Christophe has just been warned you are here with me now."

His face grave with worry, Christophe listened to his men, then tore off toward the castle, his own men racing to keep up with him.

"Think you he believes Robard is alive and intends to lock the chief out of his castle?" Eanruig asked.

"Mayhap. Let us see that it doesna happen." James spurred his horse on.

James's men took chase.

They had nearly caught up with Christophe and his men when they reached the gates and Christophe shouted, "Close the gates after us!" As if the devil was after him and he needed protection.

And as if they'd have time enough to keep James and his men out. Maybe Robard also if he had not already arrived.

But Ahearn, the guard in charge of the others, commanded no one to do so. Instead, he called out, "Our chief has returned!"

Which one? Christophe or Robard?

***

In the inner bailey, Gunnolf helped Robard down from his horse as gently as he could. The old chief wanted to walk under his own power and waved him away after Gunnolf ensured he was standing on his own. He stuck close though in case Robard faltered.

"I wish to speak with the elders at once, Lorn," Robard said to one of his men, an older man with graying temples, his sharp black eyes taking in everything.

"Aye, in your chamber?"

"Aye."

"Christophe has been staying there," Lorn said, "since we had word you had died. But once we learned from Rory you hadna, we kept things the same as you wished until you could return."

"The word of a traitor." Robard seemed to ponder the matter, then said, "You know my wishes. Gunnolf will be chief. He will stay in my quarters. I will move to the guest chamber that looks upon the inner bailey. Christophe can choose one of the others."

"Aye." Lorn cast a wary look in Gunnolf's direction. "He is a Viking?"

"Aye. We will celebrate my daughter's marriage to Gunnolf on the morrow." Then Robard turned to Gunnolf. "You will accompany me to speak with the rest of the elders. I wish you to hear their objections and explain why you would be a good choice as chief of the clan."

Gunnolf didn't feel he had to prove anything to anybody. His deeds spoke volumes. Then again, these people didn't know him. Brina looked so lovingly at him as if it meant the world to her for him to agree. He realized then that she needed this. To manage the household staff as she'd done in the past. And maybe to forge a better relationship with her father.

"*Ja.*" He would do this for Brina.

Before they could enter the keep, Christophe rode into the inner baily as if he was ready to rescue someone, or fight a deadly battle.

Gunnolf immediately shielded Robard to

protect him in the event Christophe thought to fight him for the position.

"We are so glad to hear you are alive." Christophe stopped his horse only inches away from Gunnolf, his comment directed to Robard, but he sliced a glower Gunnolf's way. "I ensured Seamus couldna return to the keep."

"But you didna track him down and eliminate him like Gunnolf did," Robard said.

Christophe's face reddened. "My place was here. To ensure I kept our people safe."

Lorn looked like he wasn't sure which way to turn. To take the lead from Robard or from Christophe.

"The elders?" Robard said to Lorn.

Several were watching to see the exchange. Not just because it might be entertaining, but all their lives could be affected by who led the clan.

"You canna think to take over the clan in your condition. I will continue to rule in your place until you are ready to retake your position," Christophe said, but the gleam in his eye said otherwise.

Gunnolf was certain he meant to keep that position, not turn it over to Robard when the old man was fully recovered. If he did a good job, the elders would most likely keep things the way they were.

Christophe dismounted and handed his reins over to a stable lad. "Here, let me help you inside."

"I need no help from you, nephew. When I was wounded on the battlefield, I could have used your aid then. Had you been here. Had you fought with us. Mayhap you could have killed the traitor who didna come to my aid and left me to die."

Robard headed into the keep, but Christophe hurried after him. "You canna rule the clan. It is my right now. No one will agree that you can lead. The elders said I was the one who would take over. No one else was brave enough to fight against Seamus."

Gunnolf only smiled. If Christophe thought hiding behind curtain walls made him appear brave, Gunnolf assumed the elders would think otherwise.

Before Gunnolf could go with Robard up the stairs, Brina pulled him into her arms and kissed him. "Whatever happens, I love you, my braw warrior. If we stay here or we leave, all that matters is that I am with you. I am glad my da is recovering. My people will take care of him."

Gunnolf wrapped his arms around her and kissed her soundly on the mouth. "You are everything to me. I know you wish to stay. I will do everything in my power to make that happen." He kissed her again, saw the tears well up in her eyes, and he said, "You are happy, are you not?" Tears meant so many different things for women, he had to be sure. He didn't want to plead his case that he should be in charge and then learn Brina wanted to leave this place behind. He didn't think so, but women were mysterious creatures, and he just had to be sure.

She smiled up at him through her tears and nodded. "I am. But no matter what, I will be happy as long as I go where you go."

"Come, Gunnolf," Robard said, pausing to ensure he was joining them in his chamber.

Christophe ground his teeth, his eyes narrowed. "Why does he have to come?"

"Because I said so." Robard headed up the stairs, his pace slow and Gunnolf was certain he was in pain.

He wanted to aid him, but he knew he could do nothing but follow behind him on the narrow, curved stairs.

When they were assembled in Robard's chamber, Robard sat down on the bed as if the effort of returning home had exerted him overly much, his face pale. Four elders stood in his chamber also, but only one that Gunnolf knew by name as if he didn't need to know the rest of their names.

"I have led the clan in Robard's absence," Christophe said, immediately advocating his right to remain as chief of the clan. "I protected you from Seamus and his mercenaries."

Gunnolf had every intention of letting Robard handle the matter, but he couldn't be silent on this issue. "*Ja*, you kept Seamus out, but what would happen when any of your people had to leave the castle? What of those living in outlying areas that would have to fend against Seamus's wrath? They were not afforded your protection. They were left to manage on their own."

Christophe folded his arms. "They owe an allegiance to the clan. They were safe enough where they were."

"How do you know when you are hiding behind these walls? I give you that you believed Seamus's lies that Robard was dead. But what of Brina? And Lynette? You sent no one after them to ensure they were safe, did you?" Gunnolf asked, angry that the man who wished to be in charge hadn't done anything to see that the women were safe.

"I had naught to do with their leaving. Besides, I knew they would find refuge and didna need my help."

"Two women alone? Against Seamus and his men?"

"Who are you to speak before those assembled? You are naught more than a Viking! Our enemy. Mayhap you killed Seamus, I will grant you that, but you have no place speaking here."

"He has every right as I advocate that Gunnolf leads the clan next," Robard said, though weary, he spoke with forcefulness.

Christophe looked shocked.

"You canna be serious. When you were wounded, your mind must have been addled as well," Christophe said.

Robard proceeded to tell all that he knew of Gunnolf from the time he was a lad, wounded, and found on their lands to what he knew of him as a grown man, fighting for the MacNeill clan. He told the elders that not only did he have James's support, which meant a great deal of men to fight with them if they had issues with other clans, but he would also have the support of James's brothers and cousin, all of whom treated Gunnolf like one of their own. He also intended to work with Inga and her people to end the hostilities.

"Gunnolf's kin nearly killed our chief," Christophe said. "They need to pay. Every last one of them."

"And we have killed them. Gunnolf was never involved. He didna even know his kin lived here. He has been living with the MacNeill clan all this time," Robard objected.

Christophe opened his mouth to speak, but one of the elders said, "Hold your tongue. Let Robard speak without interruption."

The others nodded in agreement.

Gunnolf realized just how much the elders believed in Robard as their chief. How much his words meant something to them.

Robard said, "With no thought of reward, Gunnolf rescued my daughter from Seamus after one of his men had struck her with an arrow. Gunnolf rid us of a mistake of my own making when I brought Seamus into the clan. I am no' about to make another with recommending my nephew take my place. No' when he has never proved himself loyal or capable of leading our men."

Gunnolf still couldn't believe that Robard had known so much about him, as if he'd admired him all these years after wanting to kill him when Gunnolf, as a lad, had been lying wounded on his lands.

"Brina will continue to manage the household staff?" one of the men asked.

"Aye. She has been trained, knows everyone, and knows how to make things work the best for everyone concerned." Robard looked like he was about ready to give out, he appeared so exhausted.

"Mayhap we can discuss this further later. The hour is late." Gunnolf didn't want to comment on Robard's health and make him feel like less of a man.

"We will make our decision on the morrow," Lorn said.

"And we will have a celebration on the morrow with regard to Brina's marrying Gunnolf," Robard announced.

"I have wed as well," Christophe said as if he suddenly remembered it.

"And you have no doubt been celebrating in my absence. 'Tis time for me to celebrate my daughter's marriage."

"They said you had commanded Gunnolf to wed Brina. Was it because he had forced himself on her?" Christophe asked.

"Did you force yourself on the lass you wed?" Gunnolf asked.

One of the elders chuckled.

"Of course no'. But I wasna commanded to marry her either."

Robard gave Christophe a steely-eyed glower. "I wished it because he had protected my daughter when no one else would. And I knew it would be a way to unite our clan with James's."

"I had the utmost respect for the lady," Gunnolf clarified, just in case anyone had assumed otherwise. Because the elders would now be involved in deciding who would be chief and it was between Gunnolf and Christophe, he didn't think Christophe would make an attempt on Robard's life. Unless out of vengeance for his uncle suggesting that the elders choose Gunnolf over his nephew.

"Who would be your choice to be your second?" Lorn asked Gunnolf, before they left.

"Rory, because all this time he and Cadel and his wife have kept Robard alive and safe. He was loyal to the chief when no one else had come to his aid."

That seemed to satisfy the elders who nodded, most likely pleased to hear he would have someone from the clan at his side and not someone from James's clan instead.

"Rest, Robard. We will inform you of our decision on the morrow," Lorn said.

***

Men were posted as guards for Robard as he slept in his own chamber while Christophe had to move to another and Gunnolf retired with Brina to

314

her chamber. He had never imagined sleeping with the lass in her own chamber. He wondered if she had.

He ran his hand over the pale blue curtains hanging from the bed rails as she sat on the mattress and leaned down to untie her shoes.

"Allow me," Gunnolf said, crouching in front of her.

She ran her hand over Gunnolf's windswept hair. "I canna believe Seamus was my half brother and intended to wed me. Knowing who he was, I am sorry with the way things ended."

"I am too. But it was a good thing that I rescued you." Gunnolf removed her other shoe, then slid his hands up her leg to pull down her sock.

A knock at the door sounded. He instantly rose and unsheathed his sword. "*Ja?*"

"Robard ordered a bath for you and the lady," Lorn called out.

"*Ja.*"

Brina was up on her feet in an instant and had her bow and an arrow readied just in case someone had other notions.

Gunnolf was ready likewise and opened the door.

Lorn smiled a little at them. "Just a bath. No battle here."

Then men hauled in a tub and more came with hot water. When they were done, both Brina and Gunnolf thanked them.

A maid asked if she could help them, but

Gunnolf declined. She handed him cloths and soap. Then he shut the door and bolted it.

"I feel badly that we thought we were going to have trouble. I hate for my people to think we dinna trust them."

"'Tis better to expect trouble than to be surprised by it."

"Aye, which is why you will make a great leader."

"For now, I only want to be a dutiful husband." He sheathed his sword and removed his belt, then set them aside. He lifted her face to his and kissed her.

"Thank you for bringing my da home."

"You helped just as much." Then he began to pull off her clothes and when she was standing only in her chemise, he jerked off each article of his own clothing until he stood fully naked before her. And aroused. And wanting her in the worst way, desire filling him with need. But he wanted to make love to her like she deserved, after they both bathed. He pulled off her chemise and helped her into the tub.

***

Brina sighed as she sank into the hot water, glad to be home, and having a bath, but if Christophe was chosen over Gunnolf, she knew she could be happy with James's clan too. As long as Gunnolf was there. "This feels so good."

"You look so good," Gunnolf said, crouching down next to her with the cloth in hand.

She thought he was going to hand her the cloth,

and couldn't believe it when he ran the soft material over her body. Not just the cloth, but his large hand, massaging her back and neck, and then lower, her breasts, waist, and even lower. Never had she envisioned her husband washing her. The other way around, maybe, but not this.

When he moved the cloth between her legs, then dispensed with the fabric and began to fondle her into a fevered pitch, need burned deep inside her. She couldn't believe a bath could turn into something so deliciously special, so hot and blissful. Arching against his fingers, she held onto the tub with a fierce grip. Feeling as though she could melt into the silky water with his stroking her into rapture, she tightened her hold. Every caress took her higher, made her want to go even farther.

Though the water was cooling, he was making her feel delightfully hot. She wanted him inside her then, wanted to be in the bed giving him pleasure too, but he leaned over and kissed her mouth, and she forgot everything but his touching her.

Sparks of excitement skittered across her skin as she let go of the tub and clasped his face in her hands and kissed him back. His tongue stroked hers as she felt as if she were soaring into the heavens. He kissed the water droplets on her cheek, then licked her neck and she didn't think she'd ever felt anything so wildly passionate in her life.

Pleasure blossomed deep inside her and her world tilted. She cried out, overwhelmed.

He kissed her, his mouth on hers, pressuring

and eager. She noted he was ready for her, his staff steel hard, if she wished it. But she wanted to bathe him first.

He finished washing her legs and feet, his expression intense.

"Let us switch places." She was tired and ready to fall asleep in Gunnolf's arms.

"You can retire to bed and I will join you as soon as I am clean."

"Nay. I will wash you, my husband, as you have washed me."

He helped her out of the tub and then was eagerly drying her, kissing her again, and she didn't think he would have time enough to bathe himself before the night was through. Not the way he was caressing her skin gently with the cloth, licking droplets he'd missed, and kissing off others, making bathing a true pleasure.

Then she said, "Now your turn."

He climbed into the tub, and she began to wash him, but he wasn't playing fair as he reached up to caress her naked breasts, and he kept kissing her on the mouth and shoulder. She loved the way he made the bath time fun and sexy.

She washed his chest and lower, amused at how his staff jumped in her hand beneath the cloth when she stroked it.

"Do that anymore and I will not make it inside you, if you are able to accept me again so soon," he said, his voice ragged.

She chuckled, and finished cleaning his legs

and feet. Before she knew what he was up to, he pulled her into the tub on top of him. She squealed out in surprise, her heart beating wildly, and then she laughed.

"Are you able to accept me?"

"How?" She couldn't imagine making love in the tub.

He kissed her neck and said, "Like this. But if you are too uncomfortable, we can wait. Just stop me if you need to."

He penetrated her tight sheath and she rocked on top of him, creating waves in the water, some splashing over the side. But she was getting used to him, loving the feel of him inside her, loving the way he made love to her.

He was gentle and passionate. She was glad that she had met him again and that they had become husband and wife. She had never truly imagined what it would be like to make love to Gunnolf in the privacy of her chamber. What she didn't expect was for him to place his hand between her legs and as he was pumping into her, he began to stroke her again. She couldn't imagine coming apart in his hands like this, and yet she did, felt the excitement all over again, the thrill of reaching the pinnacle, and the final feeling of total elation as she collapsed in his arms and kissed his mouth hard, then soft.

She didn't think she could climb out of the tub the way she was feeling so satiated and sleepy.

He smiled at her and assisted her to stand, then

quickly climbed out of the tub and helped her out. They began drying each other and she smiled as his staff began to take on a life of its own again.

He just smiled at her and kissed her. "You make that happen." And then he lifted her in his arms and carried her to bed. "I bet you never considered you would have a man in your bed."

She laughed. "Nay. Never. My da would have killed him. About tomorrow, should the elders choose Christophe over you, we will leave. Take Da with us if he wishes, or leave him if he feels he will be safe."

"You will not miss your people too much?"

"My home is with you, a new beginning, a new life."

"We will worry about it after we learn what the elders decide."

Brina snuggled against Gunnolf that night, trying to sleep, but sleep would not come. Not when she was so unsure of the elder's decision.

***

Early the next morning, Lorn knocked on their door, saying, "The decision has been made. Gunnolf, if you will come with me, we will meet with the elders in Robard's chamber."

Gunnolf noted Lorn didn't call Robard the chief.

Brina looked worried. He knew she wanted to stay here, and maybe they would even if Christophe was in charge. If she found him and his wife intolerable, they could still leave.

"I will be but a moment." Gunnolf turned to grab his clothes and dress.

Brina was already hurrying to dress and he helped her on with her socks and shoes. "No worries," he said. "Whatever way this goes will be the best for us."

"Aye." She kissed Gunnolf and then he finished getting dressed.

"While I am in there, what will you do?" he asked.

"I will go downstairs as I usually do and take charge of managing the household staff."

He was glad she had not given up on her duties in anticipation that they would be leaving.

He gave her a sound hug, kissed her just as soundly, wishing already they were back in bed and he had time to make love to his lovely wife again, then he opened the door. Lynette was standing just outside, waiting for him to leave, he suspected.

"I thought I would stay with Brina."

"Good," Brina said. "Come. We have much work to do." She led Lynette down the stairs to get to work on the morning meal.

Gunnolf went to Robard's chamber where the elders and Christophe had assembled. Robard was seated, looking tired.

"We understand the way Robard feels about you being in charge, Gunnolf," one of the elders said. "Like Robard, we have heard of your successes and your failures. But we havena seen you lead our people."

Christophe was quiet, smug.

Robard listened quietly.

"We have had good campaigns and bad under Robard's leadership. For the most part, he has led us well. By his own admission, he needs time to recover before he can lead us again," Lorn said.

"Christophe was Robard's first choice, but his leaving the clan as he did for no good reason and not protecting our people from the likes of Seamus when we learned of his deception, didna bode well. Would he lead our people to meet the challenge head on? Or would he always close the gates and hide within?"

Christophe's face reddened, but he wisely didn't speak.

"We canna hand over the clan to a man whose family has been fighting ours for years"–Lorn raised his hand to stop Robard's objection--"until he has proven himself worthy. The best way that we can see this happening is for Robard to continue to lead. Gunnolf will be his second-in-command and as such, he will do everything Robard asks of him. If this means Gunnolf will lead our men into battle, so be it. If he can handle alliances with other clans until Robard has recovered enough, he will do so. Is this acceptable?" the elder asked Robard.

He looked to Gunnolf for his consent. Gunnolf bowed his head, thinking it was the best of options. He would prove his worth while Robard recovered and if someday Robard no longer wished to rule and his people trusted in Gunnolf's leadership, he would lead.

"Nay, this isna acceptable," Christophe said, his face red with anger.

"'Tis the lot you chose when you abandoned the clan," Robard said. "If we are done here, I wish to get on with the feasting."

Gunnolf thought Robard needed to rest further, but he realized this was important to Robard and the news would be shared with the clan then.

It turned out to be a grand feast, with alliances made between Robard and James, the elders knowing the only reason for it that Gunnolf was staying on to help lead the clan. Even though the celebration was about Brina's marriage to Gunnolf, everyone seemed to be celebrating the fact she was in charge of the management of the staff and made the feast happen.

Christophe and his wife attended, Guennola, angry at the world. Gunnolf had overheard her pitching a fit. But Christophe assured her that Gunnolf would never earn the clan's favor and as long as they remained here, he would prove his own worth.

Gunnolf wondered how long that would last. Would they really stay and see if Gunnolf couldn't sway the elders to his cause and hope to still take his uncle's place? Maybe his wife would learn how to manage the staff in the meantime. Or would he leave like he'd done in the past?

In any event, Gunnolf was delighted that his Highland lass was so excited to be home among her people, singing, dancing, and enjoying the revelry as much as anyone else. And he was caught up in the moment just as much as she.

James spoke to Gunnolf as they watched Brina and Lynette dancing with several others.

"This was the best thing that could have come out of the situation, dinna you agree?" James asked.

Robard joined them. "Aye. I finally have my son." He smiled darkly at Gunnolf.

James laughed.

Smiling, Gunnolf inclined his head toward Robard in concurrence. He'd never expected Brina's father to call him son. And he would do what he could to prove to him his support was fully warranted.

"But what I really want to know is when I will have my first grandson to bounce on my knee."

"That is something we are working hard at," Gunnolf said.

Just then, Brina joined him and pulled him out to dance. "Working hard at what?"

"Loving you."

EPILOGUE

A Year Later, Anfa Castle

Gunnolf held his infant son in his hands as Brina smiled up at him. She lay on the mattress, the covers pulled up to her waist, exhausted but happy. "He is beautiful, is he no'?"

Beowulf was eager to see the baby too, his paws on Gunnolf's leg, his tail whipping back and forth.

Gunnolf smiled down at Brina. "As beautiful as his mother."

Lynette brushed Brina's hair and said, "Aye, Hagen is."

Brina couldn't have been happier to have a son, that Gunnolf was now chief of the clan, having proved that he had what it took to lead them, and that Lynette had decided to stay and everyone knew her as Brina's sister. And her da —

"Where is my grandson?" Robard asked,

stalking into the room. "Are you going to hold him and no' let anyone else see him? We must show him to the gathered clan at once." He reached out his hands to hold their son.

"Hold him close to you," Gunnolf said, like a midwife teaching Brina's father how to do it right.

"I have done this with my daughter, your wife, I might add," Robard said, and took the bairn and admired him. "He has my eyes."

Everyone laughed.

But she loved how close she'd become to her da who had worried enough for all of them that she would survive the pregnancy and that her son would too. "Bring him back soon," Brina said.

"I will go with them to ensure they dinna lose him in the crowd." Lynette kissed her cheek. "He is beautiful, Brina."

Gunnolf kissed Brina before he left. "Will you be all right?"

"Aye, I will sleep for a while. I know you will wish to celebrate. Enjoy yourself. You and my da have been so worried about this bairn—"

"And you."

"Aye, that it is time for you to celebrate."

"I will return soon."

And she knew he would, because when other men would rather drink and celebrate good news, he'd rather be with her, and now the bairn, to enjoy them as a family.

***

Gunnolf couldn't have been more pleased at

how things had worked out. Some still grumbled about his leading the clan, but for the most part, the clan members knew he was doing the best he could. Inga had even married the man who had confronted Gunnolf and they'd had peace for this past year between Brina's clan and theirs.

Lady Akira, Lady Eilis, and Wynne were coming with James to see the baby after a few weeks. Eilis's own baby was a girl and was several month's old, and their son, Ian, was eager to see Brina and the new baby too. Christophe and his wife had left the castle that morn as soon as they learned Brina had survived the birth of their bairn and their son was perfectly healthy.

Gunnolf knew Christophe had only stayed to see him fail. But Gunnolf would never fail when being here for Brina was so important to her and her people.

He caught up to Robard holding up his grandson, proud as could be. And for a moment Gunnolf folded his arms, watched, and smiled, Beowulf sitting beside him, a couple of months older than a yearling, so not quite full grown, wagging his tail as he watched Robard and Hagen too.

The Highlanders and the Norsemen had finally made peace, and Hagen was the result of it—a beautiful son bringing their two worlds together.

It all began with Gunnolf believing he had died and the goddess had come to take him away. Brina was that goddess, and she had taken him away all right. To a place that was perfect for the both of them and for their newborn son.

ABOUT THE AUTHOR

Bestselling and award-winning author **Terry Spear** has written over sixty paranormal romance novels and seven medieval Highland historical romances. Her first werewolf romance, *Heart of the Wolf,* was named a 2008 *Publishers Weekly*'s Best Book of the Year, and her subsequent titles have garnered high praise and hit the *USA Today* bestseller list. A retired officer of the U.S. Army Reserves, Terry lives in Spring, Texas, where she is working on her next werewolf romance, continuing her new series about shapeshifting jaguars, writing Highland medieval romance, and having fun with her young adult novels. When she's not writing, she's photographing everything that catches her eye, making teddy bears, and playing with her Havanese puppies. For more information, please visit www.terryspear.com, or follow her on Twitter, @TerrySpear. She is also on Facebook at http://www.facebook.com/terry.spear. And on Wordpress at:

Terry Spear's Shifters
http://terryspear.wordpress.com/

ALSO BY TERRY SPEAR

Romantic Suspense: Deadly Fortunes, In the Dead of the Night, Relative Danger, Bound by Danger
The Highlanders Series: Winning the Highlander's Heart, The Accidental Highland Hero, Highland Rake, Taming the Wild Highlander, The Highlander, Her Highland Hero, The Viking's Highland Lass
Other historical romances: Lady Caroline & the Egotistical Earl, A Ghost of a Chance at Love
Heart of the Wolf Series: Heart of the Wolf, Destiny of the Wolf, To Tempt the Wolf, Legend of the White Wolf, Seduced by the Wolf, Wolf Fever, Heart of the Highland Wolf, Dreaming of the Wolf, A SEAL in Wolf's Clothing, A Howl for a Highlander, A Highland Werewolf Wedding, A SEAL Wolf Christmas, Silence of the Wolf, Hero of a Highland Wolf, A Highland Wolf Christmas, A SEAL Wolf Hunting; A Silver Wolf Christmas, A SEAL Wolf in Too Deep, Alpha Wolf Need Not Apply, A Billionaire in Wolf's Clothing
SEAL Wolves: To Tempt the Wolf, A SEAL in Wolf's Clothing, A SEAL Wolf Christmas; SEAL Wolf Hunting, SEAL Wolf in Too Deep
Silver Bros Wolves: Destiny of the Wolf, Wolf Fever, Dreaming of the Wolf, Silence of the Wolf; A Silver Wolf Christmas, Alpha Wolf Need Not Apply
Highland Wolves: Heart of the Highland Wolf, A Howl for a Highlander, A Highland Werewolf Wedding, Hero of a Highland Wolf, A Highland Wolf Christmas
Billionaire in Wolf's Clothing

Made in the USA
Monee, IL
02 November 2023

45709230R00194